THE DARK SIDE OF BLUE

A Novel

DICK ELLWOOD

ISBN: 1530126789
ISBN 13: 9781530126781
Printed in the United States of America

ACKNOWLEDGEMENT

I would like to thank my friends and family who encouraged me to push forward with this book. A special thanks to my wife, Sharon, who did a tremendous job editing the book.

I would like to make a special acknowledgement to a dear friend, retired Maryland State Trooper, Ray Leard. Ray passed away before I could finish the book. I will cherish the many hours of conversation with him discussing our police careers. His background and expertise in certain areas of law enforcement were helpful with my writing.

I would also like to acknowledge all the men and women in law enforcement who put their lives on the line every day to keep us safe. May God watch over you and protect you.

CHAPTER 1

The view from the window was breathtaking. It was just another beautiful, warm, and sunny day in California. The cool breeze was a reminder of how nice the weather can be in this part of the country. The trees were bending slightly as if they were performing or dancing to "*California Girls*" by the Beach Boys. Fluffy clouds that looked like marshmallows dotted the beautiful sky.

Standing there inhaling the air made you want to pull the steel bars off the window and run out screaming. But the steel bars don't budge and never will. They have been in place at Pelican Bay Prison in Crescent City, California, since 1989. The inmates see the same view from the windows every day. The supermax prison lies on a sprawling two hundred and fifty acre complex on the Pacific Coast. The facility houses over four thousand maximum security inmates, the worst of the worst as reported by the media when the facility opened.

The prison got its name from the Pelican, a bird that prowls the waters of the nearby Pacific Ocean. The bird is huge and has a long beak that allows it to catch its prey and keep it in a very large pouch. Whoever named the prison came up with that name figuring that if the bird can hold his prey, then a well-constructed, maximum security prison can certainly hold its prey.

The "Pincher" was a big man. He stood at least six feet, five inches, weighed in at about two hundred and fifty pounds and was solid as a rock. He could be the poster boy for prison guards. He was feared by most prisoners in the Security Housing Unit, most commonly referred to as the SHU at Pelican Bay. His name was Oscar Mandez and his rank was lieutenant. The new prisoners called him Lieutenant Mandez. Those who had served some serious time on the SHU simply called him, The Pincher. He earned his nickname from the way he escorted prisoners from their cells. He handcuffed them through the cell door. As he directed them where they are going, he pinched them on the neck. He told new inmates that he pinched them so that he can easily get to their jugular if they broke bad. If you had a red mark on your neck, it was assumed by other inmates that you had taken a walk with The Pincher.

Life on the SHU was hard. The only real rules were that you keep your mouth shut, do what you are told, and make no waves. There were also some institutional rules that are provided to all new inmates, but keeping your mouth shut and doing what you are told pretty much covers it all. The SHU is no place for the weak. Nothing in the prison rules state that the guards couldn't beat the shit out of you when they feel you need it, so thus the main rule of making no waves is important.

The guards in the SHU made sure you knew who was in charge. The twenty-two hours spent in your cell were torture enough without putting up with the occasional beatings. Somewhere in the real rules, it was stated that you were entitled to five hours a week outside in the courtyard. For most in the SHU, it very seldom came close to five hours. Whatever time they did get outside was cherished by the inmates.

Although the SHU was definitely the toughest section in Pelican Bay, word was circulating among the inmates that a new unit was being formed. The guards referred to the new unit as the CLEO Unit. Over time, the inmates found out that CLEO stood for Corrupt Law Enforcement Officers.

Most inmates when they came into the SHU never really knew what anyone was in for or what they did on the outside. There was very little time for communication among the inmates. When in the yard, as many as two hundred inmates could be out there at a time. If any talking took place that appeared out of line to the guards, it was stopped. It was well known by the inmates that listening devices were placed in the walls surrounding the yard. The towers were manned by guards who were downright nasty. If they thought you were getting friendly with another inmate, they would first announce over a speaker to break it up. If it looked like you were ignoring them, the guards did not hesitate to fire a shotgun blast in your direction to scare the shit out of you. Some of the shotgun blasts wounded inmates, but no one bitched or their yard privilege would be taken away. Fights very seldom occurred in the yard. Fighting meant you did not come in the yard for six months, no disciplinary hearing or appeal process. The guards had the final say.

The prison rules stated that a new inmate would be housed in the SHU until such time that the staff deemed him to be ready for general population. It was known to some on the SHU that inmates had spent upward from eight to ten years in the SHU. The only time anyone knew that someone was leaving, was when The Pincher took them from their cell and paraded them by other cells and announced, "Gentlemen, this fine inmate has obeyed all the rules. His reward is that he is going to general population. Maybe someday you will get there, too."

CHAPTER 2

The CLEO Unit would be much different than the SHU. The inmates would be all former law enforcement officers who had been serving time in federal correction facilities in every state. While being members of law enforcement, they had committed a variety of crimes from racketeering, bribery, perjury, and narcotic violations. These were not just your typical bad cops; these inmates were convicted based on their strong involvement in organized crime. All of the inmates that would be in the CLEO Unit had been convicted in federal courts.

The inmates coming to the CLEO Unit were convicted under the Racketeering Influenced and Corrupt Organization Act or most commonly referred to as the RICO Act. The act was adopted in 1970 to prosecute the Mafia. The law carries a twenty year maximum sentence. The inmates that would be coming to the CLEO Unit would have started their sentences in federal prisons around the country. Pelican Bay was selected by the Justice Department to house fifty of the most corrupt law enforcement officers in the country, one from each state. It was thought by the powers in the Justice Department that this might be a deterrent to police corruption; the theory being that corrupt law enforcement officers would know that they could wind up in one of the most dangerous correction facilities in the nation.

The process for selecting the inmates to go to the CLEO Unit at Pelican Bay was done in secret by the Justice Department. The inmates selected were removed in the middle of the night from their current facilities and under heavy guard were taken to Pelican Bay. This procedure received no publicity and was conducted in complete secrecy. The families and attorneys for the inmates were not informed of the move. No explanation was given to them about where they were going. They were secured with handcuffs, leg irons, and hoods placed over their heads during the trip. Depending on the state the prisoner was in, most were flown to the West Coast in military transport planes. The cost for moving the fifty former law enforcement officers was very expensive. The plan and the cost were not made public until all fifty inmates were in the CLEO Unit. Families of some of the inmates threatened lawsuits stating that the move to the West Coast caused a hardship.

The Justice Department selected Mike Hubbard, a retired FBI agent to run the CLEO Unit. He had been with the Bureau for thirty-two years. His credentials were impeccable; he had risen through the ranks at the Bureau to deputy director. Prior to his retirement, he headed the Civil Rights Unit within the FBI. He had also supervised some very high profile investigations of police corruption around the country. Hubbard was known as a no-nonsense person who despised those in law enforcement whom he investigated for corruption.

When asked to take the position at Pelican Bay, he at first balked at the idea. He lived in Washington, D.C., and although his children were grown and out of the house, he cherished his family life. It would be a huge challenge to take the leadership of the CLEO Unit, but Mike Hubbard had always loved a challenge. The attorney general convinced him that the Justice Department needed someone like him to run the unit.

The salary for the job was also something he could not turn down. The move to the West Coast included many incentives and an agreement that he and his wife could fly back to D.C. at the government's expense for family functions.

Mike did confide in his wife about the proposed position, and reluctantly, she gave the okay; she always supported his assignments.

Although they had been planning for his retirement for several years, she knew that when it came to fighting law enforcement corruption, he would not turn the job down.

Mike and his wife decided that they would keep their home in the Washington suburbs. He also told her that after getting the CLEO Unit up and running, he would consider a real retirement. If the position created a challenge for him, she knew they would be on the West Coast for quite some time.

CHAPTER 3

M ike Hubbard's appointment to run the CLEO Unit was no surprise to the warden at Pelican Bay. Jonathan Scope had been in charge at Pelican Bay since it opened. He knew Hubbard was coming. He had been briefed about the establishment of the CLEO Unit by the Justice Department. Scope was a proud man who had put his life's work into making Pelican Bay a tough and well-run prison. It was also a maximum correctional facility that was respected around the country. Warden Scope embraced the accolades about it being the toughest prison in the nation; he intended to keep it that way.

Prior to the arrival of Hubbard, Scope had oversight of the construction of the CLEO Unit. He decided that the unit would be located at the farthest section of the two hundred and seventy-five acre complex. His theory for the location was that neither the regular Pelican Bay inmates nor the public would know what was happening for quite some time. The construction consisted of a two-story brick building looking similar to the other buildings, except for the inside. The interior of the building had fifty cells. The cells were eight by ten feet with no windows. In addition, the building had five additional cells that were ten by twelve feet and had windows. The five larger cells were set in an area that could not be seen by inmates in the main fifty cell section. The facility was state of the art. Scope made sure that the camera system was the most sophisticated available. The guard stations were outside the area of the cells.

Each cell could be viewed on a high-tech monitoring station twenty-four hours a day.

The warden was tasked with the job of providing guards for the CLEO Unit. He knew that some of the guards would balk at working in a unit that contained only corrupt law enforcement officers. Many of his current staff of guards were former law enforcement, and some of the guards had aspirations of leaving Pelican Bay to go into police work. Selecting the guards, however, would not be as much a problem as staffing the unit with supervisors.

Scope knew that he had a highly qualified supervisory staff. It took him a few years to get the right people in place to where he felt comfortable. He also did not want to dump guards and supervisors who were not performing at a high level into the CLEO Unit. He knew that when Hubbard arrived on the job, he would want to interview potential supervisors.

In all, the warden had allocated for the CLEO Unit to have twenty-four guards, three sergeants, and three lieutenants. The plan put together by the Justice Department outlined that Hubbard's title would be deputy warden.

When Mike Hubbard arrived on the West Coast he was picked up at the airport in a car sent by Warden Scope. He had traveled to California alone. His wife was making arrangements back in Washington to have some of their belongings put into storage. She would be joining him after he settled in the temporary residence that was pre-arranged by the Justice Department. He instructed the driver to take him directly to Pelican Bay.

The driver was a prison guard, but he was not in uniform. After putting some luggage into the trunk, the driver introduced himself to Hubbard. "Sir, I'm Sergeant Ron Sanders. I'm one of the assistants in the warden's office at the prison. It's a pleasure to meet you. We have heard a lot about you."

"Thanks Ron. I hope whatever you heard was good. I'm looking forward to meeting everyone at the prison. As I do not have a vehicle yet, would you be available later to take me to the residence they have for me?"

"Sir, I would be glad to assist in any way I can. I do believe they have a vehicle that will be assigned to you back at the prison. It's a little tricky getting around town. I'll be glad to direct you to your new residence."

When Sanders and Hubbard got to the car, Sanders opened the back door of the shiny black Chrysler. Hubbard shut the door and asked him if it was okay if he rode up front. "Ron, I want to fit in with the staff at Pelican Bay. My background was in law enforcement with the FBI. I have a lot to learn about the corrections system."

"Sir, I think you will fit in just fine. You will have the support of the warden and the personnel assigned to your new unit. Information has leaked out about your unit. We are a proud bunch at Pelican Bay. Warden Scope always preaches integrity, loyalty, and honesty. Obviously, the inmates that you will have in the CLEO Unit have violated all those principles."

"You're correct. The inmates that will be in the CLEO Unit are the worst cases of police corruption in the nation. I do not intend to make this a picnic for them, but I will treat them fairly. They chose to violate their oaths and now they must pay the price."

The ride to Pelican Bay was fairly quiet. Hubbard took in the sights and occasionally asked questions about the area. When the car was approaching the prison, Hubbard leaned forward to take in the imposing edifice. Sergeant Sanders could see both excitement and curiosity in Hubbard. "Have you ever seen a prison this big, sir?"

"I have been in quite a few correctional facilities, but I don't think I have seen any this big."

CHAPTER 4

After driving through a series of prison gates, Sergeant Sanders and Mike Hubbard were still not in the main section of the prison. As Sanders pulled the vehicle to a stop after passing through the gates, a guard about thirty feet up on the wall hollered down, "Exit the vehicle and identify yourself."

Hubbard thought identifying yourself was a little unusual—didn't they know Sergeant Sanders? He was one of them. When they exited the vehicle Sanders said, "Sir, this is the same procedure for anyone coming into the prison. Before this gate opens into the main section of the prison, a guard will come over and ask for our identification. He will ask if we are armed with a weapon. He will then do a body scan on each of us before we are allowed into the prison. He will also ask me to open the trunk of the vehicle. I know opening the trunk seems time consuming, but the procedure has been in place for quite some time. The prison guards do not bring their vehicles into the prison; they have a parking lot nearby. They have a separate entrance and they are also searched before they come in."

"Have there been any escapes from the prison?"

"We did have one escape about two years ago. A prisoner got in the back of a delivery truck and got through the gate. We had him back in the prison in less than two hours. The prisoner forced the driver out of the truck. The driver had a cell phone and called in the theft of his truck. The state police apprehended the guy after a short chase. We had a couple other attempts, but they didn't get out."

After all the entry procedures were completed, Hubbard got into a golf cart for a short ride to meet the warden. Hubbard thanked Sergeant Sanders. "Are you still available later to provide some directions to my place?"

"Yes sir, I have some paper work to do. I'll find you later or just have someone call me."

Hubbard's ride to the main building was short. Along the way he could see some inmates in the large yard. As he passed them, he noticed that some of the inmates moved closer to the fence to see who the new guy in the suit was. The guard driving the golf cart did not speak during the short drive. He was an older man. Hubbard assumed that he had been at the prison for some time. When they stopped at the entrance to the administration building, the driver said, "Sir, I wish you well in your new job. I have been around this prison since it opened. Be very careful. There are inmates in this place that don't give a damn. You can go in that door; someone will take you to Warden Scope."

"Thanks for the good advice. This is all new to me and I will be careful."

Hubbard walked into the building and was greeted by a very attractive female. "Hello, Mr. Hubbard, my name is Carla. I'm the administrative assistant for Warden Scope. He is waiting for you. Please follow me."

Carla led Hubbard into a very large outer office and then into the warden's office. The office was expansive and very well decorated. Scope was sitting behind a beautiful mahogany desk, in a large leather chair. The rest of the furniture was quite nice and this surprised Hubbard. He didn't know why he was surprised, except that he assumed it would be standard government furniture.

The warden walked around from behind the desk. "Mr. Hubbard, welcome to Pelican Bay. I have heard a lot about you. It's a pleasure to finally meet you."

"Thank you, warden. I'm excited to be here. I have also heard many good things about you and this facility."

The warden motioned for Hubbard to sit on a huge leather couch. He asked Carla if she would get some coffee. Hubbard sank into the leather couch. He moved forward to sit on the edge. He would rather have sat at the large conference table, but this was not his show; it was the warden's.

Scope sat on the couch, too; the sinking did not seem to bother him. He asked Hubbard how his flight was. They exchanged some small talk until the warden slid to the edge of the couch. He told Hubbard that the job ahead of him would be daunting. He assured Hubbard that he would have the full support of all the personnel at Pelican Bay. The coffee arrived. Scope waited for Carla to exit the office before he continued talking. "Can I call you Mike?"

"Please do. Can I call you Jonathan?"

"Most of my close staff at the facility call me, Jon."

"Then Jon it will be. I'm excited and anxious to get started as soon as possible."

"Good, I will have Carla direct you to the people who will issue you your credentials. She can also provide you with all the manuals, special orders, and policies pertaining to Pelican Bay. I would assume that most of this material will be what you implement in the CLEO Unit, but that's up to you."

"I will review the material as quickly as possible. I'm sure we will use whatever procedures that are already in place. If it works for you, why would I change it?"

Carla escorted Hubbard out to the main office where a large box was waiting for him. "Sir, all the manuals you will need are in this box. I have also provided you with all the forms used here at Pelican Bay. I know it seems like a lot, but most of the people that will be working for you already know the procedures. I'm sure they will get you up to snuff in no time at all."

"Well, Carla, without my wife being with me I will have a lot of extra time to do some serious reading. I'm not the kind of guy that runs out of the office at the end of the day. You will probably see me in the office late into the night. Until such time that I feel the CLEO Unit is functioning like I want it to, I won't be satisfied."

After a couple hours of fingerprinting, photographs, and meeting members of the warden's staff, it was time to leave the facility. It was getting late, but Hubbard noticed that Sergeant Sanders was still hanging around in the main office. "Well, Sergeant, do you think you have time to get me to my residence? I know I would never find it. I don't even think I could find my way out of the prison."

"No problem, sir. I'm free tonight. I will make sure we get you out of the prison first and then we will find your new residence. If you're hungry I can direct you to a very good restaurant."

"If you're free for a while, it would be my pleasure to buy you dinner. I think that is the least I can do for you after all the help you have given me today."

"You let me know what you prefer to eat. I can assure you I will take you to a place you will like."

Chapter 5

The fifty inmates who would be housed in the CLEO Unit gradually arrived over a period of two weeks. In no particular order, each was placed in one of the fifty cells. The CLEO Unit under corrections guidelines was considered a maximum security facility.

The guards being picked from the staff at the main prison would be assigned to the unit until Hubbard could check them out, give his approval, and make the assignments official. The supervisors assigned would need to go through an interview process with Hubbard.

The order was given that no inmates in the unit were allowed to go into the yard until Hubbard felt all procedures were in place. They were on lockdown until he decided the unit was functioning as outlined in the initial set-up guidelines.

As the inmates arrived at the CLEO Unit, they did not talk to each other; most did not even know where they were. Having been moved in total secrecy, they were still trying to figure out what the move was about. The unit was quiet compared to the main section of Pelican Bay. The guards were not used to the silence. They could tell that these inmates were not the usual run-of-the-mill street criminals. They would eventually find out that these inmates at one time had been well-respected law enforcement officers. Most had worked for many years in their police agencies before they chose to change directions and go for the easy money. The records of many inmates were very impressive. Some were supervisors in their agencies; many had even received citations for heroism. They had stood out in their agencies at one time as the cream of the crop.

In law enforcement, the positions that could lead to corruption usually dealt with assignments to units that investigated gambling and drugs. Some of the law enforcement agencies the inmates came from were notorious for having corruption problems. CLEO inmates had all been convicted in Federal Courts under the RICO Act.

It was a definite that whatever they did, it was serious. In some states when law enforcement officers committed crimes that were considered corruption, they might just be fired after an internal investigation. Whether or not they were referred to the judicial system depended on the degree of corruption. No matter what level of corruption you committed in your agency, you knew you would never work in law enforcement again. The CLEO inmates had lost their careers, their income, their trustworthiness, and in many cases, their families. The money they received that led to the corruption charges cost them a most precious thing—their freedom.

Corruption in law enforcement was a big problem in large cities, such as New York, Detroit, Chicago, and its tentacles also reached into smaller cities in the nation. No law enforcement officer ever started on the job thinking he or she would get wealthy taking money to allow illegal activity to take place. Corruption usually started from a series of happenings, such as being assigned to a unit that exposed them to the opportunity to accept money and gifts and look the other way. The corruption by the men in the CLEO Unit towered over all degrees of corruption.

Veteran law enforcement officers most likely had heard of the movie, *Serpico*. It came out in 1973 and starred Al Pacino as a NYPD officer who went undercover to expose corruption in the department. From 1960 to 1972, Serpico uncovered a hidden world in the department that had officers being paid off to allow drugs to be sold openly in certain sections of New York City. Serpico was shot in the face during a drug raid. It was determined that the drug dealers were tipped off by members of his unit that the police would be conducting a raid. Serpico was the first officer in the raiding party to go through the door; that's when he was shot.

The movie concluded with Serpico testifying before a grand jury to expose all that he knew. Large scale indictments were issued, and it was the start of ridding the department of corruption. After his retirement from the NYPD, he had to move to Switzerland because of all the threats on his life.

It would be a good bet that there were no Serpicos in the CLEO Unit.

Chapter 6

Mike Hubbard was in his office early on his first day on the job. He had received accurate directions from Sergeant Sanders on how to fight through the heavy morning traffic. Leaving his residence at 5 a.m. also helped. He knew where to park his new official vehicle that had been delivered to his residence late at night.

The sign in his parking spot read, *Deputy Warden—CLEO Unit.* He was unsure of the procedure on how to enter the prison through the employee gate. As he neared the entrance, it was still dark outside. He made sure that he had all his credentials out before he approached the guard. He was the only one going through the gate. No one else was reporting that early; it was not shift change. "Good morning sir. Can I help you?"

"Good morning, I'm Deputy Warden Mike Hubbard. I'm in charge of the new CLEO Unit. I have all the cards that were issued to me. Which ones do you need to check?"

"We check all three of your cards at this entrance. I know you will probably be coming through here each morning, but we still need to check the cards. It's just our procedure, so please don't think we are making you produce the cards each morning for no reason. It's a pleasure to meet you sir. I wish you success in your new job. We have heard a lot about the new unit. Is there anything I can do for you this morning?"

"Thank you. I will know to have my cards ready each morning. Have a nice day; I'll be heading down to my office."

"We have a golf cart and it would be no problem driving you down to your building."

"Thanks officer, but I think I will just walk on my first day. I want to take in the awesomeness of this prison. Will I be violating any procedures if I walk to the building?"

"Sir, you're a deputy warden, if you want to walk that's fine with us. I suggest you walk about ten feet away from the fence. It has an electrical charge that will be on until about an hour from now."

"Well, that's something I should know. I don't want to be fried on my first day."

Staying far away from the fence as possible, Hubbard started the walk to his office. It was much longer than he thought. The cool air felt good on his face as he gazed at the massive structure that was Pelican Bay Prison.

The walk was refreshing, even if there was a slight chill in the air. As he walked, he thought about his new job. *What will my first day bring? I have some thoughts on how I want to proceed, but I have never worked in the corrections field. I will play it by ear and listen to the professionals before I make any changes. I have been entrusted with a huge task. I am sure the far reaching eyes and ears of the Justice Department will know every move I make in the beginning.*

Entrance to the CLEO building was simple; no more cards to show. The administrative office was separate from the unit. Hubbard had to pass through two large steel doors to get into the unit. The outer office was empty when Hubbard entered. He saw a sign on a door at the far end of the main office that read, *Deputy Warden*. He entered and flipped on the lights. It was a very large office with what appeared to be new furniture. He put his briefcase on a chair and walked behind his desk. He noticed off to his right and sitting on a conference table was a large vase with a beautiful arrangement of flowers. He closely examined the vase and pulled a note from the top. *Who in the world would be sending flowers to Pelican Bay for me?* He opened the envelope:

Good luck on your first day. I know you are the right man for the job…
I miss you.
Love, Donna

He was savoring the moment when he heard some commotion in an area adjoining his office. He wanted to call his wife and thank her for the flowers, but he knew she would not be up this early. He slowly opened a door that was marked.....OFFICIAL PERSONNEL ONLY. The door led to the guard center that overlooked the CLEO Unit. He had been so quiet that when he entered, he saw two guards with their feet up on their desks, and they were sleeping. Another guard was over by a refrigerator; startled, he faced Hubbard and said, "Who the hell are you?"

"I'm Deputy Warden Mike Hubbard. Who the hell are you?"

"Sorry sir, I knew you were coming in today. I didn't expect you this early."

"Apparently not...what the hell is going on?"

The two guards who were sleeping were now wide awake. One of them almost fell off his chair when he heard the words..."deputy warden."

"I take it that you are the shift lieutenant on the CLEO Unit?

"Yes sir, I'm on duty until 8 a.m."

"Lieutenant, do you call this being on duty? Two of your men are sleeping. Is this the way it is around here? When those two are off duty have them report back to the main section of the prison. They will not be working here. As far as your position, when you are relieved this morning, I want to see you in my office. Do you understand?"

Hubbard did not wait for a response. He left the room, went back to his office, and pulled out a large leather binder. In all of his years at the Bureau, he had used the binder to record almost all of his daily activities. He reviewed the material at night and would transfer what was worth keeping to a program on his laptop. He intended to do the same at Pelican Bay. He knew that very detailed notes would be a must in this new position until he felt comfortable.

Hubbard took time to make a call to his wife. Over the years, no matter what investigation he was involved in, and no matter where he was, he always found time to call his wife. "Hi honey, I guess you're at the gym. I just wanted to leave a message to let you know I received the beautiful flowers you sent. That made my morning. I will call you later. I love you."

Hubbard settled behind his new desk. He looked through all the drawers and made sure they were empty. He was known at the Bureau as a neat freak; everything had its place. After checking the desk, he looked at the file cabinets. He actually looked behind them. He proceeded to check out the furniture. A funny thought crossed his mind. *Do you think anyone would bug this office?*

All the years in the FBI made him think of almost any scenario. He knew what the Bureau and the Justice Department were capable of. He just wanted to make sure. He was very qualified to find any bugs; he had planted a few in his days at the Bureau.

Hubbard was getting familiar with some procedures from the many manuals he found in the cabinets. He was also entering several new phone numbers into his cell phone. He wanted every number of anyone who would be associated with the CLEO Unit or Pelican Bay. There were locks on the desk and the cabinets. He made a note to call a locksmith; he wanted to watch them change all the locks. He decided against using the prison maintenance section. He was not paranoid. He just knew that coming into a new position he wanted to make sure his documents were secure.

A knock on the door interrupted his reading. He hollered for whoever it was to come in. The night shift lieutenant came in and stood at attention in front of Hubbard's desk. "You wanted to see me sir?"

"Yes, have a seat. What's your name, lieutenant?"

"Sir, I'm Lieutenant Jesse Wilson. I have been here at Pelican Bay for twelve years. I've been a lieutenant for the past two years. Sir, before you start, I do want to apologize for what happened this morning. Over in the main prison, when we work the night shift we get a little lax in the middle of the shift when all the inmates are locked down."

"Lieutenant, let me stop you right there. I'm not a highly trained corrections person yet. I have a lot to learn. I do know that sleeping on the job in any profession is a violation. Sleeping on the job while working in a prison should be considered a very serious violation. In the CLEO Unit, we have the most corrupt former law enforcement officers in the country. These are not nice people—many have been involved in some pretty nasty crimes. They are no different from the inmates that are in the main sections of Pelican Bay. Lieutenant, do you have a family?"

"Yes sir, I'm married and I have two boys."

"Are you the sole bread winner in your family?"

"Yes sir, I am."

Hubbard came around from his desk and told the lieutenant to have a seat. The lieutenant sat on the new leather couch and sank into it. Hubbard sat on the other end of the couch. "I don't know what they paid for this couch, but it doesn't seem to have any support for our big bodies."

Both of them laughed and for a moment it seemed to put the lieutenant at ease. "Lieutenant, I inquired about you before you came in my office. I talked to the deputy over in the main section. He said that you are one of the most experienced people here at Pelican Bay. He was surprised that you allowed two of your men to sleep while on duty. He said your record while at this institution has been nothing but exemplary. I could recommend some type of disciplinary action. For some reason, I don't think that is what I want to do. I don't think it would bode well for my first day on the job. I would rather look at it as a learning opportunity for you. How do you feel about that?"

"Sir, I'm embarrassed about what happened this morning. I guess I let my guard down a little with the men. I did not appreciate being moved from the main section where I had been a shift commander since getting promoted. I would appreciate it if you would give me a chance to prove that I am trustworthy. I assure you that I will not let you down."

"Lieutenant, for some reason I believe you. Let's forget about what I saw this morning. If you want to stay in this unit as a shift commander, I think I can live with that."

The meeting ended with Wilson talking about his kids. Hubbard talked about his family and his time with the Bureau. He wished the lieutenant well, and told him that he looked forward to working with him.

Chapter 7

Deputy Warden Hubbard showed up for the morning meeting in Warden Scope's office. After coffee, they sat at the very large conference table along with Carla and Scope's top assistant, Marcus Dent. They were preparing for a teleconference from Washington with Assistant Attorney General John Thompson. Dent had been the assistant to Scope for about one year. He was known to be tough. Some supervisors felt that Dent made most of the decisions coming out of the warden's office.

Hubbard knew John Thompson from their days in Washington. They had worked some high-level investigations when Hubbard was with the Bureau. The meeting agenda called for both Scope and Hubbard to brief Thompson on the delivery of the CLEO inmates, the facility they would be housed in, the staffing of guards, selecting supervisors, and some time would be allotted at the end of the agenda for open discussion. Noticeably on the agenda at the bottom was the word – CONFIDENTAL.

The meeting started on time; this was a trait of Thompson. He was well-respected at the Justice Department, or depending on who you talked to, more feared than respected. It had been rumored that he could possibly be appointed attorney general in the near future. Thompson started the meeting by thanking Warden Scope for all his help in the smooth transfer of the inmates to the CLEO Unit. He thanked Hubbard for taking the new assignment. He kidded Hubbard about leaving his wife back in Washington. "Don't get to comfortable on the West Coast... Donna is a very attractive young lady. She might just find a young agent from the Bureau to keep her company."

"I don't think I have anything to worry about. Most of the younger agents were scared to death of me when I was there. I have plane privileges and could be back there in a matter of hours to kick some butt."

Thompson took on a more serious tone. "Warden Scope, I'm going to get right to the reason for this conference. First, I would like to politely ask if Carla could be excused from the rest of the meeting. What I have to say will be classified and only for you and Mike. No disrespect Carla, I'm sure you understand."

Carla got up to leave the room. "Warden, I will be right outside in case you need anything."

"Thanks, Carla. Mr. Thompson, I also have Deputy Warden Marcus Dent in the room."

"I'm sorry, Warden, but Deputy Dent will have to leave the room also."

"There is very little that goes on at Pelican Bay that Deputy Dent is not involved in."

"Warden, I'm sure Dent is your main man at the facility. You can brief him later about certain parts of this meeting."

Deputy Warden Dent did not say anything. You could tell from his expression he was not happy as he left the room.

Thompson thanked the warden and proceeded. He told them that what he had to say for the rest of the meeting would be confidential and recorded.

"Warden, I'm not sure how you run your prison. What I mean is that I don't know how you get information from the inmates to quell disturbances or just get much needed information. I do know that most prisons have a system in place to interrogate inmates. It should be no different in a prison than it is on the outside. You need to do this to find out about gangs, potential uprisings, and everyday threats. Prison life is probably the most dangerous atmosphere that I can think of."

Hubbard and Warden Scope, now alone in the room, listened intently as Thompson continued.

"The reason that I am saying this is that Mike will be tasked with attempting to get information from certain inmates in the CLEO Unit. I know that in today's world when you mention the word interrogate, some people want to associate it with torture. I am not suggesting that we are going to actually torture inmates. We are, however, going to use some methods on certain CLEO inmates that might be different. Do either of you have any questions so far?"

Scope said that he had questions, but he would save them for later. Hubbard agreed with Scope and asked Thompson to continue.

"Mike, I'm sure you're familiar with coercive techniques. I won't go into them all right now. The CIA has used this means of interrogation for many years. Very few people know them, but this type of obtaining information is covered under a law that dates back to 1983. The law is called the Human Resource Exploitation Act. It is outlined in the Human Resource Exploitation Manual. Mike, I know that you're familiar with this manual."

Hubbard looked at Scope, and with somewhat of a frown on his face, acknowledged that he was familiar with the manual.

Thompson, after getting a verbal acknowledgement from Hubbard, continued. "Warden, some of the methods used and outlined in the manual are prolonged restraints, extreme heat or cold, threats of pain, drugs, lack of food, lack of sleep, and one that is a no-no lately—water boarding. In contrast to these methods, we have also found that when certain inmates or prisoners are treated well, they may also provide information. It's a toss-up on how an individual will respond under these conditions. It's on a case-by-case basis, and that's where Mike's expertise comes into play. I hope I'm not going too fast. Are there any questions?"

Hubbard seemed to know where the conversation was headed. The warden seemed a little confused. He was, however, very attentive and taking notes. Hubbard could tell by the expressions on the warden's face that he would certainly have questions. Thompson waited for questions, and when there were none, he proceeded.

"I know that I'm laying a lot on you today, but the Justice Department needs to move quickly. Mike, we all know that running the CLEO Unit will be a daunting task that you have graciously agreed to take on. You served the FBI well, and could have gone off into the sunset. Everyone at the Justice Department is grateful to you for taking on this very important assignment. I also want to thank Warden Scope again for his assistance in setting up this unit. I know that we will need his total cooperation in the future."

Warden Scope had known about Hubbard's career with the Bureau. It was now very obvious after listening to Thompson, that Hubbard was selected for the position based on his exemplary background. Scope assured Thompson that he would provide whatever was needed to make the CLEO Unit a success.

Thompson cleared his throat and continued. "The second part of what I have to say deals with actually getting information from some inmates in the CLEO Unit. I know that the unit is just getting off the ground. Mike, you are running the unit, but I have been instructed by the attorney general to stay in constant contact with you. I have also called upon a well-respected CIA agent to come out there and work with you. This agent is one of the top interrogators at the CIA. I will tell you that he is very familiar with the Human Resource Exploitation Manual. He was one of the best at getting information in certain areas of the world when we needed him. His name is Andy Brewer. He's as tough as they come. He should be showing up out there in about a week."

Thompson went on to say that Brewer would have the title of Chief of Internal Investigations. He would not be a uniform person. He would be known around the CLEO Unit as the guy who investigates inmate violations. After a period of time, he would conduct more serious interrogations, and he would do them his way. Thompson said that he would talk more about Brewer at another time.

"The last thing I want to cover on this conference is that at first we want the CLEO inmates to feel like they are being treated well. I know they are basically kept in their cell now, but let's plan on them spending more time in the yard. I know that with all the sophisticated cameras, we will know who is buddying up with whom."

Thompson paused for a moment and jokingly asked if everyone was still awake. "I know I have given you a lot to think about. We will have more conferences and phone calls in the future to go into more precise details. I have one last thing that I almost forgot to mention. There is an inmate in the CLEO Unit that we have tremendous interest in. At one time he was a highly respected undercover cop in Camden, New Jersey. His name is Tony Spitlato. He was so good undercover that he penetrated deep into the Camden Mafia. It took him quite some time, but he was accepted and went through the ritual of being a trusted mob soldier. He was presented to the Camden Mafia by a long time member. He went through the rituals. You know, the one where he has his finger cut and the blood spilled onto a card of his patron saint. The card is then set on fire and passed around to members until it goes out. He actually took the Mafia oath of loyalty and silence; that's how well he was accepted. The problem is that he forgot he was working undercover for his police agency.

Thompson took a breath, exhaling into the phone and stated that Spitlato may have been involved in some killings of rival Mafia members. He said that Spitlato was indicted in federal court after he was heard on wiretaps discussing his involvement in several shootings. Thompson said that Spitlato was undercover for so long that he got sloppy, and probably didn't care about the phones being tapped. Thompson paused a few moments and continued.

"Mike, he's a tough guy. He thinks we at the Justice Department framed him. He has a lot of information that we need. Now, I'll stop talking and take any questions you guys have. I hope I haven't bored you to death."

There was silence in the conference room. Hubbard and Scope just sat there and looked at each other. What they had listened to for the past twenty minutes was a lot to absorb. Warden Scope motioned to Hubbard that he wanted to speak first.

"Mr. Thompson, now that I have caught my breath, let me say a few things. As the warden here at Pelican Bay, I have run a prison system that has the respect of other institutions around the country. I am sure what you have told us has been cleared at the highest level of government. I will cooperate with your plan, but I will not stand by if I feel that there are illegal things happening. Although the CLEO Unit is a separate building, it's on the grounds of Pelican Bay. I will meet with Mike on occasion, and I know he will keep me informed. I understand that this meeting was being recorded. I want to be on the record that I have concerns. Mike, it's your turn, do you have anything you want to say?"

"Thanks, warden, I too am a little surprised at some of what I have heard. John, I wish we would have had this conversation before I accepted this position. I have known you for a long time, and I think I understand what you and the folks in your department want to do. I hope that your plan goes well. If you think this Spitlato fellow was a trusted man in the Mafia, it won't be easy to get anything from him. We have fifty inmates in the CLEO Unit. I have the responsibility for all of them, not just a few that you want information from. Is there anything else we should know?"

"Thanks Mike, I know that this was sprung on you after you accepted to run the CLEO Unit. I really don't have anything else at this time. I do want to remind you that this conversation is confidential. It is not to be discussed with anyone at Pelican Bay or in the CLEO Unit, other than Andy Brewer when he arrives. Warden, you may brief your deputy. I will close this meeting by saying that getting information from Spitlato is a top priority to all of us at the Justice Department. I think that I failed to tell you that one of the murders that we think he knows about was the murder of a federal judge who was presiding over a trial of a Mafia member. The judge was gunned down when he got out of his car returning home from dinner with his wife. His wife was shot, but she has recovered. If there are no further questions, we can end this meeting. You guys have a nice day, and I'm sure we will talk again soon."

When the warden knew that the phone conference was definitely ended, he stood to leave. "Mike, I'm sure that while you were with the Bureau you were involved with some crazy investigations. How does this plan compare to the ones you've had over the years?"

"Sir, I have to say that this is up there with some others. I would have liked to been the one who told you about this plan, but I didn't know anything until this conference. I guess we will just have to see how it all plays out. I have known Thompson for a long time. For him to be so committed to getting Spitlato released, he must feel like it will work. I need to get over to the unit and read the entire folder on this Spitlato guy. I will stay in touch with you. I assure you that my unit will not do anything that will discredit you or Pelican Bay."

"Mike, I have only known you for a very short time. I plan on retiring one day from Pelican Bay. When I do, I want it to be with my honor and integrity intact. You seem like an honorable man. I hope you will do the right thing."

"Warden, I have always tried to do the right thing in my career. As you get to know me better, you will find that I'm a guy who uses a lot of quotes. I will leave you with this quote from Robert Schuler. 'Tough times never last, but tough people do.'"

CHAPTER 8

After two weeks on the job, Hubbard was finding his way to work in the morning without much assistance. He had also relied heavily on Marcia, his new administrative assistant. She had been working in the Human Resource section of the prison for several years. Warden Scope sent her over to Hubbard with high recommendations. He told him that if she didn't work out, he could hire someone from the outside. Marcia was more than working out; she briefed Hubbard on all aspects of Human Resources which kept him from reading several manuals. She was very good at what she did—she was a keeper. In a very short time the office was running smoothly.

Marcia was asked to set up times for Hubbard to interview potential supervisors for the CLEO Unit. He did not want to drag out the interview process. She told him that it was procedure within the system to post the positions on the bulletin boards and the employee website. He gave Marcia a list of people he wanted to interview. "Let's set up these people. We will worry about procedures later."

The interview process did not take very long for Hubbard to decide on some people he wanted in the unit. He asked Lieutenant Jesse Wilson to continue in the unit as the daytime shift commander. At the interview he told Wilson that he believed in second chances. "I have a good feeling about you. I read your folder. You have been a real asset here at Pelican Bay. I know you will continue to do fine work in the CLEO Unit.

Lieutenant, remember this: 'The measure of who we are is what we do with what we have.' Do you know who said that?"

"No sir, I have no idea."

"He was the most famous of all football coaches, Vince Lombardi."

Hubbard had someone else in mind that he wanted in the unit. He decided that before actually conducting an interview he would ask Warden Scope for permission. He was pleasantly surprised when he received the warden's permission. He called Sergeant Ron Sanders and asked if he would come to his office. After a short interview he asked Sanders if he would join him in the unit. "I would like to have you in this unit as a shift supervisor. I'm aware that you are on the promotion list for lieutenant. I was assured by Warden Scope that it may happen soon."

"Thank you, sir. It will be a pleasure to serve in your unit. I was hoping you would ask. I will do my best."

"Thanks. I'm sure that promotion will be forthcoming soon."

Hubbard interviewed a few more that were recommended by Warden Scope. After the interviews, he made a selection of a lieutenant who had worked at Pelican Bay for many years. He interviewed very well and impressed Hubbard. Some of his answers had a military tone to them, but that was fine with Hubbard. The lieutenant knew a lot about corrections. Hubbard would need all the help he could get in that area and this person seemed to fit that mold. "Lieutenant, the warden highly recommended you. He did, however, say that you could be a little rough with the inmates at times. What did he mean by that?"

"Sir, I have been working at Pelican Bay for many years. At times, there are inmates that need to know who's in charge. I would not say that I'm rough on them; I would say that I'm persistent, and they know it. I look at coming to this unit as a career move. I don't think you will be sorry for bringing me on board."

"I like your honesty. Welcome to the CLEO Unit Lieutenant Mandez."

With the interviews completed, Hubbard knew that he needed to attempt to interact with the inmates. He had been reading personnel jackets on as many as he could. Some were quite long and very interesting.

They all dealt with corruption in some form. That was Hubbard's wheel-house; he had worked many police corruption investigations at the Bureau.

The only other person who would be coming on board as a super-visor would be Andy Brewer. Hubbard inquired of Marcia, "Have you heard anything from Andy Brewer? He should be reporting very soon. He will handle all the internal investigations for the unit."

"I have not heard from Mr. Brewer. Do you mind if I ask you a question?"

"Marcia, you are a member of the unit and a very important one. You can ask me anything you want."

"I'm typing up the transfer orders on the people you interviewed. I see that you are bringing Lieutenant Oscar Mandez into the unit. He has quite a reputation in the main section here at Pelican Bay. The word around the prison is that he can be extremely rough with the inmates. Did you know that his nickname is…The Pincher?"

"What the hell does that mean?"

"I believe that it refers to the way he transport inmates."

"Well, I'm sure if that happens here, we will hear about it."

Hubbard went in his office and continued reading the personnel jackets. "The Pincher, that sounds absurd. What a name to be tagged with."

Chapter 9

Hubbard received a text message to call his office. "Marcia, this is Mike. What's happening?"

"I just got a couple of calls concerning one of our inmates. Mr. Thompson called from the Justice Department. He wants you to call him immediately. I also got a call from a lawyer named, Howard Gibbons. Mr. Gibbons wants to come to the prison and talk with inmate, Tony Spitlato. He said that he wants to fly in tomorrow from New Jersey. It's about an appeal that Spitlato had made to the federal appeals court."

"I'm on my way to the office. Have the shift lieutenant bring Spitlato to the bullpen in about an hour. There should be no discussion with him until I get there."

The bullpen was a small secure room that was designated to be used for talks with inmates. It was located next to Hubbard's office. There was an entrance to the bullpen directly from his office and another entrance from the cell block area.

Marcia gave the information to Lieutenant Mandez. "Lieutenant, Mr. Hubbard wants inmate Tony Spitlato brought to the bullpen in about an hour. He's on his way in. He needs to talk to him."

Hubbard arrived at his office. He immediately called Thompson at the Justice Department and was put on hold for about ten minutes. He hung up and called back. "Hello, my name is Mike Hubbard. I need to talk to Mr. Thompson as soon as possible. If you tell him whose calling, he will take my call."

Thompson got on the phone. "Mike, did I give you my secure cell phone number? You don't have to call the office. Call me direct on the cell phone."

After giving Hubbard the secure cell phone number, Thompson proceeded to tell him that Spitlato had an appeal pending with the US Federal Appeals Court in the third district. The appeal was being heard by Judge Wallace Sharper. The appeal filed by Spitlato's attorney dealt with the fact that the judge did not properly instruct the jury in his corruption trial. Thompson told Hubbard that the appeal was denied. He went on to tell him that Judge Sharper was friends with the federal judge who was murdered. He said that there is a possibility that Judge Sharper felt that Spitlato may have been involved in the murder.

"Mike, you will probably get a call from Spitlato's lawyer. His name is Howard Gibbons. Between me and you, he's about as crooked as they come. He represents the Mafia in the Camden, New Jersey, area and makes no bones about it. He was indicted a few years ago for income tax fraud but was acquitted. We think that the mob got to a couple of the jurors, but we can't prove it."

"He has already called my office," Mike said. "He wants to come here and talk to Spitlato. He said that he is flying in tomorrow. I intend to meet with Spitlato today. Is it okay if I tell him his appeal was denied?"

"I think it's a good idea for you to meet with him. Yes, it's okay to tell him about the appeal. Also tell him that his attorney is coming to the prison to go over the reason for the denial of his appeal."

Lieutenant Mandez went on the cellblock to get Spitlato. He instructed a guard to accompany him. Spitlato was in cell A12. When they approached the cell, Spitlato was reading. Mandez stood close to the cell and said, "So you must be Tony Spitlato? You don't mind if I call you Tony, do you? I think that we will be getting to know each other quite well in the future."

"I really don't give a shit what you call me. If we're going to get to know each other what should I call you?"

"You can call me Lieutenant Mandez. That will work just fine with me."

"I really don't like formality. I'll call you Mandez and you can call me Spitlato. Will that work for you Mandez?"

"That will work just fine with me. Now that we have that straight, you need to come with me. I'm sure you know the routine, back your hands through the slot to be cuffed."

Tony was a big man, at least six feet tall. His muscular build testified to all of the hours of working out in prison. Mandez was a little taller and also well built. Over the years of working in the prison, he had maintained the attitude that he would be stronger than any inmate. Tony was removed from the cell. As they started to walk, Mandez grabbed Tony behind the ear and pinched his neck.

"What the fuck are you doing, Mandez?"

"Be cool, Spitlato, it's just my way of welcoming you to the CLEO Unit. I only do this to inmates that I like."

"Well, I don't want you to like me. If I didn't have these fuckin' cuffs on, I would kick your ass."

Mandez guided Tony into the bullpen. He never let up on his neck until he placed him in a chair. Tony was furious. With the cuffs still on, there was very little he could do. Mandez removed one cuff and attached it to a steel chair. He told Tony to just sit there until Deputy Warden Hubbard arrived to talk to him. Tony insisted on knowing what was happening, but he didn't get any answers.

Mandez sat across from Tony and told the other guard that he could leave. Then Mandez got up in Tony's face. "You know what, Tony? You're just another scumbag prisoner in this unit. You might have been a big shot when you were working for the mob, but in here you're just another bad cop. You're all alike. You took an oath to protect the citizens and then decided that the other side looked better to you. People like you always get what they deserve. If I had my way, all you bastards would be doing hard labor."

"Hey, screw you Mendez. You think you're pretty tough as long as I've got these cuffs on. You don't know anything about me. I was a good cop. I did outstanding work while I was undercover. I got framed. The assholes at the Justice Department know it. They set me up to make me the fall guy for a bunch of crooked cops in Jersey. If I get a new trial, we will prove that I was framed. Don't fuck with me while I'm doing my time. You treat me right, and I'll do the same to you."

"Yeah, I guess the other forty-nine assholes in this unit will say the same thing. You were around a lot of money with the mob. You could have stayed clean, but you chose to take their dirty money. You ain't that tough Tony. You sure as hell ain't that smart either or you wouldn't be here. As far as treating you right, I'll make that call."

In the middle of their conversation, the door opened from Hubbard's office. Mandez stood and greeted Hubbard. Tony just stared at him. Hubbard took the chair that Mandez was in. He motioned for Mandez to leave the room. Mandez looked surprise. "Sir, you sure you want to be with this guy by yourself?"

"Lieutenant, I think that Mr. Spitlato and I can get along just fine. If I need you, I'll call you."

Tony smiled at Mandez as he was leaving. "It will be a pleasure talking to someone with some sense. Go find somebody else that you can pinch on the neck, you piece of shit."

Hubbard introduced himself to Tony. "I'm Mike Hubbard; I'm the Deputy Warden for the CLEO Unit. I can see that you and Lieutenant Mandez don't seem to get along very well. What's that all about?"

"He's a weird fuckin' dude. I was walking peacefully out of my cell hand-cuffed, and the guy grabs me. While I'm cuffed, he pinches me on the neck around my ear. I don't think that shit is necessary, especially when you're cuffed and cooperating. You need to talk to that guy before someone gets hurt. If he didn't have that gun and badge, I'd kick his ass all over the cellblock."

"I appreciate the input, and I will check into it. If I take the cuffs off the chair, will we have any problems?"

"No, you won't have any problems with me. In case you haven't noticed, we are in what appears to be a very secure room with cameras. On the outside of this room, I'm sure there are guards that would love to beat the shit out of me. Warden, I know the ropes in prison. I was in a pretty tough one before I came here. If you take these cuffs off, I can assure you that we can have a decent talk."

Hubbard grinned approvingly at Tony. He took the cuff off that was attached to the chair. He started the conversation by asking about the prison that Tony came from. He told Tony that he read his personnel folder, and felt like he knew a lot about him, as the folder was quite thick. He told him he was a former FBI agent and had worked many investigations on corruption in law enforcement. Tony listened as he slouched down in the chair. Being out of the cell to Tony was a treat. He wanted to stretch it out. The chair actually felt good; there were no chairs in the cells, just the steel bunk with the paper thin mattress.

As Hubbard talked, Tony wondered what the meeting would be about. Surely, the guy in charge didn't just want to have a casual sit-down with one of his inmates. Although Tony was a convicted felon, he had been a pretty good cop at one time. He knew that Hubbard was setting the table, doing basic 101 interviewing techniques. Engage the person in small talk and get him to feel at ease. Throw out some key phrases and hope that there is a reaction. If there is a reaction, you know you hit a sweet spot. Listen attentively, nodding your head in agreement when necessary. Try not to take notes that look to official. Notes can always be made later when the talk is over.

Tony knew all these techniques. He also knew that he was up against a formidable foe. He knew that Warden Hubbard, having been with the FBI, obviously had received training in the field of interrogation and interviewing. You don't put thirty some years with the FBI and not come away with an expertise in those areas. Tony surmised that Hubbard was obviously a well-respected FBI agent. If not, he would not have been chosen to run the CLEO Unit.

This first meeting of two cops…one who is straight and one who is crooked, could be a complete standoff. Each person would listen and then through their prior training, try to decipher the material and have a response. The meeting could go on for quite a while. Maybe the talks would have to be continued for either one to feel they had the edge.

Hubbard talked for about twenty minutes. He wasn't telling Tony anything he did not already know. He talked about Tony's background. He talked about his family or at least the family he used to have before prison. Hubbard knew when to stop and pause by the body language coming from Tony. His training told him that looking up at the ceiling, folding his arms on his chest, gritting his teeth, and fidgeting in the chair, were signs that Tony was bored. Hubbard paused for a few minutes. He wanted Tony to jump in; he had been talking to long.

"Tony, after all this talking by me, tell me something about yourself that I don't know."

"Well Mike, you pretty much covered a lot about me. You did miss one very important thing. I'm not guilty of any of the charges that the Justice Department trumped up against me. I worked undercover in the mob. I was good at what I did. At my trial, the prosecutor even told the jury that I had infiltrated the mob better than anyone had ever attempted. He told them that the information that I provided while working undercover was all that was needed in the prosecution of several mobsters. So I guess my reward for being so good was to be charged with crimes under the infamous RICO Act."

Tony felt at ease with Hubbard. He even stretched out and put his leg up on the table. He waited for Hubbard to tell him to take his leg off the table, but that didn't happen.

"Mike, you know as a former agent that I had to completely play the game with the mob, or I would have been wacked. I lived and breathed working undercover. It was a twenty-four hour a day, seven days a week job. I could not even see my family for over eight months unless I secretly met them at a location out of the state of New Jersey. It cost me my marriage. I thought I could keep it together, but when all those lies came out at the trial, she filed for divorce. I have two kids that I have not seen for over two years. I was a good cop. I took the undercover assignment thinking that it would further my career in law enforcement. It destroyed my life and put me in this place, whatever the hell it's called. Mike, before I go any further, can you tell me why there are fifty former law enforcement guys in this damn place? What the hell is going on? Who named this unit the CLEO Unit, and what the hell does that mean?"

"Tony, you were convicted of corruption under the RICO act. You already know that. There are fifty inmates in this unit because the Justice Department has decided to have one corrupt law enforcement officer from each state confined to this unit. You all are alleged to be the worst of the worst as far as corrupt cops go. Pelican Bay was picked because of its location and security. The building you are in is new. The unit was named by the Justice Department. Get used to it. CLEO stands for Corrupt Law Enforcement Officers. You know how things work in law enforcement; everything has to have a catchy tag.

Tony laughed and for a while, he felt a connection with Hubbard, but he knew connections with prison officials didn't last.

Hubbard smiled at Tony and then got serious. "When I was with the Bureau we had names for investigations and programs that sounded downright silly. What difference does it make to you what the unit is called. You are going to be here for a long time, so live with it and co-operate. It will be a whole lot easier for you if you go along with the program here."

Tony sensed that Hubbard was now in a serious mode. "Now, before we go any further I need to let you know that we were informed that your appeal to the US Court of Appeals before Judge Wallace Sharper has been denied. I also got word that your attorney, Howard Gibbons is on his way to see you. He will probably be here sometime tomorrow. He has informed our office that we could break that news to you. I'm sure you have been waiting for some time for the decision."

"I'm not surprised about the decision. I had no real hope that the appeal would be granted. I don't know Judge Sharper. He's a federal judge, so I guess they take care of their own. I'm sure you know that the goons in the Justice Department think I had something to do with the murder of that other judge in Camden. If they had their way, they would pin the Lincoln assassination on me.

Tony pushed his chair back and stood. He was surprised that Hubbard didn't react. "Mike, you seem like a decent guy. I want you to know that I will not cooperate with any questioning about murders or anything else they think I did. I'll do my time. Nobody is going to fuck over me. For the short time I have been in this place, the guys on that tier look up to me. I don't plan to organize any clicks while I'm here. You have fifty former cops that are bitter about being convicted of corruption. Fifty might not be a big number, but you can't keep human beings in cages all the time. I'm not a spokesman for the inmates, but I have your ear now. If you want peace and tranquility while you're in command, think about letting these guys out in the yard more, allow them to communicate, and also have some type of recreation. What the hell harm would it do if we were out of our cells more during the day? This place seems pretty secure. Hell, there ain't any windows in the cells. As far as I can tell, there is only one exit from the tier. Other than going in the yard, the only exit is gained by going through the guard station, which is built like a damn fortress."

"Tony, your observations of the unit are very impressive. I'll also take into consideration what you said about having peace on the tier. Let me tell you something, I'm not a screamer. I have a sign that has been on my desk in every place I have been a supervisor. It's a simple little plaque that says, *Do Not Mistake Kindness as Weakness.*"

Hubbard stood and reached out to shake hands with Tony. "I think we had a very informative talk. I know you are in no real hurry to get back to your cell. It has been nice chatting with you. You will be allowed some time with your attorney when he shows up."

"Yeah, I want to get back to the cell in time for that slop you call food to be served. I like you, Mike. I hope it stays that way. I don't know if I can be a model inmate. It depends on how we are treated in your silly named unit."

"Let me end our meeting with a quote. Tony, you will find that I love to use quotes."

"Is this the one about—if you can't do the time, don't do the crime."

"No, but that's a good one to remember. My quote goes like this… 'The brave man is not he who does not feel afraid, but he who conquers that fear.' Do you know who said that?"

"Yeah, you just did."

"No, Tony, that was a very brave man who did what you claim you are doing now. He was falsely imprisoned for a significant part of his life. He believed in something and would not waiver. That man was Nelson Mandela."

"Well then, Mike, me and Nelson got something in common. It seems like we were both imprisoned for something we didn't do. Have a nice day. I'll be heading back to the CLEO Unit. I'm starting to like that name. I think I banged a girl back in Camden name Cleo."

Hubbard laughed as Tony was directed back through the door to the tier. He went to his office and made notes on as much as he could remember from the talk with Spitlato. Even though the meeting was recorded and videoed, he had the habit of always making his own notes and observations. His notes concluded with stating that Spitlato would not be someone easily convinced to give information unless there was something in it for him. He also noted that because of Spitlato's law enforcement background, he knew all the tricks of the trade. He had been a cop a long time. He was street-smart. Although convicted on overwhelming evidence in federal court, he would maintain his innocence; the type of guy who believed if he said it long enough, maybe someone would believe him.

Hubbard ended his notes by writing that Spitlato would be a key player in the CLEO Unit. He was tough, loud, knowledgeable, charismatic, and could be nasty.

Hubbard's last sentence in his notes, read; in a different place and under different circumstances, I could like that guy.

CHAPTER 10

M arcia answered a phone call from the front gate. Andy Brewer had arrived. She asked the guard to have him escorted to Hubbard's office. She buzzed Hubbard's conference room and interrupted a meeting with the prison medical staff. Hubbard was working on a plan that would have the medical staff respond to the CLEO Unit for routine examinations, instead of transporting inmates over to the prison hospital. The plan included responses for medical emergencies in the unit. The original construction of the CLEO building included space for such needs.

Hubbard answered Marcia and told her to have Brewer relax in his office until he was clear of the meeting.

Brewer was taking in all the sights on his way to meet Hubbard. He had been in prisons in different locations around the world. Pelican Bay looked light a resort compared to the prisons in Iraq, Afghanistan, and Mexico. Brewer was a highly motivated individual. He loved a challenge, he was just not sure what to expect on this assignment.

When he entered Hubbard's office, Marcia greeted him and offered him coffee. She was immediately struck by how well dressed he was and that he appeared to be in great shape. He sat with his coffee and asked no questions. Marcia tried to make him feel at ease. "Mr. Brewer, I'm Marcia, Deputy Warden Hubbard's administrative assistant. While you're waiting, can I answer any questions about Pelican Bay? Will your family be joining you later?"

"Thanks, Marcia, I'm single. I won't have any family coming out here. I have read a lot about Pelican Bay. I was impressed with this facility as I was escorted up to the office. As far as the CLEO Unit, I'm sure Deputy Hubbard will fill me in."

Brewer waited for about fifteen minutes for Hubbard. He read from some material he pulled from his briefcase.

"You must be Andy Brewer? I'm Mike Hubbard. It's a pleasure to finally meet you. I've heard a lot about you. Sorry for making you wait. We are all new at this, and I'm trying to get things done as quickly as possible. I have never worked in a prison, so I'm kind of flying by the seat of my pants. Can I get you anything before we talk?"

"No thanks. I had a coffee. Marcia has been very cordial to me. I'm ready to discuss my new job."

Hubbard directed Brewer to the conference room. He was also looking him over. Although they were both federal agents in their careers, the FBI and the CIA never really got along. It was always like pulling teeth to have either agency share any intelligence with the other. In many investigations in the U.S. and abroad, they sometimes crossed paths. The FBI on occasion claimed that the CIA was too secretive, and the CIA often claimed that the FBI got involved in areas that they didn't have the expertise. It was well known within each agency that sharing information would only be done by an order from a supervisor.

"Andy, I have read your personnel folder. I'm very impressed. You have had quite a career in the CIA. I'm sure you know that I'm retired from the FBI. I know our agencies have not really gotten along over the years."

"I know, and that's too bad. We were both working for the same government. I know it goes back a long way with both agencies. I personally never had any bad experiences with the Bureau. Whenever I needed something, I always got total cooperation."

"That's great to hear. I can pretty much say the same thing. When I was a supervisor in the D.C. area, I frequently attended meetings at Langley. I'm glad we are both now on the same page. We will be working very close. We need to have the utmost trust and respect for each other. I know that you have talked to Thompson at the Justice Department. I won't beat around the bush about what your job will be here in the CLEO Unit. I do have a few things I would like to talk about."

Hubbard opened a folder and flipped through some papers. He asked Brewer if he minded if they could discuss a few issues. Brewer gave the okay and Hubbard proceeded.

"In your personnel jacket, I read that you and other members of the CIA were reprimanded for some action at the Abu Ghraib prison in Iraq a couple of years ago. I'm familiar with what happened at that prison, but most of what I know I got from the media coverage. I'm sure you were cleared of any involvement, or you would not be here today. I know that in your new assignment you will be interviewing, or should I say, interrogating, our inmates. I will not be participating in that activity. Thompson was very clear that you would be in charge of that phase with some of the inmates in this unit. I do want to make you aware that this entire facility has very sophisticated cameras and listening devices. I'm aware that some of what you want to get from certain inmates might take some form of coercion. I will cooperate with you to some extent. I just want to be clear that I intend to keep my record clean by running a model unit. I know that these inmates are the worst of the corrupt law enforcement officers from around the country. I guess what I want to get across is that we will not have anything like Abu Ghraib while I'm in charge."

"Mr. Hubbard, I'm a professional, and I have been briefed by Mr. Thompson. I understand what he wants me to do while I'm here. The situation that occurred at Abu Ghraib is very different than the mission here in your unit. Most of the violations that occurred at Abu Ghraib were committed by the military police battalion. The violations had been going on for a long time. Many soldiers were charged with misconduct under the Uniform Code of Military Justice. Several of those soldiers were sentenced to prison, and some received dishonorable discharges. I'm not sure who was at fault at that prison. Were the soldiers just doing what they were told to do? Some have testified that the Justice Department sanctioned the torture, calling it enhanced interrogation techniques."

Hubbard sensed that Brewer was making a case that he had nothing to do with the torture at that prison. He stopped Brewer and told him that he merely wanted to bring it up because it was mentioned in his folder. He assured Brewer that he was not accusing him of any involvement at that prison. He asked Brewer to continue.

"I am aware that they used a medieval method of torture called strappado. This form of torture is when the inmate's hands are tied behind his back, and he is suspended in air by a rope attached to his wrists. Most of the information I have is contained in a very lengthy report conducted by the CIA."

"Andy, I'm sure you know that what happened at Abu Ghraib was a black mark on our country. I don't have all the information that you have, but I have seen the photos that were released. As a member of a federal law enforcement agency, I was appalled and embarrassed when they came out. I do know that a lot of low-level soldiers took the brunt of the discipline. It seems that the big brass is always protected in these cases. I'm sure you know that in cases like this, they use what is called qualified immunity. It protects certain government officials from liability. The law states that if they did not violate clearly established law, they cannot be charged with a crime. It's bullshit, but most people will never hear about it. I guess we will never really know who gave the orders to torture those inmates at that prison. Hell, for all we know it could have come directly from the White House."

The meeting dragged on for a long time. Hubbard was laying the ground work for what he expected from Brewer, although he knew that Brewer already had some direction from Thompson. His main reason for drawing the conversation out so long about Abu Ghraib was that he knew Brewer was there and probably knew firsthand about the torture. In the personnel jacket he read on Brewer, he saw that he was trained at the CIA Counterintelligence School. Listed in the section on training, he noticed that Brewer taught a course titled, The CIA's No Touch Torture Methods. If he had been involved in the torture of inmates at Abu Ghraib, he was putting on a good show to dispel any involvement. A good show was what CIA agents were capable of. They are sent all over the world, and one of the main characteristics of a CIA agent was to be deceitful. Hubbard had been around for a long time. He prided himself in judging people.

"Well, Andy, we have talked a lot for our first meeting. I will have someone show you around the unit. I trust that you have made accommodations for housing. If not, we can assist you. Also, there are some routine human resources procedures that need to be addressed. You will need certain badges to get into the facility. I have a spot picked out for your office. Take your time getting situated. If you need assistance, Marcia is available."

"Mike, I can probably be ready to go in a couple of days. Let me say one thing before we end this meeting. I have talked at length with Mr. Thompson in the Justice Department. He knows my background. He could have picked any number of CIA agents for this assignment. I think he chose me because I have a knack for getting information from prisoners, whether they are terrorists or bad cops. I don't always go by the book. Terrorist and bad cops don't play by any rules. They are behind bars for a reason. They are tough, and if they see any sign of weakness from an interrogator, they will play him for a fool. I don't intend to be played for a fool by anybody. I have received some information on a few of your inmates, and I will concentrate on them."

Just as Hubbard was standing to shake hands with Brewer, a security horn in the yard went off. Hubbard was not exactly sure what the horn meant. He went to the guard station and saw the inmates on the ground in the yard. They had been instructed to drop to the ground in the prone position when the horn sounded. Inmates not following that rule would be placed in confinement. If the fight or disturbance continued, the guards were instructed to fire pellet rounds from their shotguns. Hubbard called the guard tower above the yard. He was informed that a fight did break out. The combatants were identified as

Bernard Wells, Louie Tusta, and Tony Spitlato. The guard was not sure what it was about. The three men were placed in separate holding rooms to cool down.

Hubbard returned to his office and found that Brewer was still there. "Well, this is the first incident I've had since the unit opened."

Brewer walked toward the door. He turned facing Hubbard and with a slight grin, he said, "I hope it's not me showing up that got them excited. I overheard the names given to you. The Spitlato guy is one that the Justice Department is really interested in."

Chapter 11

"Let me introduce myself, Mr. Hubbard, I'm Howard Gibbons. I'm here to talk to my client, Tony Spitlato. I have cleared the appointment with Mr. Thompson at the Justice Department. I hope he told you that he has given me the approval to speak with my client. I would appreciate talking to him someplace private. I'm sure you are aware that the U.S. Court of Appeals for the third district in New Jersey has turned down his appeal. We were expecting that. The honorable Judge Wallace Sharper did not see fit to allow us to show that Tony was framed by his government. I use the word honorable very loosely when I talk about Judge Sharper. If they think Tony's a crook, they should be checking on Sharper. The guy lives too high of a lifestyle to be doing it on his salary. Hell, the guys got a mansion on Cape Cod, a yacht, two or three high dollar cars in his driveway, and wines and dines at the finest places. Mr. Hubbard, I'm not sure if you know about Sharper. He's a disgrace to the dysfunctional justice system we have."

"Mr. Gibbons, I do know Judge Sharper. I find it hard to believe that he is anything but an outstanding member of the court of appeals. I really don't want to discuss him with you. If you're here to talk to Tony Spitlato, that might be a problem. Prior to your arrival, Tony was involved in a serious violation, an altercation in the yard. He's in isolation at this time. I will give you my card and will call you when you can talk with him."

"Mr. Hubbard, I did not come all the way to the West Coast to be turned away. I told you that Thompson gave the okay for me to talk to him. I will call Thompson; I need to get this done now. I hate to go over your head. I also hate to keep calling you Mr. Hubbard. Can I call you Mike?"

"Yes, feel free to call me Mike. Call Thompson if you like, but for now I have work to do. I need to have my people talk to Spitlato and the others involved in the altercation. Violations like this need to be nipped in the bud. I want this unit to run smoothly. If you get through to Thompson, let me know, but for now, I have to excuse myself. I will ask Marcia to make sure you get back to the front gate."

Gibbons half-heartedly thanked Hubbard as he left with Marcia. He tried to get through to the Justice Department on his cell phone but was not successful. He decided to get settled in at his hotel and try to reach Thompson later.

As Hubbard was doing some paper work, he stopped and pondered why Thompson would be talking with Tony's lawyer. Gibbons seemed very sure that he would get the okay to talk to Tony. Was Thompson holding something back? Gibbons was a lawyer that was known to be mob connected. The Justice Department knows all the players in the New Jersey mob. They surely know that every time a mob figure is arrested, Gibbons gets involved. For him to come all the way out to the West Coast, without being assured that I would let him talk to Spitlato, is strange. If he only wanted to let him know about the court turning him down, he could do that over the phone. There has to be more to it.

Andy Brewer came into Hubbard's office. "Mike, I would like to get in there and talk to those involved in the fight. It would be a good time to let the unit know that we will not tolerate such violations. I have asked Lieutenant Mandez to sit in with me. I hope you don't mind."

"Mandez? He's just a prison guard. He's not trained to interrogate people. Andy, you need to discuss things like this with me. I think I told you when we met that I don't like surprises. I can get someone to assist you. Let's not start off on the wrong foot."

"Mike, I know you're in charge of the unit. I was sent here to get information from some of these inmates. When Thompson asked me to take this assignment, he clearly told me that I would have a free hand in talking to whomever I wanted to. I'm not sure how much he told you about my mission here. I'm a little confused."

"I don't think there should be any confusion. I'm in charge of the CLEO Unit. Unless I'm told different, you work for me."

Brewer stood there in silence. He watched Hubbard go back to his desk and pick up the phone. "Let me get Thompson on the phone. We can clear up exactly what your position will be here in my unit."

"Mike, can you put the phone down for a minute. I think I can clear up some things without you making a call. First of all, I talked to Thompson this morning. I have the approval to use Mandez. I guess I was just assuming that you had the same talk with him that I had. My job is to get information from Spitlato and a few others that have big time Mafia connections. Unless I misunderstood what Thompson and others at the Justice Department told me, I can use whatever method I need to get the information. Spitlato has a ton of information about the New Jersey mob. He absolutely turned on his agency. If people didn't know he had been in law enforcement, they would think that he was a born and raised Mafia guy. He participated in beatings, shootings, and may have murdered a federal judge."

Hubbard gave Brewer a look of disbelief. He moved closer to him and just shook his head. He wanted to put Brewer in his place, but he could not come up with the right words. He moved behind his desk and picked up the phone.

"If you get through to Thompson, I would like to be in the room when you talk. If I have the wrong direction on my assignment I want to hear it from him. If I'm correct on what I was told, I want you to hear it. In the meantime, Mandez and I are going in to talk with Spitlato."

"You know what, Brewer, I have been around a long time. I honestly don't believe you would talk to me like that if you were not telling the truth. I took this job because I was told I was the best man for it.

Knowing how the Justice Department works, I don't doubt that you were told something that I was not. For you to stand there and tell me you are going over my head would either take a goddamn fool, or you're telling the truth. Either way, we will have a conversation with John Thompson. Maybe in the excitement of accepting this job, I missed something, but I don't think so. Nevertheless, go ahead with talking to those guys. I will set up a conference with Thompson and others at the Justice Department. Depending on what I am told, my stay as deputy warden may be short lived."

Brewer used the phone on the conference table and called the tier to have Spitlato taken to the smaller interview room. Brewer opened the door, and Mandez was standing there. He did not have his uniform on. When he walked past Hubbard, he didn't even look his way. Brewer and Mandez went through the outer door which led to the interview room.

When the two of them left his office, Hubbard could not wait to make the call to the Justice Department. He was thinking how smooth things had run when he was with the Bureau. In all his years there he had never had anyone talk to him like Brewer did. *I'm out here on the West Coast about as far away from my former life as I could be. My main support person is at home trying to sell the great house we had. I'm spending about fourteen hours a day in this place. I'm trying to learn on the fly how to run a prison.*

"Mr. Hubbard, you have a call from the Justice Department."

Hubbard thanked Marcia and told her that he did not want to be disturbed for the next thirty minutes. He locked the door to the office, and also the door leading to the tier. He had the equipment that allowed him to record phone calls. He thought it was going to be Thompson, but it was Thompson's assistant, Pat Driscoll. He knew who he was talking to because they had crossed paths while working investigations between the Bureau and the Justice Department. He knew Driscoll well and wanted to hear his take on what was expected from him at the CLEO Unit.

He knew that Driscoll was on top of everything at the Justice Department. He was a single guy who probably spent eighty hours or more a week at work. He was a bulldog when it came to high level investigations. Hubbard asked all the cordial questions, even though he knew most of the answers. Driscoll had no family in Washington, he was from Iowa, he hardly ever socialized, and his idea of fun was to jog to work from his midtown condo. He was in great shape, and along with the three mile run to work, he frequently worked out in the gym at the Justice Department.

After exchanging some small talk, Hubbard flipped on the recorder. When he flipped it on, he knew from his experience that a recorder was also being flipped on at the other end. Both men, being federal agents, were well aware that recording someone was a crime under the D.C. laws. You had to have permission to record a conversation on the phone. Both used the device not so much that they did not trust each other; it was to make sure they were clear on what was being said. Taking notes was distracting and did not lend itself to being a good listener.

Driscoll started by congratulating Hubbard on getting the position to run the CLEO Unit. "Mike, I'm sure you are missed at the Bureau. I think it was very noble of you to take the assignment. I know about the mission at the unit, and you are the right man for the job. I'm sure Donna was against it. I know how much she was looking forward to your retirement and traveling. We can discuss whatever you want to for a few minutes, and John will join us shortly."

"Thanks, Pat, for the kind words. I'm not really sure I'm the right man for this job. I accepted it based on what John and others in your department told me. I'm not throwing in the towel, but I need to get some things straight with Thompson. What do you know about this Brewer guy they sent here?"

"I'll let John answer that. He is joining us on the phone now."

"Hi, Mike, I'm glad that you called. I guess you and Pat have been catching up on some of the old cases you both worked? I think I know why you called. I'm sorry that Brewer came on so strong. As you know or will find out, he is wired. He puts the Energizer Bunny to shame. Let me make a few things clear while I have you on the phone. You were selected to run the CLEO Unit because as I told you before, you are the best man for that job. You have some pretty bad people in that unit. Some still have ties to the mob. Some have ties to organized crime in the states they came from. Brewer was picked because he is good at what he does. He has a list of inmates in that unit that have information that can be very beneficial in stopping mob corruption in several states."

Hubbard was rolling his eyes; he had heard the accolades before. Was Thompson just throwing out some niceties to soften the blow that Brewer had thrown? Thompson told Hubbard again that he was picked from several people for the position.

"You and Brewer are about as opposite as they come. You are the boss and will oversee the unit. Brewer will handle getting whatever information he can get. Some of his tactics will be questioned by the inmates and their attorneys. I'm not concerned with any feedback I get from inmates or attorneys. My concern is to get as much information as fast as we can. Brewer is the guy that can do it."

"John, let me interrupt you for a minute. I wish I knew about Brewer before I took the job. I have already had a run in with him. He appears to be someone who will do things his way. I don't have a problem with getting information from these inmates. I do have a problem with his tactics possibly getting out to the media."

"Mike, I appreciate your concern. I will talk to Brewer and make sure he understands you are in charge of that unit. I will tell you that he does have approval to conduct the interrogation of those inmates identified that we believe can help us. I really have to run to another meeting. Call me anytime, or you can call Pat. He's fully aware of what we are trying to do."

The phone conversation ended. Both parties turned off their recording devices. Hubbard detached his from the phone and placed it in his briefcase. He wanted to play it back later in the privacy of his home. He was a little concerned that the talk ended so quickly.

Thompson slid back in his leather chair. After the talk with Hubbard, he instructed Driscoll to make a call.

"Hi, Andy, this is John. I just got off the phone with Hubbard. You need to slow down a little. We don't want to piss him off so soon. You still have the same orders, but just try to be more respectful to him. Your job is to get information from those assholes any way you see fit. I hope you're starting with Tony Spitlato. He's tough, but I think you are tougher. If you have any problems with Hubbard, call me. I'm starting to wonder if he is the right guy for that job. If he gets in the way too much, we might have to remove him. If you need anything, go through Pat. I think it is best that you and I don't talk so much on the phone. Hubbard's a good man, but he will not get in the way of what we are trying to do; it's too important."

CHAPTER 12

Shortly after 8 a.m., Howard Gibbons walked into Hubbard's office. He had told the guards that he had a scheduled appointment with Hubbard and they escorted him to the office. Marcia was not at work yet, but Hubbard was. "Is that you Marcia? You are early today."

"No, Mr. Hubbard, it's Howard Gibbons. I hope I didn't startle you, but the guard escorted me to your office. I told them I had an appointment with you. You don't mind if I tell a little lie, do you? I'm sure you know that lawyers will do most anything to get their way."

"Mr. Gibbons, I certainly do mind. Most lawyers I have dealt with have been upstanding people; maybe you should try it. Now, before I have the guards escort you out to the gate, what is it that you want?"

"I just want to get an early start and talk to my client. I need to be back in New Jersey later today to prepare for a trial. I apologize for my tactics this morning. I hope you don't hold the guard at the gate responsible; he was just trying to be accommodating."

Hubbard was upset at Gibbons, but he figured that the best way to get rid of him was to let him talk to Spitlato and get the meeting over with. He called the guard station and told the shift lieutenant to put Spitlato in the small conference room as soon as possible. He told Gibbons that he would allow him to talk to his client, but if he tried any of his so-called tactics in the future, he would not get the same results.

Hubbard motioned for Gibbons to have a seat. "When your client is in the conference room, I will let you know. You will have thirty minutes to talk to him and then you can start your journey back to New Jersey."

Hubbard started to do some paper work. He glanced up occasionally to see Gibbons smiling at him. "Mr. Gibbons, can I ask you a question?"

"Yes, but if you're looking for legal advice, I have to warn you that you will get a bill for my service. I'm kidding, of course. Ask me anything you want."

"How well do you know John Thompson at the Justice Department?"

Gibbons looked surprised, as if he were taken aback by the question. "I know him from some cases he prosecuted before he got the big job. We are not friends if that is what you're getting at. I think that he would try to go after me if he could. I make no bones about the fact that I represent some questionable characters in the New Jersey area."

Hubbard put his papers down and directed his attention to Gibbons. He was hoping that he would hear about some connection between Thompson and Gibbons.

"To be frank with you, Mr. Hubbard, I think he's power hungry. He rose pretty fast to the position that he holds at the Justice Department. He either knows someone in high places, or he's got some compromising photos of the attorney general. I think it's a little of both. I'm sure you are aware that some of his investigative strategies have been questioned in the past. He makes more deals with convicts than anyone I can remember. I think he promises them anything for their testimony against co-conspirators. He is very good at intimidating witnesses to the point that a couple of them have committed suicide."

Gibbons paused and asked Hubbard if he wanted to hear more. Hubbard said nothing, but held out his hand and made a motion that indicated that he wanted Gibbons to continue.

"I know that they love him at the Justice Department, but I think he is an accident waiting to happen. I didn't mean to go on so long with my response. Does that answer your question?"

"Yes, that more than answers my question. I was just wondering if you knew him on a personal side. You had mentioned earlier that you talked to him, and he gave you the green light to come here. You also said that if you had to, you would call him. It appeared to me that you were friendlier with him than what you just told me. So basically your relationship with Thompson has been professional, is that correct?"

"Yes, I would say that. Now if you don't mind, I would really appreciate it if I can talk to my client. I would love to chat with you some more, but I'm on a tight schedule. Can you see if he is ready for me?"

Hubbard called the guard station and was informed that Spitlato was in the conference room. He asked the guard to come to his office and escort Gibbons to the room. Gibbons thanked Hubbard for his hospitality and told him that if he ever got to Camden, he would buy him dinner.

The guard showed Gibbons to the conference room.

"What the fuck happened to your face, Tony?"

"Well, Howard, you see there was a little fight in the yard. Nothing big, just a disagreement between a few guys—you know how that shit works. Well, after the fight I was placed in confinement. A couple of other guys were sent to confinement, also. You would have thought I did something really bad. Later, two guys, I'm assuming they were prison officials take me in this room and start breaking bad with me. While I was cuffed to the chair, the one they call The Pincher, smacks me in the face. You know me, Howard; I swung the chair across the table and hit both of them. That's when they got pissed and commenced to punch me. It's no big deal. I'm used to that treatment. I'm sure there will be more."

"You look like shit, Tony. Do you want me to take some photos and make a formal complaint to the warden?"

"Nah, let this one slide. I'll let you know when to make a formal complaint. I would just like to get my hands on either one of them without the damn cuffs on. They wouldn't know what happened to them after this wop got done with them."

"Tony, I'm sorry your stay in this stupid unit has gotten off to a bad start. I kind of knew they would be coming after you. Hang in there. We are working all angles to get you out of here. You do know that your appeal was denied?"

Gibbons motioned to Tony to look up in the corner of the room. He put a finger up to his lips motioning Tony not to say anything. Gibbons pulled a piece of paper out of his suit coat. He handed it to Tony. He leaned across the table and whispered, "Read this note, Tony. They are recording our meeting."

Tony opened the note and turned his back away from the area where he thought the video was taping. Gibbons kept talking while Tony read the note, not saying anything relative, just talking, and knowing that the video and recorder were running. Tony read the note.

Tony,

I put this on paper because they are listening to what we say.

We are working real hard to get you out. The fellows back in Camden send their love. They know it won't be easy for you in this place. Several angles are being looked at. We will be putting pressure on some prominent people real soon.

When we get you out, you will be rewarded for all that you have done for us. Hang in there.

Tony winked at Gibbons and passed the note back to him. Gibbons put the note into his coat pocket. He continued talking loud on purpose, playing to the recorder and video. "Tony, it's great to see you. I wish it was under different circumstances. I wish we were back in New Jersey, eating at your favorite place and knocking down some fine wine. Everybody misses you and sends their best."

"Thanks for reminding me of the great food back in Camden. If only I could be sitting at my table at Carlo's, feasting on shrimp scampi with that special sauce that only Carlo can make. A nice bottle of my favorite red wine would be heaven right about now. I guess for now I have to settle for Italian night here in this shit-house. I had something they called Italian the other night. I almost puked it up. What they served makes a can of Chef Boyardee look like a luxury Italian meal. I think Emeril Lagasse would shoot the fuckin' chef at this place if he visited their kitchen."

Tony rubbed his belly as if the talk about a good Italian meal was being digested.

"Damn, Howard, you got me thinking about the good old days. Maybe the next time you come, you can sneak in a bottle of Ruffino Chianti. I remember the first time I drank Ruffino Chianti; I killed the whole bottle in about ten minutes. Carlo came over to the table and told me the bottle cost a hundred and twenty-five dollars. I almost shit myself when he told me the price. Hell, when I was a cop in Camden, I drank wine that cost no more than five bucks."

"Sorry that I brought up food and wine, Tony. I know it must be horrible in this joint. You're a great guy. We will do whatever it takes to get you back to Camden. You sure you don't want me to make a complaint about those assholes that smacked you around?"

"No, it will all work itself out. Thanks for coming. Keep working hard to get me out of this shithouse. I hate being in here for something I didn't do."

Chapter 13

Tony was sitting in his cell thinking about what his attorney had told him. Although he would always maintain his innocence, he also hoped that the mob back in New Jersey would do whatever they could to get him out. Even though it all came out in the testimony at the trial about Tony being a good undercover cop, it was also made very clear that he liked the mob better than being a cop.

The reports he submitted back to his department while undercover, on mob activities, were extremely valuable. Over time working undercover, the reporting started to become very vague. His supervisors in the police department were concerned that he was holding out on some activities of the mob. It became apparent to his supervisors that something was going on in Tony's personal life. When questioned, he made up stories just to appease his bosses. He started to be extremely late on reports that he was supposed to submit on a weekly basis. When he first started undercover in the mob he was very thorough in reporting; the reports were always on time. But as time went by, they became vague, with little if any information on mob activities.

When he did report to his police supervisors, he used a computer at the public library and always deleted the report after sending it. As time went by on the undercover assignment, Tony felt that something might go wrong, so he started to transfer the reports to a disk before he deleted them. He kept the disk in a safe deposit box at his bank. He knew that if anything went wrong, his police bosses would probably not back him up. It was a save your own ass mentally in the police department.

Before going undercover in the Camden mob, Tony worked in the narcotics unit. He was one of the top guys in the unit. It seemed like working drugs came natural to him. He made undercover drug buys in areas that no one else could. After a period of time in the unit, he questioned if some of the drug detectives were playing by the rules. He had been on drug raids where he believed that some of the detectives had planted drugs. He knew that some of the search warrants were just out-and-out lies, anything to get a judge to sign them. In the drug unit there seemed to be a code of silence. Tony compared it to the *Omerta* code used in the Mafia. In the drug unit, you did not report your fellow detectives for planting drugs, stealing drug money, or falsifying search warrants; you were supposed to just look the other way.

Tony was aware of some of the more egregious activity from members of the drug unit. He had first-hand knowledge that some drug dealers were operating in the open, and was keenly aware that on several occasions the drug dealers were tipped off that a raid was eminent. Rumors were rampant in the unit that most of the bosses were being paid off by the high-level dealers to allow them to operate with immunity in certain parts of Camden.

When Tony was first assigned to the drug enforcement unit, he was ecstatic. He had worked hard to get the assignment. He felt like working drugs would be a career move that could eventually lead to a promotion. As time in the drug unit went by, he became complacent and disillusioned. The fire inside of him was being siphoned out as each day went by. He was considering asking for a transfer but he knew that would not put him on the path that he envisioned. His dedication for the job had changed. Instead of the guy who was always early for work and stayed late to help anyone, he was just putting in his time.

When he had almost reached his breaking point, he requested to see the captain. He was not sure he would ask for a transfer; he just needed to talk to the boss. He loved police work, but he had lost the fire to do the job.

The captain had been in charge of the drug unit for several years. He was a flamboyant individual who was well-respected throughout the department. He dressed better than anyone. Nothing cheap about what he wore. He drove a BMW convertible; it was a vehicle that was recovered under the drug confiscation laws. He had a parking space inside the police building, and he always made sure the top was down when he approached the entrance to the garage. His dress, his vehicle, his lavish spending habits, and his overall demeanor left very little doubt that he was living a lifestyle way above the salary of a police captain.

Tony was nervous as he sat outside Captain Jerry Dance's office. He had some notes he had put together the night before. He hoped he would remember what was on them without pulling them out. The captain's secretary told Tony that the captain was ready to see him. "Come in, Tony. It's great to see you. I wish I could get together with you guys more often. Have a seat. Can we get you something to drink?"

"Thanks, captain. I do appreciate you taking some time to see me."

"Not a problem, Tony. I'll listen to what you have first. I also have something very important to discuss with you when you're done."

The conversation lasted about ten minutes. Tony fumbled at times but pleaded his case to the captain. He talked about his lack of interest working in the drug unit. He tried to be very careful not to upset the captain, or he could wind up back in patrol. It dawned on him during the conversation that he might be looked upon as a snitch by the members of the unit. He started to get into a sensitive area; he was talking about things that were clearly violations of procedures in the department. The captain was listening, but it didn't seem like he was terribly concerned about what was going on in his unit.

"Tony, let me stop you for a minute. I kind of get the point that you are trying to make. I know that some things are going on in the unit by certain individuals that are unacceptable. Those things will be addressed in time. I really do appreciate you coming in to talk to me. I would like to take a minute to talk to you about something that the department wants you to do."

The captain got up and closed the door. He told his secretary that he did not want to be disturbed. He moved back behind his desk and pulled a folder out from the top drawer. He didn't say anything for a few minutes while he moved papers around. "Tony, you have been a good drug detective for the time you have been in this unit. I have watched you grow in many ways. What I'm about to discuss with you is to be considered extremely confidential. Do you understand?"

"I understand, but if you think I came in here today to rat on any guys in this unit, that is not my intention."

"We are not going to talk about the unit right now. I have something to discuss with you. Tony, I have been working with our police chief, the attorney general's office, and the FBI on a plan to get one of our people inside the Camden mob. I want to submit your name to be the guy. It will involve a lot from you, and as you very well know, it could be very dangerous. I don't want you to answer right now. The plan would involve drumming up some departmental charges on you, like taking money from drug dealers and tipping them off to raids. We would fabricate a fake department trial board hearing and you would be fired. We would make sure we have media coverage of the firing. The New Jersey attorney general's office has a confidential informant that has connections inside the mob here in Camden. Through him, we will attempt to get you into their inner circle. I know this all sounds far-fetched right now. Trust me that there are quite a few people wanting to make this happen."

"Captain, let me catch my breath for a minute. I heard everything you said. We are talking about the mob in Camden. As you know, they may be one of the tightest groups of people in this state, or this country for that matter. I'm very familiar with the mob. As you probably also know, I have family members over the years that were affiliated with the mob. My father, my uncles, my grandfather, and other family members all had mob ties, either now or in the past. It doesn't sound like a plan that will work. You might want to get someone else for the job."

"Tony, I understand how you feel. I know all about your family's association with the mob. It will not be easy. We believe that with a good plan, you have the ability to get it done. You will have the support and backing of many people. I can assure you that nothing will happen. At any point that you feel your cover is blown, we will pull the plug. However, if it goes off as planned, we will be able to take down the Pete Calabrese family. It's no secret that they have operated freely in South Camden for many years. They need to be taken down."

"Captain, I know from my upbringings that they have been around for a long time. I also know that they have no problem killing anyone that goes against them. I have a family to protect. I just don't think I'm the right guy for the job."

"Tony, this could be the biggest break in your career. I can assure you that all the safeguards possible will be in place. I want you to think about it. I also want to let you know again that you are not to discuss this with anyone—that includes your entire family, the good ones and the bad ones. I want you to get back to me as soon as possible. Tony, we have faith in you. A lot of people are counting on you. Please do the right thing. This might be an opportunity to make the Spitlato name something your current family can be proud of."

As Tony was leaving the building with a pounding headache, he found it hard to comprehend what had taken place. It sounded like something out of a bad gangster movie. *Undercover in the notorious Calabrese crime family…what the hell are they thinking.*

Tony sat in his car for the longest time. He wondered if he should have gone into his family's past a little more for the captain. Hell, the captain had been around for a long time, and he sure as hell knew that Tony's family had mob affiliations in Camden.

Tony had been raised in a very strict Italian family. His dad, Carmen had died at an early age; he was only fifty-five years old. The smoking of at least three packs of cigarettes a day and drinking heavy had brought on the early death.

He was also gone from the home for days at a time. When Tony was young, he was told by both parents that he should not question where his dad was or what his job was. Carmen was small in stature, but he was as tough as they come. He would have talks with Tony beginning at the age of ten. The conversations usually revolved around always respecting others. Sometimes, to get his point across, Carmen would end his talk with a smack across the side of Tony's head. Although it hurt, Tony knew that he could not show any outward signs of weakness. As he got older, the smacks got harder.

Tony remembered times when relatives would come to the house late at night. Carmen had his wife, Gisella, cook up a meal for the guys, and they sat in the kitchen and ate and drank well into the early morning hours.

Tony had a sister, Roseabella. She was three years younger than Tony and was certainly the apple of her father's eye. She didn't get the talks that Tony got. She didn't get the smacks in the head either. As Tony got to be a teenager, he questioned his mother about the late night meetings. She simply told him that it was his father's business and not to question it. Some of the meetings got loud. The group usually consisted of his dad's brother Louie, Mr. Luca, who ran a flower shop in Camden, and Mr. Rosario, who had a cut-rate liquor store, also in Camden.

Tony, being true to his parents' wishes, stopped asking questions. As he got older he was allowed to stay up later, but not in the kitchen. He could hear some of the talk, and it usually revolved around money. Some nights he saw large bags of money being brought to his house and counted in the kitchen. As the men talked, it was obvious to Tony that his father was in charge. Tony was not sure what he was in charge of, but he could tell that when his dad raised his voice, the others got quiet.

The talks between Tony and his dad intensified. The theme was always about loyalty, integrity, being faithful, and protecting your family and friends. On nights when Carmen came home late, he always woke Tony up to have a talk. Tony knew that his father was a heavy drinker. He took care of his family and never was abusive with either his mother or his sister. On the nights that his dad was drinking heavy, the smacks were harder. Tony never backed up; he believed that his dad was just trying to make him tough, and he was succeeding.

By the time Tony was in high school, he knew without a doubt that his dad was mob connected. The meetings in the kitchen never stopped. Some nights, there would be men that Tony had not seen before. He would always hear them talking about money. One night he was walking through the kitchen and he heard Uncle Tomaso say that he was glad that "Pete" got whacked. He no sooner heard the word whacked, that his dad jumped up and smacked Tomaso in the head. "Can't you see my son is behind you? I don't ever want to hear anything like that coming from you. Do you understand?"

Tomaso didn't answer. Dad smacked him again, and this time Uncle Tomaso fell onto the floor. I was standing there with a soda in my hand. Dad pulled a steak knife from the drawer and put it to Uncle Tomaso's neck. Dad looked at me and said, "Get your ass upstairs before you make me cut this bastard's throat."

I was terrified by the look in dad's face as he held the knife to my uncle's throat. I ran out of the kitchen and went upstairs. Most of the night, I lay awake wondering what happened to Uncle Tomaso.

The next night the regulars showed up for the counting of the money. I didn't see Uncle Tomaso. I wanted to ask where he was, but I was afraid of what the answer might be. Before the counting of the money started I got enough nerve to ask my dad where Uncle Tomaso was. "Dad, is Uncle Tomaso okay? Why isn't he here tonight?"

"Well, my little tough guy son is worrying about his uncle. Do you think I cut his throat and tossed his sorry ass in the lake? Do you remember me telling you to never question me about anything I do?"

"Dad, I remember, but I have a right to ask about my uncle."

"You have no rights when it comes to my business. Your uncle is fine. He won't be here tonight; he is taking care of something for the business. Now, if you don't mind, we have things to do; so excuse yourself and go upstairs."

CHAPTER 14

After being up and running for several weeks, the CLEO Unit appeared to be operating smoothly. There were a few minor bumps here and there, but Warden Hubbard was getting the hang of it. When he wanted advice on operating a corrections facility, he called Warden Scope to seek out his expertise.

The daily routine for the inmates in the CLEO Unit was very simple. Lights went on in the tier at 6 a.m., breakfast was served from 7 a.m. to 8 a.m., inmates were back in their cells until 11 a.m., lunch was served from noon to 1 p.m., and forty-five minutes were allowed in the yard for those inmates who had no violations. Dinner was served from 5 p.m. to 6 p.m. and inmates were allowed to be out of their cells on the tier until 8 p.m. at which time they were ordered back in their cells. The lights in the tier were turned off at 10 p.m., but inmates were allowed to have small lamps in their cell.

Hubbard was getting accustomed to the vigorous daily grind of running a prison. He was spending a lot time at the facility. He missed his wife. He had talked to her several times about making the move to be with him. This was the first time in his career that he had spent so much time away from her. He not only missed her as his wife, he missed discussing things with her at night over dinner. She had a calming effect on him. He would at times run some things by her. She seemed to provide quality insight when asked for her opinion. Mike always told her that what she did around the house, which included raising the kids when he was away, was more important than anything he did. When he got home late at night, and she was not there, he felt lonely. He was hoping that the house in Washington would sell soon so she could join him.

The weekly meeting of the inmate grievance committee was created by Warden Hubbard to give the inmates a voice. He allowed the inmates in the unit to choose three representatives to meet weekly with him to talk about whatever they wanted to discuss. His hope was to instill a feeling in the unit that even though they were incarcerated, they could have a say.The meetings were scheduled for Wednesday afternoons. They were held in the large conference room.

"Good afternoon, gentlemen. I want to start today's meeting by thanking everyone for accepting the responsibility of being on this important committee. Marcia, I appreciate you taking notes for the meeting. Let the record show that participating in the meeting today will be Mr. Brewer, Sergeant Sanders, and Lieutenant Mandez from my staff. The inmates attending the meeting are Tony Spitlato, Donny Napolitano, and Bernie Wells."

The three inmates were picked by the other inmates, knowing they would be guys that would not be afraid to speak their mind to Warden Hubbard or anyone. They were tough, and the inmates on the tier knew it. It was a known fact on the tier that Spitlato was not terribly fond of Wells. Tony made it clear that although he didn't personally like Wells, he needed him on his side to appease the black inmates.

Warden Hubbard believed that if he could win these three over, the rest of the inmates would follow and go along with the program. The daily reports from the guards showed that the three seemed to be the go-to-guys on the tier. Wells, a black man, was one of only ten blacks in the unit. He had been a police officer in Miami, Florida. Like the others in the unit, he had been convicted under the RICO Act. He had been serving a twenty-five year sentence at the Federal Correction Institute in Tallahassee, Florida. At his trial, there was testimony that while working as an undercover detective in the drug unit, he provided protection for drug dealers. He was arrested at his home where federal agents found large quantities of drugs, weapons, and money that were tied to major drug dealers in the Miami area. He maintained his innocence during the trial, but the evidence was overwhelming. For the short time he had been in the CLEO Unit, he associated mainly with the other black inmates. He jokingly referred to the other black guys as the *Colored Law Enforcement Officers*, not *Corrupt Law Enforcement Officers*.

Donny Napolitano had come to the CLEO Unit from the Federal Correction Facility at Otisville, New York. Like the others he was also convicted under the RICO Act. He had worked in the NYPD Drug Task Force, and was a highly decorated police officer before his corruption conviction. He was indicted after a drug kingpin in New York City was arrested, and for a reduced sentence gave information on Donny and other members of the task force. The drug kingpin testified at their trials that he personally paid off members of the task force to avoid the arrest of his dealers. At the trial, it was revealed that Donny's father had retired as the Deputy Chief of the NYPD. He also had two brothers that were on the NYPD.

The meeting was quiet and reserved for a while. Tony, Donny, and Bernie were actually enjoying the time away from the tier. Hubbard provided sodas and cookies for the meeting and they were devoured within no time at all. Tony was the first to speak after Hubbard asked if anyone had anything to say. "Mr. Hubbard, I have been told by some of the guys on the tier that this prick sitting over there treats the guys like shit. I guess he thinks he is running the unit. I would like for you to instruct Mandez to lighten up or his fat ass might get something he won't enjoy."

Mandez bolted from his chair. He pointed his finger at Tony. "You piece of shit, you don't talk to me like that. I'm around here to maintain order, and I do it damn good."

Hubbard, surmising he might be losing control, stood and told Mandez to take his seat. He also told Tony that he would not tolerate any outburst like that. "Spitlato, if you have a grievance or anyone else has one, this is supposed to be the forum to discuss it in a civilized manner. Do you understand?"

"Civilized manner—that asshole don't know how to act civilized. He thinks we are a bunch of animals. I just want you to be aware that we might be inmates, but most of us have nothing to lose. We won't tolerate The Pincher's games. Yeah, and by the way Mr. Hubbard, when is that silly shit of pinching inmates going to stop? Also, his friend in crime, Brewer, seems to go along with whatever Mandez feels like doing. If this is a grievance committee, that's our first grievance. So what are you going to do, Warden? Who the hell is in charge around here anyway?"

Mandez stood again and before he could say anything, Hubbard told him to sit down. Brewer just stared at Tony. If looks could kill, Tony would have died right there. Hubbard remained standing and said, "Gentlemen, I was hoping this committee would be both beneficial to me and to the inmates. I would encourage you all to maintain your tempers, and we will get more done."

Hubbard sat back down and looked at Tony. "I need to end this meeting because I have something to do. As far as your complaint about Lieutenant Mandez, I will check into it and get back to you. Does anyone have anything else to discuss?"

Although nothing else was said, the stares from one side of the table to the other made Hubbard uncomfortable. He stood to leave, but appeared to be grasping for something positive to say before ending the meeting. Before he could get anything out, Tony stood and smiled. "Well it was nice meeting with you guys. I can't wait until we do this again. I'm sure Donny and Bernie have had as much fun as I have. Oh yeah, by the way, the cookies were really good."

Donny looked at Tony and gave him a wink of approval. Bernie was finishing the last of his cookie, but it appeared that he was in support of his sometime Italian friend. Hubbard ended the meeting and the three inmates were escorted back to the tier.

Hubbard asked Brewer and Mandez to stay in the room. He asked Marcia to leave them alone for a while. It appeared to Hubbard that Brewer was unusually quiet doing the meeting. It was also noticeable that he had a smile on his face when Tony was talking. "Andy, how do you think things went? I get the impression you didn't want to be here."

"It's not that I don't want to be here. I just think that Tony is a crock of shit and a troublemaker. Here's a guy that was involved in more mayhem than we may ever know, and we are treating him with kid gloves. It's okay to have a grievance committee, but do you really think those assholes are taking this serious? I think they'll look at it as a time for soda and cookies; it's all bullshit. I came here to do a job for the Justice Department. I think it's time I started to earn my pay. As far as Mandez pinching these guys, who gives a rat's ass? It's not like he's torturing the poor bastards. He is merely directing them to where he wants them to go. They all know that when he tells them he is taking them somewhere, they should not act up. The bottom line, Mike, although these guys were once trusted law enforcement officers, they are now convicted felons and need to be treated as such".

After the meeting, Brewer and Mendez took a walk outside the facility. "Oscar, since I have been here you have supported me. I think you and I are on the same page as far as the treatment of these prisoners. Can I trust you with some information on why I'm here?"

"Andy, I appreciate you taking up for me in that stupid meeting. I really don't think Hubbard is the right man for this job. I don't dislike the guy; I just think it takes a special kind of person to deal with inmates. He's not here to turn those bastards into model citizens. This is a prison, and unless I'm wrong, they are here to be punished. To answer your question, yes, you can trust me with anything you tell me."

"The Justice Department selected me over many others to come here and get information, mainly from Tony Spitlato. I have orders to interrogate others, but Spitlato is my main target. The Justice Department knows that Tony has a wealth of information on the mob in Jersey. He also was either in on it or knows about the murder of a very prominent federal judge. I recognized early in my time here that I need someone like you to help accomplish what I was sent here to do. You know the ins and outs of the prison system here at Pelican Bay.

I have talked to Assistant Attorney General Thompson at the Justice Department about you. Thompson is my contact person, and I report directly to him on this assignment. If you are on board with me and help me get this job done, I can promise you, it will bode favorably for your future here at the prison."

"Andy, I appreciate what you are trying to accomplish. I often get frustrated with my job here at Pelican Bay. I can assure you that I will assist you in any way that I can."

"Thanks, I knew from the first time I met you that you would be a guy I could trust. You won't regret working with me."

CHAPTER 15

The call came just after the late night news. Hubbard had fallen asleep on the couch after reading as many policy procedures as he could. He fought staying awake. The material he was reading was boring. The phone startled him. This late at night his first thought was that something happened back home. "Hello, Mike Hubbard, can I help you?"

"Sir, this is Sergeant Sanders. I hate to bother you this late at night. We have a serious incident in the CLEO Unit. I know you want to be called when anything bad happens. Lieutenant Mandez was attacked on the tier and beaten pretty bad. He's at the prison emergency room."

"What the hell are you talking about? What happened?"

"At this point, we are not sure what happened. The guards heard a commotion at the far end of the tier. They went on the tier and found Mandez on the ground. He was bleeding from a head wound and was not conscious. He was taken to the emergency unit where he is being treated. I have very little additional information other than Mandez was in civilian clothes. I'm not sure what the hell he was doing on the tier."

This being Hubbard's first major incident at the facility, he told Sanders that he would be on his way to the prison. "How in the hell did he get beat when the inmates should have been locked down at that time of the night?"

"Sir, I'm not sure at this time. There was a pipe found on the ground by the responding guards. The pipe had blood on it. I was told that when the guards got to him, most of the inmates were in their cells. You're not going to like this; the cell doors were all unlocked."

"Do whatever you have to do to protect the scene. I will be there as soon as possible."

"Just one other thing you should know…Mandez appears to have been drinking."

"Well, that's just great. I've got a lot of questions, but they can wait until I get there."

Hubbard grabbed his briefcase and headed out the door. He contemplated calling Warden Scope. As he drove toward the prison, he decided not to call him. He wanted to have more facts and hopefully some answers before making the call. Of all the policies and procedures he had read, he didn't recall any of them covering this type of incident. He knew one thing for sure; whoever hit Mandez with the pipe was in a cell on that tier. *The question now was who was it and does Mandez know his attacker? What the hell was he doing on the tier in civilian clothes? What reason would he give the duty guards that they would allow him on the tier? Did they feel that he had been drinking and still let him on the tier?*

Hubbard parked in his official spot and ran through the gate flashing his credential as he ran. He entered his office to find Sanders on the phone with the prison doctor. Sanders whispered to Hubbard that he was getting an update on Mandez. He hung up the phone, and the look on his face was compelling. "Sir, it doesn't look good. Mandez is in critical condition with severe swelling in the brain. Doctor Sullivan is having him moved to Hagler Medical Center. That facility has one of the best trauma units in the country."

"Fuck…this is not good. Can you get Warden Scope on the phone? He needs to be made aware of this before it hits the media."

After making the call to Scope, Hubbard started to document everything from the time he got the call from Sanders. He knew from past experience that in the near future, he would have to report this incident to Thompson at the Justice Department.

With Mandez being moved to a trauma unit, he wanted to make sure his family was notified. "Ron, can you get Mandez's wife on the phone for me?"

"Sir, Mandez is divorced and lives alone in a condo in Crescent City."

"Please check his personal file and see who is listed as next of kin on his medical file to see who should be notified in case of an emergency. The last thing I want is for any family members to read about this attack in the paper. Please make every effort to find someone in his files."

The conversation with Scope had gone well. Scope had made some suggestions to Hubbard on how he should proceed. He told Hubbard that he had his full support. He only asked that he be kept in the loop on the investigation. Hubbard was surprised at how calm Scope was. He assumed that Scope had probably been through situations like this in the past.

Because Hubbard had been through many investigations while at the Bureau, he wanted to call the shots on this incident. Even though he had some capable people, he wanted to get to the bottom of what had happened. He knew for his own peace of mind that he needed to stay totally involved.

"Sir, the shift lieutenant on the tier has locked down the unit. He has his guards on the tier walking and watching the prisoners. The area where Mandez was found has been roped off. He has called in additional people to assist until things quiet down. The crime scene people from the state are here and processing the scene. I'm sure you have read in the manuals that when something like this happens we use the California Highway Patrol to process the crime scene and conduct any forensics that is needed. After they are done, the investigation is conducted within the prison system with their assistance. Will you be handling the investigation, or do you want me to notify Andy Brewer?"

Hubbard paused for a moment as he took in all that Sanders had told him. His first thought was that he wanted to handle the investigation, knowing that it would get done the way he wanted it to. However, he also knew that it would be better to have someone else involved and he could be the overseer. At the Bureau he was always the boss in the background. He enjoyed having discussions with the investigators on how they were proceeding with their investigations. He also would not hesitate to make suggestions when he thought things were not proceeding in a timely manner or if he felt the investigation was going in the wrong direction. With all the eyes being on him as the Warden of the CLEO Unit, it might be best to proceed with appointing someone to lead the investigation. "Ron, get in touch with Andy Brewer. Tell him what happened and ask him to report to work immediately. Brewer has a pretty good background. I will assign the investigation to him."

CHAPTER 16

The phone in Hubbard's office was ringing non-stop. Marcia had been called in to help in anticipation of the humongous amount of reports that would be needed for different entities. Hubbard knew from his past experiences that there was never enough reporting; someone always seemed to be left out. Anyone in a position above the primary investigator wanted a report. It seemed endless and stupid on how high up the chain the reporting went. At each level of reporting, the paper work would come back down the chain asking for more information; most of the time, there was no more. At times, trying to keep up with the request for information got crazy. You dare not miss anyone in the pecking order, or the failure to include somebody, could come back to bite you in the butt.

It never failed in any level of law enforcement that the most important person, the primary investigator, caught all the flack. It was usually a case of damned if you do or damned if you don't. There were times in an investigation that you did not want to speculate and put something in a report that was not verified. It was a practice of good investigators to put just the basics in a report. They knew that there would be follow-up questions, but if you had put something in the initial report, it was hard to change it later. Investigating was one thing; putting it in a report that made clear sense to the recipient was another.

Some of the best investigators on a crime scene could have problems reporting in a manner that left no questions from the reader. Before a report would go up the chain, several levels of approvers would be involved. It was frustrating to investigators, knowing that the effort they put into making a good and thorough report would be looked over by so many eyes—for no other reason than them being a supervisor. Bosses had the attitude that they simply wanted to add their touch to the report. Investigators were very thankful for programs on their computers that could quickly make changes. In the old days, having a good size bottle of white-out on your desk was a commodity.

Brewer arrived in Hubbard's office and was briefed by Ron Sanders on what had occurred. Hubbard had remained on the tier observing the work of the crime lab detectives. Many of the inmates who had apparently slept through the incident wanted to know what had happened. Hubbard instructed the guards simply to tell them that a guard was assaulted. He also told the guards to let all inmates know that at some point, they would be interviewed.

While on the tier, Hubbard could not help but eyeball certain people. He occasionally glanced in the direction of Tony Spitlato's cell. Tony was lying on his bunk, but Hubbard could see he was awake. Hubbard made a point to glance over at Donny Napolitano who was in the cell next to Spitlato. Donny was intently watching the crime scene people at work. Hubbard could not help but think that at some time in the past, these guys who were all former law enforcement were probably on similar crime scenes. A serious assault was nothing new to most of them.

Hubbard made some mental notes as he looked around the tier. Bernie Wells was in his bunk, but Hubbard could not tell if he was sleeping. With all the excitement on the tier, Hubbard found it hard to think that anyone would be sleeping. Even if they were former law enforcement officers, an attack like this one was not an everyday occurrence, even in a prison. You would think they would be watching intently for something to do on another boring day behind bars.

As Hubbard was leaving the tier to go to his office, he walked by the cell of Louie Tusta. "Hey Mr. Warden, how is Mandez doing? Is he going to be all right?"

"We will be conducting interviews shortly. If you have questions you can discuss them with whoever interviews you."

"I hope he's okay, but you do know the guy's a real prick. I don't know what happened, but I would bet he fucked with the wrong guy."

"Louie, you can have any opinion you want. Lieutenant Mandez is a prison guard under my watch. I can guarantee you and the others in this unit that we will find out what happened."

"I wish you luck Mr. Warden—have a nice day."

Hubbard's law enforcement background was kicking in. He wanted to talk more to Louie and some others. He fought the urge and returned to his office. He needed to supervise the investigation, not conduct it.

As he walked into his office, he saw Brewer on the phone. He asked Sanders if he had briefed Brewer on the situation. Sanders nodded his head, affirming that he had. He also nodded his head motioning for Hubbard to walk to the other side of the office. "Sir, you ain't going to like this. He's on the phone with Thompson from the attorney general's office."

"You're right, I don't like it. Did he call Thompson, or did Thompson call here?"

"After I gave him a short briefing, he made the call."

"When he gets off the phone, stay in this office. You might have to pull me off this bastard."

Hubbard walked toward Brewer. He just stood there staring at him. Brewer covered the phone. "I'm talking to John Thompson, letting him know what happened."

"Give me that fuckin' phone right now."

Brewer held the phone up in Hubbard's direction. Hubbard ripped it away from him and almost took part of his hand. Hubbard sat at the desk and attempted to compose himself before he talked. "John, this is Mike…what the hell is going on?

"That's exactly what I was going to ask you."

"John, you of all people know about protocol. You don't get information on what goes on in this unit from Brewer; you need to get it from me. In case your next question is why haven't I called you…my answer is that I am running a fuckin' prison and overseeing a complex investigation. I wanted to have some concrete facts before calling you. I don't know what the hell he told you. He just walked in this office and had a short briefing from one of my guys. He doesn't know the entire picture of what happened. This really pisses me off, and Brewer knows it because he is sitting right here listening to me."

"Mike, you need to calm down. I don't think Andy meant any disrespect toward you by calling me. I do agree with you that he may have jumped the gun. I'm sure you will have that conversation with him. Just go easy with him. He's a good man, and you will need him to work with you on this terrible incident. Now, let's talk about how we will proceed with the investigation. How is Lieutenant Mandez?"

"The last report I got was that he was moved from here to the trauma unit at Hagler Hospital. He's in pretty bad shape. I will have to get an update on his condition as soon as we hang up. I'm not sure what Brewer told you. We have the California Highway Patrol guys here doing the crime scene processing. I have called in additional guards to assist. The unit will remain on lockdown until we conduct interviews and view the surveillance tapes. My initial intentions were to put Brewer in charge of the investigation. Before I do that, I need to have another talk with him about his position here in this unit. I will have a more detailed report for you shortly. Is there anything else you need before we hang up?"

"Mike, I have confidence in you. I do agree that Brewer should be assigned the investigation. You have too much on your plate to be handling this investigation. If you need anything, please do not hesitate to call me. I would like a report on the incident in a couple of hours. I will need to brief my boss."

Hubbard slammed the phone down and looked at Brewer. Brewer had moved over to the couch. He had the look of a schoolboy who got caught cheating on a test and anticipating the teacher was about to scold him. Hubbard pulled a chair up close to Brewer. He gathered his thoughts. He was biting his upper lip. He wanted to make sure whatever came out of his mouth would be meaningful. He looked at Sanders. "Ron, would you leave the room so that Mr. Brewer and I can talk?"

Sanders was glad that he was asked to leave the room. He could tell that what was about to take place might get ugly. When the door was closed, Hubbard stood up. He paced the room before he said anything. "Andy, let me start by saying that I do not appreciate you circumventing my position and calling John Thompson. I think we had this conversation when you first got here. Let me again explain to you how things work around here and in most places. I'm in charge of this unit. Reports that have to go to people above my pay grade must come through me. I work directly under John Thompson; you work directly for me. I need to make sure that any reports or information relating to the running of the CLEO Unit get to Thompson directly from me. I'm not sure why you had the urge to call him. I want to make it perfectly clear to you that in the future, any reporting you need to do will come to me.

I assume you are an intelligent man, or Thompson would not have sent you here. I also understand that your mission here is to attempt to get information from some of our inmates. I have direction from Thompson that I am to allow you to proceed with that mission. I also know that in your short time here you have developed a relationship with Mandez. I'm not sure what happened on the tier. I hope you share my intentions to get to the bottom of this attack. Even though I'm pissed at you for going over my head with the call to Thompson, I will go along with you being assigned to handle the investigation. I just want to make it clear one more time that although Thompson sent you here, you report directly to me. Do you understand me and do you have any questions?"

"Mike, I understand you perfectly. I know what I was sent here for. I will continue to work toward that mission. I appreciate you giving me the lead on finding out what happened to Mandez. Maybe this will give me the opportunity to do two things at the same time. It's not like we have to roam the streets of Crescent City to find out who injured Mandez. He's right here in the CLEO Unit."

Brewer stood and extended his hand for a handshake. With no hesitation Hubbard shook his hand, the same hand he almost tore from his arm just a few minutes earlier.

The two men sat at the large conference table. Hubbard called for Sanders to return to the office. Hubbard also asked Marcia to return. He stood and started to pace around the table. Both Sanders and Marcia had heard some of the prior conversation between Hubbard and Brewer. The silence in the room was broken when Hubbard asked Marcia to take some notes and to keep a running account on paper of the progress of the investigation. "I do not want to make reports that are confusing to my superiors here at the prison or further up the line. I want you to find out what happened to Mandez. If while doing that, you obtain information relative to your main mission that's fine, but I do not want reports to be confusing. Do you understand what I'm saying?"

"I understand. I'll make sure there is no overlapping of reporting. I will separate the reporting on what happened to Mandez from my attempts to get information from certain inmates in this unit."

"I want you to start immediately. I need you to talk to the crime lab guys, the guards on duty at the time, inmates in that general vicinity, and if possible, we need to talk to Mandez."

Hubbard walked back to his desk, but no one moved away from the conference table. "Well, don't just sit there. Let's get to the bottom of this."

Brewer started toward the tier door. He stopped, "Mike, can I ask for the assistance of Sergeant Sanders? I was working close with Mandez, but I don't think he will be back for a while, if at all. I just need someone to sit in on some of the interviews."

"I have no problem with Ron working with you. Please don't try to corrupt him...I'm just kidding. We do need to act quickly. I want to report back to Thompson by this afternoon."

As Brewer and Sanders started towards the tier door, Hubbard said, "Andy, I trust that you will do a good job. I do want you to know that I am by nature a person that stays involved in high profile investigations. I am also a guy full of crazy quotes, so let me leave you with this thought, which is actually one of my own—*Follow your strengths, manage your weaknesses, and don't let your babies grow up to be cowboys.*"

CHAPTER 17

As Brewer and Sanders sat in the small conference room, Brewer started to tell Sanders how he wanted to proceed. "I know you are an intelligent guy. I would, however, like to call the shots on this investigation. Any input you have will be greatly appreciated. As you know, we are dealing with guys that had been involved in criminal investigations when they were good cops. They know all about the *good guy/bad guy* routine, so that shit won't work with these dudes. Most of these guys are in here serving long sentences. If we are to find out what happened to Mandez, we will need to either put the fear of God in them or make some promises. Somebody on that tier knows what happened. You know from your experience working in this prison that nobody is going to say anything unless it benefits them. I'm sure you realize that some of our interviews might get a little nasty or even physical. That's when I need you to back me up."

"I may only be a uniform guard in this institution, Andy, but I won't stand by and see guards mistreated. I have made this job a career, and although Mandez had some weird ways, he was still a respected guard. We cannot have the guards attacked viciously like he was. I will assist you in any way I can. If at some point I think your tactics cross the line, I will tell you."

Brewer reached out to shake hands with Sanders. "What do you say, partner? Let's get started. We can begin with some interviews; we can always catch up on the forensics later. It's not like we have a tremendous crime scene. We know where Mandez fell, we think we have the weapon, and the best part is that whoever did it is locked in a cell."

Sanders was excited to finally get his chance to sink his teeth into a meaningful investigation. He was impressed with how Brewer handled himself. Brewer could sense the excitement in Sanders. He wanted to keep Sanders on a high, now that Mandez was out of the picture. As they were leaving the room, Brewer continued to brief Sanders.

"One of the main prisoners in the unit is Tony Spitlato. Right now he is probably thinking we will talk to him first. I want him to stew for a while. Let's start with the guy in the cell next to Tony. I have read a little about Donny Napolitano. He comes to this unit from the Otisville Federal Prison in Upstate New York. Like most in this unit, he's a tough guy and, thus, the nickname, The Brick. He was an undercover drug guy with the NYPD. His trial was an open and shut case. He was indicted for feeding information to the mob in New York. The prosecutor had tons of evidence on him. They had surveillance video, a wiretap on his home phone, and bank statements showing he was living way above the means of a cop."

As they walked, Sanders was taking it all in. The investigations that he had handled in the prison were nothing compared to what Brewer was laying out. The briefing continued.

"Halfway through the trial, Donny told his attorney to make a deal, and he would plead guilty. He knew from the start that he would be found guilty, so he went for a deal. As part of the deal, he was asked to give the names of other cops who were involved with the mob and on the take. He refused. Not having much to bargain with, he stuck with the guilty plea and requested leniency. At his sentencing he asked the judge to consider the fact that at one time he was a good cop. The judge did not buy the good cop plea and hit Donny with a twenty year sentence with no chance of parole, unless he decided to cooperate and provide information on other cops."

Like a little kid hearing a good story for the first time, Sanders spoke up.

"I assume that because he is still with us in the CLEO Unit he has not made the choice to give information."

"Yeah, Donny has stuck to his guns, and he's here for the long haul. He won't be easy to talk to. He still has the attitude that he didn't do anything wrong. In his pre-sentence report, he told the court that he was only doing what half of the NYPD was doing. I want to start with him because he gives me the impression that although he is tough as nails, he is always looking for the deal he didn't get at sentencing."

"Okay, Andy, I'll get the guards to bring him in and let's see what happens."

Donny was sleeping when the guards woke him. They told him he would be questioned about the beating of Mandez. Brewer told the guards to talk loud when they went to get an inmate. He wanted the others to start thinking about what, if anything, they would say.

Donny didn't bitch; he went without saying a word until he passed Tony's cell. "Hey, Tony, if I ain't back in a little bit, make sure they leave my dinner."

"Yeah, Donny, I'll make sure you get fed. Get them pricks to buy you some McDonald's Big Macs and fries. Tell them you ain't saying a damn thing until you get a treat."

Donny and most of the other inmates close by laughed. As Donny walked by the cells, he got a greeting from each inmate. Some reached out and tried to slap him on the shoulder. One inmate hollered out as Donny walked by. "I saw the whole thing. Mandez slipped and fell on that pipe. It couldn't have happened to a nicer guy."

As former cops, the inmates knew that the game was on. They knew that when a guard got hurt, all the stops were pulled out. It was the same in the law enforcement world on the street. If a cop got injured, all hell broke loose. The shit would hit the fan, and ass kicking would start—lots of ass kicking. If a cop got seriously injured or even killed, the neighborhood where it happened would turn into an open season on the bad guys or anybody who looked like a bad guy. It was an unwritten law on the street that you didn't fuck with the guys in blue. After a cop was injured or killed, the streets were bare. The bad guys knew the creed and wanted no part of the boys in blue kicking ass and taking names.

Donny was led into the conference room. The cuffs were removed, and he was instructed to sit in a chair facing Brewer and Sanders. The uniform guards left the room and said they would be outside the door. Donny rubbed his wrists, and as the guards left, he said, "If I need you guys, I'll holler."

As Andy Brewer started to talk, Donny put his hand up. "Is there any chance that I can get a soda?"

"Donny, this is not a social visit. You know why you are in this room. Don't get cute with silly shit. We will be talking to your buddies later, and I'm not starting sessions with sodas, candy, or anything you guys ask for. Make sure when you go back on the tier you don't bullshit the guys and tell them you got something."

"Wow, just a lousy soda. I guess a bag of chips is out of the question."

Brewer looked at Sanders. It was the kind of look that said, *See, I told you these assholes won't be easy to talk to.* For Sanders, the confrontation was a learning experience. He had conducted smaller investigations on the Pelican Bay side, but they were nothing compared to this. He waited for Brewer to start the questioning. Sanders knew this was a great opportunity to hone his skills in interviewing techniques.

The interview didn't last long. Donny was not in the mood to provide any information; maybe the soda would have loosened him up a little. He squirmed in his chair, looked out the only window, cracked his knuckles, and smiled a lot. At points during the interview he shook his head giving Brewer the impression that the line of questioning bored him. At one point, he looked at Sanders and said, "You've been awful quiet. Did Mr. Brewer tell you that you don't have a speaking part?"

Sanders smiled at Donny. "Let me tell you something, Mr. Napolitano. I have dealt with prisoners a whole lot nastier than you. I've been in this prison system for a lot of years. People like you always amaze me. You think you're mister tough guy because you were a cop. Then when you disgraced that profession, you went in the mob. I guess because you're a fuckin' dago, you think we will shake in our boots. Well, Donny, we're in control in this place, and you got a lot of years to figure that out. Now, unless Mr. Brewer has any further questions, I'm sending your ass back to the tier. Make sure when you get back that you tell everyone how you fucked over us. Tell them you got a soda and chips; tell them anything you want. It's going to be hard for you to play tough guy for all the years you got to serve. I would suggest you make every effort to stop acting like the asshole you are."

Brewer just sat there during Sanders' dressing-down of Donny. He thought about interrupting, but he was actually impressed with Sanders. He hadn't heard much out of him, but he liked what he was now seeing.

Sanders called for the uniform guard. "Take Mr. Napolitano back to his cell. He doesn't want to miss his dinner. He's hoping they have soda and chips with this evening's meal."

Donny got up from the chair and actually looked a little pissed. He was cuffed, and as he was going toward the door, he turned with a smile on his face. "I like your style, Mr. Sanders. You would have been a good cop, but you would not have lasted long in the mob. If you would talk to some of my Italian compadres in Benson Heights like that, they would put your ass in the Hudson River. Salute!"

Sanders pushed his chair away, stood, and said to Brewer, "I'm sorry that I went off on him."

"Hey, you did good. I was really impressed. The fun has just begun. I would love to be a fly on the wall when Donny goes back and tells the guys he screwed all over us. While you were talking to Donny, I had this thought; you and I are going to leave this prison tonight. We are going to have a nice meal, see our significant others, and pretty much do whatever we want to do. The only thing Donny is getting tonight is a prison meal and the sound of a cell door slamming shut. Now, who do you think wins these verbal battles we have with these guys? Let's move on. We've got a lot of inmates to talk to."

Chapter 18

The interviews of the inmates continued late into the night. Brewer was holding up pretty good, but Sanders was fading. Most of the interviews were very quick. It seemed that the majority of the stories were about the same. Nobody saw anything or heard anything. The main theme of the interviews was that Mandez got what he deserved. It was clear after several interviews that nothing would come from them. These guys had to live on the tier, and the last thing they needed was to be harassed for giving information to the guards.

After getting nowhere, Brewer told Sanders that they would break for the night and start back up in the morning. When they left the interview room, they were surprised to see Hubbard sitting on the couch talking to Warden Scope. There were two other men in the room. Neither Brewer nor Sanders knew who they were. Warden Hubbard walked over and asked how they were doing. Brewer shook his head, and with a scowl on his face said, "It was like they rehearsed what they would say. I guess because we are dealing with ex-cops, we are up against the wall. We still have some of the more interesting inmates to talk to. I think we will start back up early in the morning, if that's okay with you?"

"Yes, that will be fine. Andy, I want you to meet the warden of Pelican Bay. Warden Scope, this is Andy Brewer. He's working here on a special assignment from the Justice Department. I think I briefed you on it a few weeks ago. I'm sure you know Ron Sanders. Ron has agreed to work with Andy on these interviews."

Warden Scope shook hands with Brewer and acknowledged Sanders. Hubbard introduced the two other men in the office. "Gentlemen, this is Lieutenant Josh Mahoney and Sergeant Paul Larson. They are with the California Highway Patrol Homicide Unit. We have been briefing them on what we know up to this point about the attack on Lieutenant Mandez."

Hubbard asked that everyone have a seat at the conference table. Before Brewer took a seat, he asked if he could get a drink. "I have been talking non-stop for quite a while. I feel like I have cotton mouth. If I have to talk to these gentlemen from the Homicide Unit, I want to be able to speak clearly. I'm sure Ron needs something to drink, also."

Hubbard said that he would have someone bring drinks into the office. He then took a deep breath. "Guys, I have the very unpleasant task of informing you both that Lieutenant Mandez passed away earlier tonight at the hospital. His wounds were quite severe. After two emergency surgeries, he passed away. We are all very saddened by this loss. I will let Lieutenant Mahoney fill you in on what he learned at the hospital."

Mahoney was a large man. He stood up to address the group, and it appeared that he kept getting up; he was at least six foot five and weighed about two hundred and fifty pounds. He cleared his throat as he pulled out some papers from his sports jacket.

"Gentlemen, we are sorry for your loss. We were called to Hagler Hospital earlier this evening after Lieutenant Mandez had passed away. I talked to Dr. Donald Wirtz who is the chief at the trauma center at Hagler. He reported that they performed two very delicate surgeries on Mandez. The second surgery he did not survive. I was told by Dr. Wirtz that they performed a craniotomy. During that surgery they removed part of the skull to relieve the pressure on the brain. Dr. Wirtz felt that the surgery was the only chance he had. Wirtz is a renowned trauma surgeon. He has worked wonders at that trauma center. Unfortunately, they could not save Mandez. He passed away in the operating room."

Mahoney paused to allow the news to be taken in by the group. Even though he had given bad news to loved ones and family members over the years, this was different; Mandez was considered a law enforcement officer. When Mahoney saw how they were taking the news, he allowed a few minutes to pass before he continued.

"That is basically what we were told. I'm sure there will be an autopsy later today when the body is sent to the medical examiner's office. The only other thing I want to mention is that we do have jurisdiction in this investigation which is now a homicide. My office will work with the prison investigators. I have been briefed by Warden Hubbard concerning some of the inmates in the CLEO Unit. I know this will be a difficult investigation because of who we are dealing with."

Andy got up from the table and walked toward the window. The death of Mandez was not what he had expected to hear. Even though he had only worked with him for a short period of time, they had hit it off almost immediately. The drinks were brought into the room. Andy grabbed a Coke from the table. "I wish I had some Jack Daniels to put in this. Damn, Mandez dying has hit me like a ton of bricks. I didn't expect this, but I'm not sure why I didn't expect it. Hell, getting hit in the head with a pipe sometimes is worse than getting shot or stabbed. I'm really pissed. I could go back in there and beat the shit out of a few of those assholes. I think I know who I would start with. It would big Mr. Big Shot, Tony Spitlato. That bastard knows who beat Mandez, or he did it himself. The stakes have just been raised. Mike, I want to yank Tony's ass out right now. I want to get into his shit, and it can't wait until tomorrow."

Hubbard, who had dealt with many very serious situations at the Bureau, was almost speechless. He popped open a ginger ale. The room was very quiet. Lieutenant Mahoney broke the silence.

"Gentlemen, I would suggest that at this very difficult time for all of us, we just pause for a period of time before any interviews proceed. Let's allow my crime lab guys to finish and report on their findings. I understand that you have cameras on the tier. Let's review the cameras, and we can collectively make a wise decision on how to proceed. One thing is for damn sure; whoever hit Mandez with that pipe is in your CLEO Unit. I like our odds. I have worked murders where we thought we had several people who had witnessed the act, only to find out nobody saw anything. In this case, not only do we have our suspect confined, we know we have people who probably saw what happened. Time is on our side. Hell, we could take a week away from this case knowing that when we resumed the suspect is still in the same spot."

Sanders had been quiet; as he also had popped open a Coke. He stood and walked over toward Brewer. As Brewer stared out the window, Sanders whispered into his ear. "When I first met you I thought your tactics were wrong. After what has happened, I now think that you're right."

Brewer patted Sanders on the back and thanked him. Hubbard moved to the center of the room. "I agree with Lieutenant Mahoney. Let's all get some sleep. We can meet here early in the morning. With clear heads, we can discuss how to proceed. I also want to mention that we are not to tell any inmate on that tier that Mandez is dead. I feel we have the upper hand if they continue to think that he may not be severely injured. Once we tell them that Mandez is dead, the game changes. They might be serving lengthy sentences, but none of them wants to take on a murder charge or an accessory to murder charge."

As the group was looking to break up and head out for the night, Mahoney got a call on his cell phone. After a very short conversation, he asked for everyone's attention. "Gentlemen, it appears that the news gets worse. I just talked to my technician, and there are no legible prints on the pipe. There is no evidence in the area where the attack took place. He also said that after examining the surveillance cameras, he found that they had been turned off. They were turned back on after the guards responded to the commotion. My technician said that he asked your guard who turned off the camera. The guard said that Mandez had ordered that they be turned off."

Hubbard was furious. He smacked his desk with an open hand, and threw his soda can across the room, almost hitting Sergeant Larson. "Jesus Christ, why the hell would anyone turn off the damn cameras.

I need to talk to the guards on duty at that time. Somebody's ass is in trouble."

Lieutenant Mahoney put his hand up as to stop Hubbard from speaking. "Mike, before you go looking to fire some guards, Mandez ordered the cameras to be turned off; they were just following orders. My technician examined the control board for the cameras. Your guard made a manual log that Mandez ordered that the cameras be turned off before he went on the tier."

Hubbard flopped down in his chair. He grabbed his head and ran his fingers through his hair. At one point, he looked as if he would pull some out. "Why in the fuck would Mandez order the cameras to be turned off? What the hell was his reason for that move? Damn, we are really in the hole and starting from square one. Mahoney, what the hell else did your guys find out?"

Mahoney moved over toward Hubbard. Everyone in the room was still a little shocked from all the negative news. "Mike, after my technician found out about the cameras being turned off, he talked to your guard. I know he's a crime lab technician, but he is a sworn police officer. He questioned the guard who was on duty when Mandez ordered the cameras turned off."

Hubbard jumped up. At first it appeared that he was going to attack Mahoney. He only got up in his face. "You can't possibly have anything else. You have already told us everything negative that might hinder us in ever finding out what happened. Go ahead, Mahoney, what did your man find out from the guard?"

"I hate to tell you this…Mandez was drunk when he went on the tier. Your guard said that he questioned Mandez on why he was going on the tier and why he wanted the cameras turned off. Mandez told the guard that he was a lieutenant and not to ask any questions. I'm sorry Mike; it appears that Mandez was going on that tier to do something that he did not want to be seen on camera."

Hubbard was stunned. While all the bad news was being presented by Mahoney, he could not help but notice that Brewer was silent. Brewer shook his head a few times. He did not seem like what he was hearing bothered him. He basically stayed near the window drinking his soda. Hubbard walked over to him. "Andy, you don't seem like any of this is bothering you. Did you know ahead of time that Mandez was going on the tier? Do you have any knowledge of his intentions? When you were with him earlier in the day, did he talk about going back on the tier for anything? You and Mandez have become very close in the short time you have been here. Do you know anything?"

"Mike, I did not know anything about him coming back tonight to go on the tier. I do know that he had become very involved in the interviews. He worked very hard reading about the background of some of the inmates. He was always very itchy to get started with assisting me. I had to hold him back a few times when he wanted to talk to Spitlato and others. He didn't like Spitlato. I think that if anyone on that tier is a genuine suspect in this murder, it has to be Spitlato."

With all the bad news, Hubbard said that he needed Brewer and Sanders to stay back in his office for a while. He told them that he needed them to help with the reports. Mahoney and Larson said that they would return in the morning. Hubbard went to his desk, made some notes, and said, "I dread this phone call. Thompson's going to think I'm bullshitting him. I can't believe so much could go wrong in such a short period of time. It's times like this that I wish I was back in Washington enjoying my retirement with my lovely wife. When she hears about this terrible incident, I know her reaction will be exactly what I am feeling right now—tell the Justice Department to shove the CLEO Unit where the sun don't shine."

CHAPTER 19

Hubbard made notes on his desk with Post-its. He strategically placed them in an order of importance and timelines. He dreaded the phone call to Thompson. Over many years with the Bureau, he had to make calls to his supervisors that were nerve-racking. He had reported on some blunders concerning highly classified investigations. The perception of the FBI was that they were infallible, but that was far from the truth. Just because an agent was required to have a college degree did not make them any smarter than the average cop on the street. Agents, over time, were weeded out just like anyone would be in any business. Hubbard had discovered that an agent that had some prior law enforcement experience usually shined over the fresh out of college agents. He had always said that you can teach law, but you can't teach experience.

Hubbard knew that the phone call would not be pleasant. He picked up the phone at least three times and put it back down. After writing one more Post-it and sipping some water to clear his throat, he was ready. The natural response from the body would be a dried out throat. He had a lot to tell Thompson and hoped that he would be allowed to finish before Thompson began the bombardment of questions. It was not the time for more Post-its; it was crunch time.

The call was put through to Thompson. Hubbard started with some very brief niceties. It was time to get to the point, leave nothing out, hope for the best, and if it didn't go well, he could pack his bags and go home to someone who loved him no matter what.

"Mike, how in the hell could something like this happen? What the fuck was Mandez thinking when he went on the tier? I hate to be so nasty at a time when you're mourning the loss of a guard, but the shit is going to hit the fan at all levels over this. The last thing we need is to bring attention to that unit. We were hoping that in time this would be a project that would receive acclaim for a forward thinking initiative. This is the brainchild of a lot of people here at the Justice Department. Hell, we even had the President sign off on the CLEO Unit. I'll look over the report you sent me."

While Thompson was talking, Hubbard knew that he should not interrupt. What could he possibly say that would ease the situation?

"Mike, while we are talking, how the hell we can proceed? I know it will be tough to find out exactly what happened. I don't want to downplay this horrendous killing. I definitely need to have Andy Brewer continue what he was sent there for. Let me ask you this—I know it's early in the investigation, do you think Spitlato was behind this?"

Most of the Post-it notes had been pulled from the desk. The water bottle was empty. Hubbard felt like he was in the hot seat and it was getting hotter. The strangest of thoughts came over him as he listened to Thompson. *I don't need this shit.* I am financially sound. I have a beautiful home back in Washington. I still have my health. My kids are grown and successful. The most precious thing I have is back in Washington.

"John, at this point in the investigation, I can't say that I know who might have killed Mandez."

After the phone call with Thompson, it was time for Hubbard to take a deep breath, review the situation, and muster his many years of experience to move forward. The office was a little quieter. The lieutenant and sergeant from homicide had gone. The forensic people had finished. The tier was locked down and very quiet, and the area where Mandez had been found was cleaned up. For a moment it seemed to Hubbard that in the quietness, all was well. It was time for report writing.

Hubbard asked Brewer if he would compile a list of those inmates that had been interviewed and a brief statement about what they had to say. Hubbard said he would start a complete report outlining what had transpired from the time of the attack.

Brewer was working at a computer banging out his reports, when he stopped and threw his hands in the air. "Goddamn it, Mike, let's stop playing pansy with these guys. You got a fuckin' guard dead. Let's pull the rug out from under these guys. Let's start playing hard-ball. I think that if Spitlato didn't actually hit Mandez with the pipe, he sure as shit knows who did. I want to talk to this asshole as soon as possible. I'll bring his butt out of his cell every hour just to piss him off. What do you think, Mike? Do I have your backing to put some heavy duty pressure on Spitlato?"

Hubbard let Brewer spout off. It had been a long night, and the last thing he needed was another confrontation with him. It kind of made sense to him that maybe Brewer was right. Maybe he had been too soft on Spitlato. His concern was that if he gave Brewer the okay with Spitlato, it could get ugly real fast. He knew that Brewer was probably talking with Thompson and reporting on the slow progress of getting anything from Spitlato or anyone else. He needed to remind himself that although they now had a murder investigation, Brewer was sent there to primarily deal with Spitlato. He slid his chair away from the desk. He looked at Brewer and nodded his head.

"Mike, I hope that nodding your head means I have the go ahead with Spitlato. If it does, I want to let you know that I will use every tactic I have in my bag of tricks to break that guy. I'm sure you know that Thompson wants the same thing. We are up against time, but I think Spitlato will talk. He's a tough guy, but I think I'm just as tough. I think this guy can tell us a lot. I know his kind. He will play tough guy as long as it works in his favor. The minute he is offered a deal or at least a promise of a deal, he will purr like a kitten. Mike, I need you to give me the full reigns on this guy. You have a lot on your hands, so let me deal with Spitlato."

"Andy, when you first came here, we did not see eye-to-eye. I'm not sure we are on the same page now. I'm not going to fight you any longer.

It's obvious that Thompson has given you your marching orders with Spitlato. Starting tomorrow you have my permission to move forward with whatever it is you want to get from him. I know you think I'm too soft of a guy to be running this unit. I have been around a long time. I'm getting older and looking forward to retirement. Now that I have given you permission to move forward on Spitlato, let me bore you with one of my many quotes from the one and only, Groucho Marx—'Getting older is not a problem; you just have to live long enough to enjoy it'."

Brewer and Hubbard enjoyed a much needed laugh. They shook hands. The fatigue was setting in and the reports needed to be done.

Chapter 20

The funeral service for Lieutenant Mandez was held on a chilly, gloomy, rainy day. The skies mimicked the somberness of the mood of the many attending the service. As customary for funerals of law enforcement officers killed in the line of duty, the men in blue turned out in record numbers. It was also the occasion for politicians to turn out. They wanted to show their faces, especially if an election was in their future. The governor attended and took the opportunity to stand in the rain on the church steps and denounce violence against prison guards. He stated that he has confidence in the system and justice would prevail. It was interesting to hear him address the large gathering of the media. It was only months ago that the same governor introduced legislation to abolish the death penalty. His bill did not include the death penalty for killing law enforcement officers or correction guards. He ducked questions from reporters if this murder would change his mind.

Several people got up to talk about Lieutenant Mandez. It was a far cry from what the inmates thought of him. Each speaker talked about his dedication to his job. His son talked lovingly about his dad, and other relatives praised him as a good family man—a man who would do anything for his family and his neighbors. Noticeably missing from the service was his ex-wife from whom Mandez had had been divorced for several years.

Approaching the end of the service, the preacher asked if anyone else wanted to speak. Mike Hubbard stood and walked toward the altar.

He pulled a paper from his suit coat pocket and cleared his throat. Nervously, he looked out over the very large gathering. He had prepared some notes on Mandez's career at Pelican Bay, and was hoping that it would not appear to be such an official act. He wanted his remarks to sound sincere. As the most senior official at the prison other than Warden Scope, he knew he needed to say something. He acknowledged the family members and offered his sincere condolences for their loss.

"My name is Mike Hubbard. I'm the warden of the unit that Lieutenant Mandez worked in. We are all deeply saddened for the loss of such an outstanding corrections officer. I have heard some wonderful things about him in the past couple days. On behalf of the warden at Pelican Bay, the secretary of public safety, and all of Lieutenant Mandez's fellow correction officers, I pledge to you that we will tirelessly continue to investigate his senseless death."

Hubbard left the altar and hugged several members of Mandez's family. He had much more on his notes, but he thought it best to be brief and allow others to say something. He left the church with Sergeant Sanders and Andy Brewer.

On the way back to the prison, nobody did much talking. Finally Brewer broke the silence. "Mike, I have scheduled Spitlato for this afternoon. I guess this is as good a time as any to tell you that I talked to Thompson."

"Andy, normally I would be pissed at an employee that goes over my head. I guess I should get used to you talking to Thompson. I don't like it, but obliviously Thompson's okay with it. I'm glad they pay me well for this job, or I would pack it in and go home. Okay, what have you two schemed up that I should know?"

"It's not that we are scheming up anything. I think Thompson feels that you have your hands full running the unit. I'm just keeping you up-to-date on anything that goes down between Thompson and me. It seems that he is getting some direction from his boss. I have been told to change my plan of action with Spitlato. We at first thought that strong arming him would be our best approach. I have now been directed to see if I can convince Spitlato to work with us. I have been given the leeway to make any deal that will convince him to cooperate with the attorney general's office. I'm not sure how far I can go."

Hubbard was listening, but his thoughts were wandering. *How far is this guy going to push me with these conversations with Thompson? Should I have another talk with this guy? Hell, I'm kind of getting intrigued about these talks he has. I guess I will just let it go. Maybe Brewer will piss off Thompson at some point.*

Brewer continued, "During the conversation with Thompson, he sounded like the Justice Department was desperate to get Spitlato back on the street working undercover for them. I think that the tough persona will fade away if Tony thinks he can get out of prison. He's no fool. The tough guy approach is something he wants to maintain in a prison setting. I might be wrong, but I think that if he was offered a deal, he would jump on it."

Hubbard was looking out the window. He was obviously not happy about the conversation between Brewer and Thompson. He was left out again. Before he could pull the plug and tell Thompson to shove the job, he wanted to make sure he did it as professionally as possible. He knew that with his impeccable reputation, there might be other employment opportunities for him.

On the other hand, if he pissed off Thompson, the word would get around. He definitely wanted to resign on good terms. He thought that if his wife pushed the retirement button real hard, he could simply tell Thompson that he wanted to be with her and travel. Many thoughts were running through his head as Brewer was talking. Amazing how you can listen to someone and your thoughts are off in another world.

"Mike, say something. I need you to be on board with the new plan. I don't think it would take long to convince Spitlato that there might be a remote chance that he could get released. I think that after that's done, you will have smooth sailing running your unit."

"Andy, I don't fault you for anything. I intend to have smooth sailing in my unit with or without you or Spitlato. I know that you are following orders. We are in the midst of trying to find out who killed Mandez and you're talking about getting one of the prime suspects out of prison. I'm not sure it's a good time to talk to Spitlato about him getting released. With Tony being one of the top dogs in the unit, he most likely knows who beat Mandez. It sounds like the Justice Department has already forgotten about the murder of a prison guard. I would like to see the interviews completed before there is any talk about getting Spitlato out. I would definitely like to see someone charged with Mandez's murder."

The remainder of the ride back to Pelican Bay was fairly quiet. Hubbard asked Sergeant Sanders to come to his office. Brewer asked if he should also come. Hubbard told him that he wanted to talk to Sanders alone. He asked Brewer to get in touch with the homicide investigators. "I want to know if they have any additional findings uncovered by their investigators and technicians."

When they got back to the office, Hubbard asked Marcia if she would order some lunch for him and Sanders. He asked Sanders if he thought the murder investigation would lead to a successful conclusion. "I want your honest opinion on this. I get the feeling that when Brewer is around, you feel a little intimidated. I know that he's a CIA agent, but don't let that prevent you from voicing your opinion. What do you think of him?"

Sanders adjusted himself in the leather chair. As he did, there were the screeching sounds. He maneuvered himself again, there were more screeching sounds. Hubbard smiled at him. "I get the same thing when I sit there. I need to get that chair replaced."

The lunch came. Hubbard insisted that they eat before they continued their talk. Sanders nibbled on his sandwich. He was wondering what needed to be discussed without Brewer. Marcia came back in the office. She told Hubbard that he had several calls while he was at the funeral. Marcia read off a list of the calls. She said there were a few other calls, but she had handled them. Hubbard thanked her for the lunch and taking care of the calls. He told her that he would like some quiet time with Sergeant Sanders for the next half hour.

"Ron, I wanted some time alone with you. I'm not trying to pick your brain about Brewer or the investigation. I want to let you know that I appreciate all that you have done since I stepped into this position. You have stayed in the background. You have also contributed when called upon. Your record here at Pelican Bay is impressive. I have talked to some command officers and also to Warden Scope about you. So without me making your head so wide that you can't get out that door, I have some good news for you. As of today, you are now Lieutenant Sanders. I have your new badge and promotion papers right here in my desk. Congratulations—I wish you continued success, whether it is here or back in the main prison."

Sanders had long ago stopped nibbling on his sandwich. He stood as Hubbard handed him the bright new gold badge and a promotion certificate. They shook hands, and for a moment, it appeared that they were going to do a chest bump. Ron stared at the new badge as if it were a gold nugget, instead of a gold badge. Speechless for a few seconds, he took a deep breath, cleared his throat, put the badge into his pocket, and reached out to shake hands again with Hubbard.

"Sir, I don't know what to say except thank you. I have waited a long time for this to happen. I promise you that I will continue to work as hard as possible. I hope that it's in this unit working under you for a long time."

"Well, I think you might be here a little longer than I will. I wanted to do the promotion as soon as possible. With the death of Mandez, I was allowed to get it done. I'm sure you want to get out of here and celebrate with your family. Before you go, I want to let you know that you will continue to work with Brewer. I only ask that you be very careful. He sometimes flies by the seat of his pants. I know that you and Brewer seem to get along, so just be careful. Also, if while working with him you feel that he is heading in the wrong direction, I want you to come to me. We both need to remember that one day Brewer will be gone. You and I will still be here, or at least, you will."

CHAPTER 21

A week after the death of Mandez, Warden Scope announced his retirement. It would be effective immediately. It was also announced that Deputy Warden Marcus Dent would replace Scope. Dent wasted no time in calling Hubbard. He left a message saying that he wanted to meet with him and discuss the CLEO Unit. By the tone of his voice in the message, it was obvious to Hubbard that the relationship he had with Scope would not be the same with Dent.

In the short time that Hubbard had been at Pelican Bay, he had heard stories about Dent. It seemed like there was not much love or respect for him among the prison personnel. It was also a known fact around the prison that Dent had been the hatchet man for Scope. Dent seemed to make all the media announcements that pertained to activities at the prison. He testified before the California legislature on pending legislation on prison reform. He presided over the disciplinary hearings of prison guards accused of violations of the rules and regulations.

At the command level in the prison, Scope was more of an administrative guru. He had been a political appointment. He had been appointed by the governor based on his good work in other positions at the state level. Dent, on the other hand, was known as a tough guy. When Scope informed the governor he was retiring, he strongly suggested that Dent be appointed to the position. The governor, who routinely talked about prison reform and mandatory sentencing, agreed that Dent was the right man for the job.

When Dent showed up in Hubbard's office, he was dressed in full uniform. Hubbard was surprised; he had never seen Scope in a uniform. Dent looked very military, and he had taken the liberty of placing two stars on his uniform. As the deputy under Scope, his official rank was colonel; a colonel wore a silver eagle. Dent also had a chest full of medals. When Hubbard saw him, his first thought was that he looked like General Patton.

For the short walk from the main prison to the CLEO Unit, Dent had brought along a uniformed prison guard who now had the silver eagle on his collars. Dent shook hands with Hubbard and immediately introduced the colonel as his new deputy warden. The new deputy warden appeared to be in awe of Dent. He followed so close that Hubbard was thinking that if Dent stopped too quickly, the new deputy would be right up Dent's butt.

"Mr. Hubbard, I appreciate you finding time to meet with me. As the new warden of Pelican Bay, I want to make myself knowledgeable of all that goes on in your unit. I was saddened to hear about what happened to Lieutenant Mandez. I had known him for a few years. He was a good supervisor and will be missed. I'm sure you are actively pursuing his killer. If there is anything I can do, or provide you with, please let me know."

From the appearance of these two, and the formality in Dent's voice, Hubbard knew that this visit would not be pleasant.

As Dent continued, the Colonel did not take his eyes off of him. "I also know that your unit is unique and has the backing of the Justice Department. I want you to be aware that as long as your unit is on the grounds here at Pelican Bay, I insist that I be kept up to date on any issues or problems. When the Justice Department approached Warden Scope about putting this unit here at Pelican Bay, the stipulation that Scope agreed to was that he would be briefed periodically on how the unit was running. I know that Scope gave you a lot of leeway on running your unit. I, on the other hand, want to be involved. I want you to brief me at least once a week."

While Warden Dent was talking, Hubbard was going through some papers on his desk. On occasion, he nodded his head indicating that he at least heard what he said. Dent and his new colonel never budged from their standing position the entire time. When it was apparent that Dent was finished or at least taking a pause, Hubbard stood and walked from behind his desk. He walked within a foot of Dent, usually an uncomfortable distance. Hubbard knew this from his many years of interviewing people. The closer you got to a person the more threatened they felt—that was Hubbard's intentions.

He looked Dent squarely in the eyes. "Mr. Dent, oh excuse me, I mean Warden Dent, I appreciate you taking time from your busy schedule to come and visit me. Now that you have said your spiel, let me say something. I fully understand that you are now the warden here at Pelican Bay. I'm running this CLEO Unit under a federal mandate from the Justice Department. I have no intentions of briefing you weekly on what goes on in this unit. I will let you know of any serious issues that would bring any discredit to Pelican Bay. As you well know, my orders come directly from the Justice Department. I'm sure you are also aware that the Justice Department sits way above the bureau of prisons in the pecking order. With all due respect to you, Warden Dent, I can assure you that this unit will be run with the utmost integrity and professionalism."

Hubbard thought of stopping, but he could see that Dent was getting upset. He savored the moment and moved even closer.

"Warden Dent, I have been around for a long time. I was hand-picked to run this unit, and that's what I intend to do. I'm sure we can get along just fine. You have a huge responsibility in running a prison as large as Pelican Bay. You can rest assured that this unit will not cause you any concerns. I hope our relationship can be both friendly and professional. I'm easy to get along with, and I will make it a point to talk directly to you when necessary."

Warden Dent raised his hand as if to stop Hubbard from continuing. It didn't work; Hubbard got a little louder as he continued.

"You are welcome to visit my unit whenever you want. I only ask that you give me a call to let me know you're coming. I think we have made ourselves perfectly clear. Thanks for the visit. I do wish you success in your new position."

Hubbard backed away from Dent and was surprised when Dent extended his hand for a handshake. "Warden Hubbard, I'm glad we had this talk, even though I didn't get to say much. Let's keep the lines of communication open so that we can both be successful in our positions."

Dent motioned to his colonel, and in a somewhat military maneuver, they turned and exited the office. Hubbard called for Marcia. "Marcia, from this day forward I want you to record all phone calls that come in from the prison side, especially from Warden Dent. I'm not sure how you feel about him, but I don't trust him."

"Sir, I share your lack of trust. I worked over on the prison side for a few years. I know that the guard force doesn't like him. He lacks social skills. He is a former military guy and has brought that attitude with him to this prison. You should be very careful when dealing with him or any of his new staff."

Hubbard retreated to his desk and was hoping for a quiet afternoon. After the funeral, the pending murder investigation, and the discussion with Dent, he needed some time to gather his thoughts. He started to list things he wanted to do on a sticky note. He no sooner slapped a note alongside the phone, than it rang. He thought about ignoring it until he saw that it was Thompson's number. He clicked on his recorder and answered the phone. "Hi John, I hope this is not something that will add to the miserable day I'm having."

"I will try not to add to your obvious hectic day. I just wanted to call and see how things are going. I got your report on the investigation. I know that finding out what happened to Mandez might be tough, but we need to keep trying. You would think that a murder in a prison would be easy to solve. Somebody on that tier is going to come forward with the name. You have talked to Brewer concerning our new approach to dealing with Spitlato. I know you have a lot going on, but this is a priority. I'm getting some heat from my boss. He wants to make sure every effort is tried to get Spitlato to agree to work with us. We need to get him back on the street...we have plans for him."

"John, I understand what your goal is, but do you really think Spitlato could ever be trusted to work with you if he got released. He turned on his police department. What makes you think that he wouldn't do or say anything to get out? This guy is a made Mafia man; his allegiance is to them. He's a hard core guy who only thinks about himself and would probably say or do anything to get out of prison."

"Mike, we are well aware of Tony's allegiance to the mob. He is facing a long time in prison. He's no dummy. I'm certain that if we approach it the right way, he will jump at the opportunity to get on the street. We would have safeguards in place to make sure he worked for us. The slightest hint that he wasn't working with us, and he would be back behind bars in the blink of an eye."

Hubbard mad sure the tape recorder was running. He was thinking that this is a hell of way to be operating. I'm taping the second- in- command at the Justice Department.

"Mike, there are some things that you do not know about why we want him out. I'm not at liberty at this time to tell you, but I do want your cooperation. I have given Brewer the authority to make a deal with Spitlato. If he accepts, you will be needed to work with us to make it happen. I hate to say it, Mike, but the murder investigation is secondary to getting Spitlato out and back with the mob. If we find out who killed Mandez, that's a plus. If Spitlato had anything to do with the murder, we will cross that bridge when we come to it."

Hubbard was thinking that it actually was a good thing that the conversation with Thompson was not in person. He was grinding his teeth, biting his lip, shaking his head, and rolling his eyes. He felt like pounding his fist on the desk. When Thompson said that getting Spitlato out of prison was more important than solving the Mandez murder, he almost shouted into the phone, *"Fuck it, I quit."* He had mustered every emotion in his body to keep from just screaming and telling Thompson to shove the job.

Hubbard had been involved in investigations in the past at the Bureau where the powers above him had made some asinine decisions, but this one topped them all. He was listening to a man who wanted to get an inmate out of prison over solving the murder of a prison guard. What was the motivation at the Justice Department that would warrant such a decision? Was Spitlato such an important spoke in the big wheel of justice? Weren't there other ways to bust the mob without letting a thug like Spitlato out of prison? What would Mandez's family think if they ever found out that we had released the guy who killed their loved one?

"Mike, you haven't said anything. I need to hear it from you that you won't stand in our way. I'm not saying that releasing Spitlato will work. What I am saying is that we don't have many other avenues to pursue. Our information that is coming in from different reliable sources is that some mob guys that are high up in the chain think that Tony took the fall and kept his mouth shut. We think that if we figure a way to get him released, they will accept him back. If that happens, it would be up to Tony to make a life changing decision to work with us or piss away the opportunity to have a new life. If getting him released works, we will guarantee him witness protection in any part of the country he wants. I honestly think that if he works with us, he might even have the opportunity to get his family back. Mike, he would be an absolute fool to turn us down."

"John, I understand what you're goal is, but I'm concerned that he would get out and make fools of us. I don't like it because I don't think this guy would work with you. I'm totally against releasing him before he serves his time."

"Mike, getting Spitlato out of prison is on me and will never reflect badly on you. I promise you, the plan has been cleared at the very top. Do I need to provide you with names, or will you take my word? If you say no to me, I will respect your decision. I will, however, have to replace you in the CLEO Unit. I don't want to do that because I think you're the best man to run that unit. If your only beef about letting him out is that it's just wrong, then you need to get over it."

CHAPTER 22

Brewer phoned the tier supervisor. He asked that Tony Spitlato be brought to the interview room. In preparation for the interview, he had thoroughly reviewed and damn near memorized the extensive file on Tony. He was confident that he knew everything about his career in law enforcement. He also had the transcript from the federal trial that detailed Tony's involvement with the Mafia in New Jersey. Brewer had briefed Sanders on how the interview would proceed. He was sure that Tony would think he was only being interviewed about the murder of Mandez. They would talk about the murder, but the main emphasis would be to feel Tony out on whether he would want to accept a deal to go back in the Mafia.

"Sit down, Tony. I will have the guard take off the cuffs if you promise to be a good boy. Can I get that from you?"

"Well, I guess I have no other choice than to be a good boy. I mean you have some Hulk Hogan looking guards right outside the door. I can handle myself, but I can't compete with those dudes. So the answer is yes, I will be a good boy."

Brewer laughed and seemed amused at Tony's friendly attitude. Brewer was also relaxed, and his attitude change was quite different from the Brewer who came to the CLEO Unit to use any methods possible to get some answers from Tony.

Agent Brewer had been an expert in using methods that made the toughest detainees talk. He had honed his skills while conducting unconventional methods on so-called enemies of the United States. He was used in foreign countries that most people could not even pronounce. He was good at what he did. His tactics were mostly methods of inflicting pain to obtain information or get a confession by causing severe mental or physical anguish. Brewer was everything that liberal Americans thought of when they envisioned a CIA agent torturing someone. He was the master of delivering pain. He could handle these cynical duties because he believed it was being done in the name of freedom, justice, and the American way. He knew from the history of the CIA that he was not the first agent to be designated an inflictor of pain.

"Tony, can I get you something to drink before we start?"

"If you think you can get me to say something for a soda, you are on the right track. Yes, I will take a soda."

"Let me start by telling you that we are going to solve the murder of Mandez, no matter how long it takes. We are in the position to offer a deal to anyone that wants to come forward with a name. There are forty-nine other inmates on that tier. I feel confident that in time we will get the information we need. Let me start our talk today by me simply asking you—who hit Mandez with the pipe?"

"Listen, I know you got a job to do. I'm serving a long sentence in this joint. I only know a handful of the dudes on that tier, and I have my circle of friends. We pretty much keep to ourselves. I appreciate you bringing me out for a visit, and I'm enjoying the soda."

Tony sat back in his chair. He savored the flavor of the soda. He sighed after each sip from the can. He put the soda on the table and continued.

"I know you're thinking that I'm going to sit here and give you the tough guy routine. Brewer, you've been around for a long time, so I'm not going to play games with you. I'll get right to the point. Yeah, I've heard some rumblings on the tier about what happened. Let me ask you a question. What was Mandez doing on the tier in the first place? He wasn't working, or at least, that's what we've been told. Why did the on-duty guards allow him to come onto the tier? We know for a fact that he had been drinking. Think about this—did he bring that pipe with him when he came onto the tier? I'm not a cop any longer, but let's get real about what happened. Mandez was a nasty dude. He disliked anyone that questioned his tactics. That shit about pinching people to get them to move along, what the fuck was that all about? I'm not trying to solve your case, but you need to at least put all those questions up front and work from there. Did he come on the tier drunk, looking for someone in particular? Was he going to work them over with a pipe to show he's the boss?

Tony picked up the soda and in one big gulp finished it. He sat up in his chair and burped. He knew he had Brewer's attention.

"Because he was drunk, did somebody defend themselves and take the pipe away and use it on him? Do you have a case of an inmate just trying to ward off an attack by Mandez? Is there some poor soul sitting in his cell right now that is only guilty of trying to stay alive? You worked with Mandez for a while; you know that he could be violent when he wanted to. You're sitting there thinking that I'm just throwing out a bunch of bullshit. I've had time to think about what happened. I talked to some of the inmates. I would strongly suggest that you direct your investigation along the lines of what I have told you. I really believe you have a case of self-defense. If my memory from my law enforcement days is correct, that would make the death of Mandez a justifiable homicide. I don't mean to run my mouth. This is your show, and you got me out here to ask some questions, so fire away."

Brewer was actually listened intently to Spitlato. He took some notes, and on occasion he nodded as if he might even be agreeing with him. Sanders was stone-faced during the spiel. He appeared to want to jump in and say something, but being new at the interrogation game, he decided it best to leave the questioning to Brewer.

Tony was squeezing the soda can. He knew that he had thrown out a lot of information. Being a former law enforcement officer, he thought that he made a pretty good case of self-defense for whoever hit Mandez. The facts could not be ignored. The autopsy had revealed that Mandez's blood alcohol level was high. The on-duty guards probably let him on the tier because he was a lieutenant. For an inmate to be in possession of a pipe that size would be unlikely. The tier and cells are inspected on a regular basis. How would someone get a pipe that size onto the tier? Where would they even come in contact with a pipe?

The interview was moving along without any confrontations. Tony seemed to be at ease. For being a tough guy, Brewer was actually pleasant toward Tony. Brewer told Tony that he appreciated him providing some insight in what might have happened to Mandez. He told Tony that all investigative avenues would be checked out. He did agree with Tony that Mandez going on the tier while he was off duty was unusual. The fact that he was drinking did not look good. Where the pipe came from was being checked out.

"Tony, while we are together I would like to bring something up that might interest you. What I'm going to discuss with you is sensitive. It's something that you do not want to discuss with anyone on the tier or, for that matter, with anyone at all. If you do share what I'm going to talk to you about, any deals we might make would be out the window. Do you understand?"

"You've got my attention. I'm not going anywhere. I have no other appointments today, so I'm all ears. Can I get another soda?"

"Tony, I want to get right to the point. I have thoroughly reviewed your background. I think I know all about you from the time you went on the police department, up to and including the federal trial that put you in this place. You were actually a good cop before you turned. If you didn't already know, I will tell you that I'm working directly with the Justice Department. What I want to discuss with you comes from a very high position at the Justice Department."

Tony was smiling at Brewer; he could tell that something good was going to come soon. No more requests for sodas, no more smiles... Tony perked up and wanted to hear more.

Brewer continued, "I will also tell you that when I initially took this assignment I was prepared to come to Pelican Bay and get information from you by any means it took, including some very nasty pain inflicting methods. If you're thinking that something like that could not happen in a prison, you are sadly mistaken. Warden Hubbard knows why I'm here. Even though his mandate here is to run a fifty man prison unit, he has instructions from the Justice Department to cooperate with me. I know I'm telling you a lot. Let me throw this out to you—do you ever think about getting out of this place?"

Tony sat up in his chair. Whatever Brewer was about to get to intrigued him. His thoughts were...*what the hell could the Justice Department have in mind that they wanted me out of prison?*

Tony was tough, but he could turn on the charm when needed. He was also very smart...very street smart. He had the benefit of growing up in a bad neighborhood. To stay out of trouble in that neighborhood, you had to be somewhat of a con artist and a quick thinker. He was a typical teenager who got in trouble, but nothing that would prevent him from getting into law enforcement. He somehow avoided being arrested while many of his buddies weren't so lucky. When he chose law enforcement, the guys that he grew up with were shocked. They knew about his quick temper that got him into many fights. After Tony finished the police academy and was working the Camden streets, he often told his old friends that he was always one step ahead of the authorities. His future could have gone either way for him.

Tony was relaxed and he was controlling his emotions. It was not the time to even attempt to put the bad guy role into motion.

"I would be lying to you if I told you that I don't think about getting out of here every day, just like the other forty-nine guys on that tier. That's what gets us through each day. Being confined in a cage like an animal is not something I would wish on my worst enemy. You guys get to go home tonight. I get to go back to a miserable life in which every move I make is monitored. To get back to your question, hell, I would do anything to get out of here."

Knowing that he had Tony in the palm of his hand, Brewer continued. "Tony, my instructions are to talk to you about agreeing to work for the Justice Department if we get you released. Our intelligence that we get from reliable sources is that you are endeared by the mob guys in Camden. They feel that you took your licks and never ratted on anyone. At your federal trial, you consistently pleaded that you were not guilty, but you never asked for a deal to put any mob figures away. You know by doing that, you remain in good standing with them. It may sound far-fetched to some, but at the Justice Department they are willing to take a chance on you."

Tony now had the biggest smile on his face since the birth of his first child. "Keep talking; this is getting real interesting. I would like to hear more about your plan. I'm not saying that I would look forward to getting out and living my life in the mob again. You do know from reading about me that I lost everything when I was convicted. Would it be possible, if I agree to your plan, to somehow make my wife aware that I'm doing something good for a change? I don't know if she would ever take me back, but it would be something I would want to explore."

"Tony, if you agree, no one, and that includes your wife, can know about this. If down the road, it worked out where you provided enough information to take down some of the Camden Mafia, I'm sure the Justice Department would provide you with protection and a new identity. If and when that happens, it would be up to you to convince your wife to take you back. I would think that if she knew you agreed to work with us and do something right for a change, she might consider it. I must reiterate to you that if this happens, absolutely no one other than the people you would be reporting to can know about this. You know how this works. You also know what would happen to you, if working with the government got out to the people we want you to provide information on. I don't have to tell you about the mob. They don't play fair; they would take you out in a Camden minute. Do we understand each other?"

"I'm well aware of what would happen to me. I was undercover long enough to have seen what happens to people who rub the mob the wrong way. Now you have to understand something. I led that life at one time, and it cost me everything. If those guys have any inkling that I was back in the organization to rat on them, they would get rid of me in a way that you would never find the pieces. I have to weigh my options. I can spend my time in prison and hope for an early release for being a good prisoner. I can also hope that the pending appeal before the federal judge goes in my favor, or I can agree to work for you guys."

"Tony, your chances of getting an early release are slim at best. As far as Judge Sharper even hearing your appeal, it just ain't going to happen. I would think that by the process of elimination that leaves you with our plan. Let me tell you something, Tony. I'm kind of glad I didn't have to go the route of daily doses of fuckin' with you. I can't say that I like you. I do want everything on the table before you agree to work with the Justice Department. The mere fact that we want to offer you this deal means that if you accept, you will be between a rock and a hard place. By that, I mean you will be totally under the powerful wing of the almighty Justice Department. I'm not going into some of the details that would have to take place, to get you out. I will say that if we do get you out, and you screw it up in any way, your ass will be right back here in the CLEO Unit."

Brewer was now taking the lead. He let Tony talk earlier, but now he was in charge and laying the ground work. Sanders said nothing; he was trying to act calm. This was all knew to him.

"Tony, you do realize that out of the three options we mentioned, we control all of them. Your failure to cooperate would mean no possibility of any early release from prison. You being a smart guy, you have to know that the Justice Department at the highest level has control over Judge Sharper. He is very close to his lucrative federal retirement. He will do what he is told to do. Besides that, Tony, Judge Sharper really believes that you and your mob guys killed a federal judge. So, I hope that I'm making myself very clear. I want to make your decision a little easier for you. Remember what they say about us Feds. We are here to help you, or am I stealing the line about the IRS?

Tony smiled; he knew Brewer was using the power of the almighty government to make his case. He also knew that Brewer was right; his choices were not really choices at all.

"Tony, I think I know what your answer will be. Do you want to go back to your cage and think about it? I'm sure the mushy, stinking dinner will be served soon. Just think Tony, if you're out of this shithouse soon, you could be sitting in the LaPatorre Restaurant in downtown Camden with all your wop friends eating like a king. Close your eyes and think of the smell coming out of Chef Lugi's kitchen at LaPatorre. So what's it going to be, Tony? Do you want curtain number one, curtain number two, or curtain number three? I'm betting my money that you take curtain number three."

"Brewer, I do have to say that you can be very convincing. I love the part about a fabulous meal at LaPatorre. You left out the very expensive wine that the wops drink. By the way, if we were out on the street and you called me a wop, I would kick your ass. I just want to make that very clear to you. Now, let's get back to the curtains. With much thought and having actually taken a peak into curtain number three, I think I'm going to take that number three curtain. Can we celebrate by having a nice Italian meal brought into the prison from LaPatorre? Is this the part where we shake hands and slap each other on the back?

"Tony, there will be no slapping on the back. I want to again warn you that if you discuss this with anyone, the deal is off. I know how you like to talk to your compadres and play the big cheese role. From the minute you leave this room, if I find out that you talked to anyone about this, you'll never see LaPatorre or for that matter, you'll never see a fuckin' Burger King. You have a great opportunity. Don't piss it away or your wop ass, oh, excuse me, I mean your Italian ass will be behind bars for the remainder of your sentence. We will also make sure if you return to prison you will never have the chance of parole.

Brewer stood up and Sanders followed suit. Tony stayed in his chair, but he knew the meeting was over; he just wasn't ready to go back to his cell.

"Tony, there's one more thing before you go back to the tier. Because your buddies' think you are a tough guy, they are expecting you to come back looking like you got fucked up a little. Is it okay if I punch you in the face and draw a little of that Italian blood?"

Tony cocked his head back and frowned at Brewer. He stood up and started for the door to the tier. He stopped, threw his hands in the air, and told Brewer to take his best shot. Brewer started to walk toward Tony. "What side of your face would you like the blood?"

"Whoa, you look like you want to draw a little more blood than I care to give. Let Mr. Sanders do the honors. He looks like he might be a little more compassionate than you."

Sanders stood by the table, he wasn't sure if Tony was serious. He didn't appear in any hurry to fulfill Tony's request. When he realized that it would be him doing the bloodletting, he approached Tony. "I would have never thought that this would be part of my job as a lieutenant in this unit. I will do the honors."

Tony stood tall and put his arms down to his side with the palms of his hands open. "I'm all yours Mr. Sanders. Let it happen."

Sanders made a fist and lunged at Tony striking him in the face. There was a loud thud, but the blow didn't move Tony at all. He shook his head. He touched his face. "Mr. Sanders, I've had woman hit me harder than that. How about if I smack you in the face to show you how it's done?" With a fluent motion, Tony reached out smacked Sanders in the face. Sanders was shaken for a minute by the blow but rebounded. Without saying a word he hit Tony with a right hand to the face. He missed a lot of the face and caught Tony in the nose. Blood poured out of Tony's nose.

Sanders made a move as if he were going to take another shot at him. In a move reminiscent of a professional wrestler, Tony grabbed Sander's arm and put it behind his back. In the same motion, he had his arm around his throat. Brewer stood back and wanted to see how Sanders handled the situation. Then Tony released Sanders. "Okay, you got the blood. I was not going to let you continue. You had that look in your face that you wanted to mess me up. I can't allow that; I hope your arm is okay. I'll let this blood just run down on my shirt. Maybe we should scream at each other and throw the furniture around so that the guys on the tier think we really went at it."

"Tony, I think we have established what we set out to do. I don't think your nose is broken. When you get back on the tier and after everyone sees you, let me know if you need medical treatment. I'm going to make some phone calls. I'll probably get back to you tomorrow to talk some more."

Tony walked to the door leading to the tier. When the guard was cuffing him to take him back, he looked at Brewer and Sanders. "I'm not done with you two assholes. Get me in this room with you two again and I'll fuck both of you up so bad that your mother won't recognize you."

Tony said it loud enough so that it could be heard on the tier. As he was being led away, he turned and winked at Brewer.

Chapter 23

Judge Wallace Sharper lived in a gated upscale community just outside the city limits of Camden, New Jersey. He had been a judge for over thirty years. He moved up the judge ladder to his present position as judge of the U.S. Federal Appeals Court for the Third District.

His home looked more like a castle. It sat on five acres of land that overlooked the Cooper River. He lived in the home with his wife of forty years. They had a son who was a high-profile criminal attorney in Camden. When not on the bench hearing appeals, the judge spent most of his time gardening and sailing. He very seldom socialized, but when he did, it was usually with other judges. He had a reputation of possessing a brilliant mind when it came to all aspects of the criminal code. He also had somewhat of a temper in the courtroom and had been admonished on a few occasions by the governing body of federal judges. He was very abrupt with attorneys whom he thought were not as understanding of the law as he was. He often lectured them to the point at which it appeared to be a scolding.

The judge had received a phone call earlier in the day from Assistant Attorney General John Thompson. He had known Thompson for a few years, but not on a personal basis. Their interactions always involved cases that Thompson's office prosecuted. Thompson had requested to meet Judge Sharper at the judge's home. He told him that it was a serious matter that needed to be discussed away from the federal building. The judge agreed to meet Thompson after dinner.

Judge Sharper had finished dinner and was relaxing with his favorite drink, Crown Royal over ice in a small glass. His wife often commented that he was so predictable—a good meal, the Crown Royal, and a good cigar. She knew when he was awake because she could hear him scream. He usually fell asleep with the cigar in his mouth. The cigar would fall down onto his chest and burn him. She had asked him not to smoke after dinner because it was the same result every night. Patching the holes in his shirts where the cigar had burned through was a regular chore.

After the scream, he was awake. He heard a voice on his security intercom coming from the front gate. It was Thompson requesting to be buzzed in.

After some brief polite chitchat, Thompson asked if they could talk business. Sharper directed him into a small office just off the living room. The walls had plaques and some paintings of what appeared to be family. The desk was a mess with papers and a few empty glasses. Sharper asked Thompson if he could get him a drink.

"Judge, I will take a raincheck on the drink. I have an issue that I want to discuss with you. As the deputy attorney general, I want to first let you know that the attorney general has been briefed. He is in full agreement with what I will discuss with you. I'm sure you know that what we talk about is considered confidential. I would like for you to hear me out before you respond."

"Mr. Thompson, I'm fully aware that what I talk about with the deputy attorney general who comes to my house at night is confidential. I'm sure that it is something that you all have placed a high priority on, or you wouldn't be here. So tell me what's up with the AG's office and let's see how I can help."

"Judge, you recently took under review an appeal from federal prisoner, Tony Spitlato. I'm sure you remember the circumstance of why he is serving time in prison. You might not know, but he is serving his time on the West Coast at Pelican Bay. He was recently transferred there under a new program started by the Justice Department. He is in a unit called the CLEO Unit, which stands for Corrupt Law Enforcement

Officers. We have fifty convicted former law enforcement officers in that unit at this time, one from each state."

The judge sat and massaged his face with his fingers. He was stroking his face and puckering his lips as Thompson talked. It was the same expressions he took when presiding over cases in his courtroom. Defense attorneys knew that when the face massaging started, some verbal backlash was about to come from the judge.

Thompson knew the facial expressions of the judge; he had seen them earlier in his career. Thompson continued, "Tony Spitalto is why I'm here tonight to talk to you. Prior to his sentencing under the RICO Act, he was embedded deep in the Camden, New Jersey, mob. After some time in the mob, he became a made man. Even with the mob now knowing his background in law enforcement, we have reason to believe they would welcome him back in their organization with open arms. We have intelligence information that backs this up. We have also intercepted phone conversations that make us feel that if Spitlato was released from prison, they would make an effort to get him back in the mob."

Judge Sharper put up his hand to stop Thompson. He asked if he wanted something to drink. Thompson said he would like to have a cup of coffee. The judge dialed a number on his phone which was an intercom to his kitchen. His wife answered and he asked her to bring come coffee to his office. He then asked Thompson to continue.

"Judge, the simple reason I'm here tonight is that we want Spitlato out of Pelican Bay. You hold that power. We could try to work some other ways to get him out, but granting him an appeal and the media playing it up would be our best shot. It would require you to sign off on conducting a hearing on his motion and then granting him the appeal. We would also want him to be released from prison pending a new trial on the appeal. Do you have any questions so far?"

"Mr. Thompson, I want you to know that I don't like that Spitlato guy. I remember the trial; he's a bad actor. Do you really think he would work with you after all that he has done? He's a full-fledged turncoat. You do know that he is a suspect in the killing of a federal judge. I really don't think this guy is someone you want to work with. I understand why you want him out. I just don't think he would go back to that mob life and be of any help to you."

Thompson sensed that the judge wanted to play hardball; it was his nature. He could not separate himself from the courtroom. It was all about the law. He asked Thompson about any safeguards that would be put in place if Spitlato got out. Thompson, thinking that the judge would have said yes to the plan already, was prepared to push a little harder if necessary. He explained that all precautions that the Justice Department deemed necessary would be in place.

The judge leaned forward on his desk. "Mr. Thompson, I think you know how long I have been a judge. I plan on retiring very soon. The last thing I would need that might upset my retirement plans would be a scandal. While you were talking, I could only think of all that could go wrong. There must be a better way to accomplish your goal of going after the mob. This Spitlato guy is bad news. I'm not sure I want to go along with a plan to release him."

"Judge, with all due respect to you and your position, I came here to get your blessing. I do not want to go back to my boss and tell him that you do not want to cooperate. The mere fact that you will be retiring soon should be more reason to help us. You have the easy part in this plan. My office will have the task of putting all the hard parts together to make it work. Do you really want me to go back to the AG and tell him you refused to cooperate?"

The judge finished what was left of his drink and put the empty glass with the other empty glasses. He came around from his desk, and Thompson followed his movement. "Well, Mr. Thompson, I will give you the okay. Let me tell you something before you leave. If at any time your masterful plan appears to go south, I will be the first to let the newspaper know that I opposed it."

"Judge, I don't think you would do that. I will have the lawyers at the Justice Department get in touch with you to work out the date for the appeal hearing. I want to again tell you that what we discussed is confidential. You should not discuss it with anyone. Your job is to simply have the appeal hearing and order that Spitlato be released pending a new trial."

"I'm not really used to people telling me what to do. Like I told you, if this goes bad, I will protect my retirement at all cost. I just hope I can control my temper in court when I tell that piece of shit he has won his appeal."

Thompson knew that he should quit while he was ahead. He put some papers back into his briefcase and got up to leave. He extended his hand to shake with the judge, but the judge, however, did not return the gesture. He told Thompson he would show him to the door. "Mr. Thompson, I did not shake hands with you for one simple reason. I'm an old guy. I have been around for many years. Shaking hands to me means a deal has been made. I'm not making a deal with you. I will pull out of this at any point I feel it is detrimental to me or my family."

"Judge, I think I know where we stand. When Spitlato gets out of prison, we will be dealing with some of the most dangerous people in Jersey. I would hope you would think long and hard before you make any decisions you might regret. I would hate to see anything happen to your retirement or to you."

Chapter 24

The law firm of Howard Gibbons was located in downtown Camden, one block from the district courthouse. Gibbons could be seen in the morning walking to the courthouse with several court papers stuffed in his coat pocket. His first stop before court was at Vilano's restaurant, where he was a morning fixture. The owner was a former client whom Gibbons had gotten off on a numbers racket charge. Nick Izzini worshipped Gibbons and raved about him to his customers. Gibbons loved the attention and picked up some new clients by simply showing up each morning.

He always sat in the back booth facing the front door. He would kid Nick that if anyone wanted to kill him, he wanted to see the shots coming. He would have his usual each morning—coffee and a dragon fruit cannoli with whipped cream on the top. Nick had the reputation of making a variety of cannolis that drew people to the restaurant. Originally from Vincenza, Italy, he came to America with his family when he was ten years old. He went to school for a few years and quit to help support his family. He worked in a few Italian restaurants for a while and then realized he could make more money in the numbers racket. When he had enough to buy a small restaurant, he purchased Vilano's. After Gibbons worked a deal to get him probation on the numbers charge, he decided to go straight.

Gibbons was enjoying his cannoli when he was approached by two men impeccably dressed. They looked a little out of place with the morning clientele at Vilano's. The booth where Gibbons was sitting was small. One of the men slid into the booth, the other just stood by the counter.

"Good Morning, Mr. Gibbons. I hope you don't mind me sitting in your booth. My name is Pat Driscoll. I work in the Justice Department for the Deputy Attorney General, John Thompson. My friend near the counter is a federal agent. I asked him to come with me. I always err on the side of caution. I don't carry a weapon, but he does."

"Mr. Driscoll, I didn't say you could sit in my booth. However, I get the feeling that I really don't have a choice of sharing my morning relaxing time with you. You can tell your gun-toting friend that he is welcome to sit with us. Standing there will scare the shit out of Nick's customers. Just so you know, I would venture to say that some of the customers in this joint are carrying also. What brings the Justice Department to see me without calling my office?"

Driscoll motioned for the agent to sit at the counter and then pulled some papers from his suitcoat. Gibbons continued to finish his cannoli. "Mr. Driscoll, I would hope this doesn't take long. I have several cases this morning in the district court."

"Can we do away with the formalities? Can I call you Howard? Please call me Pat, and we can pretend that we know each other. I'm here this morning to talk about Tony Spitlato. As his attorney, I want to discuss something with you that is very private. I would ask you not to discuss this with anyone. Can I get your word on that?"

"If what you want to discuss pertains to Tony's well-being, I'm all ears. I'm actually in the process of filing another appeal for Tony. I think he got a raw deal at his trial. We were hoping that his last appeal would have provided us an opportunity to get a new trial. As you know, the federal judge turned him down."

"I'm aware that his appeal was turned down. I have something that might interest you as far as getting Tony out. I must first tell you that we know that you have an affiliation with the mob in New Jersey. You have represented several of them over the years. I'm here today to talk to you about a plan we have for getting Tony out. We want to get him out and have him agree to go back in the mob. In turn, after a period of time, we would consider placing him in a Witness Protection Program. He would have to work with us to get indictments on mob members. Everything will depend on Tony agreeing and also on any results he gets while working back in the mob. We have confidence in him that he could pick up where he left off before he was indicted."

Gibbons put down the cannoli. He looked at Driscoll and smiled. He wiped his hands on a napkin and said, "Please tell me this is some kind of a weird joke."

Driscoll smile back at him and said, "Our sources in the field feel that the mob would take him back with no questions asked. This is where you come in. As his attorney, you would also need to work with us. We are confident that the federal judge will grant the appeal and release Tony until a new trial can be set."

Gibbons was now squirming in his seat. Even though he had been around for a long time, he had never been approached to participate in anything like this. "And what if I tell you to go to hell?"

"Howard, let be upfront with you. When I said that we know you have mob ties, I mean we have enough on you to indict you under the RICO laws. I'm not going to go into all that we have. Let me just say that you don't really have much of a choice. If you think you are going to put on the almighty lawyer spiel, I would suggest that you don't do that. If you work with us, we will work with you at a later time. If you do not work with us, I guarantee you that your ass will be in a federal prison real soon."

"Are you threatening me, Pat?"

"You bet your ass I'm threatening you. If you work with us fine. If you don't, then this conversation never took place. What's it going to be?"

Gibbons loosened his tie. Sweat beads were forming on his forehead. He was getting very uncomfortable. Nick came over to the booth and asked if everything was okay. Gibbons waved him off and said he was fine. Driscoll stared at Gibbons. He had a smile on his face; he knew he had the upper hand. He was enjoying watching a prominent lawyer squirm. It was like the tactics that lawyers used in court on witnesses. They loved to grill witnesses and watch them sweat and squirm in the chair. This was what Gibbons was now going through, and he didn't like it.

"Pat, I have a family to think about. If any of my clients that I have represented get wind that I had anything to do with Tony getting back in the mob, they would kill me. They would probably kill my family. I'm sure you know that some of my former clients are pretty nasty people. What assurances can you give me that any involvement I have in getting Tony out will never be disclosed?"

"Howard, if you work with us and everything goes as planned, I can guarantee you that your involvement will never be released. On the other hand, I have to be very frank with you. If you agree to work with us and turn on us, you will spend a lot of time in prison. I promise you that you will not see that family you talked about. Howard, your involvement in this will be minimal. You already represent Tony, so anything you do to get him out would be a plus in the eyes of your mob friends."

Gibbons asked Driscoll if they could go back to his office to continue the discussion. Driscoll said there was not really much more to talk about. He told Gibbons that all he had to do was file a motion for an appeal before Judge Sharper. When Gibbons heard that name, he pounded his fist on the table. "That prick won't grant us our appeal for a new trial; he already turned us down once. What makes you think he would grant the motion?"

"Howard, all you have to do is say you will work with us. We will take care of all the rest. Your job as Tony's lawyer would be to file the motion. We will tell you what you have to do after that. I know you have to get to court. So what's your answer?"

"Damn, I ain't got many options here. I feel like some of those poor bastards that I'm going to represent today. Most of them are guilty as hell. I will go to court and come up with some bullshit defense, but they're all going to jail. Now I know how they feel. If you're waiting for an answer—the answer is I will do whatever I have to do to stay out of prison. You know what, Pat? You guys should change the name of the Justice Department. There is no justice in what you are doing to me. You think the mob is cruel, but you bastards make the mob look like *Mr. Rogers' Neighborhood*"

CHAPTER 25

Tony was treated like a hero when he got back on the tier. As he passed the inmates, he smiled and gave the thumbs- up. The blood continued to pour from his nose. He had a towel, but he made no effort to stop the bleeding. There were chants of *Tony...Tony...Tony.* Slaps on the back came from just about everybody. Tony loved it. He was playing out the alleged beating like a real actor. He got to his cell and found Louie, Donny, and Bernie waiting for him. They were all smiles. It was as if Tony had taken a beating for all the men of the CLEO Unit.

Louie Tusta gave Tony a bear hug. "My man Tony, you showed those bastards how tough we can be. I gotta ask you Tony, did you do some damage to those pricks? I'll bet you fucked somebody up pretty good. I wish I could have been in there with you. We would have taken on the whole bunch. Tony Spitlato and Louie Tusta, we certainly would have been a deadly duo. We'd wipe the floor with those assholes. I'm real proud of you Tony and the rest of the guys are also. We might be inmates in this hellhole, but we ain't taken any shit off those guys."

Tony was glowing as the accolades kept coming. It was Napolitano's turn; he grabbed Tony and kissed him on the cheek. He made sure it was a spot where there was no blood. "Damn Tony, how in the hell did they get that close to you? They were trying to break your fuckin' nose. How many of them was it? I know one guy could not have done that kind of damage to a big dude like you. Did you mess'em up real good? Come on, Tony, stop the suspense. What the hell happened in there?"

Before Tony could say anything, it was Bernie's turn. "I ain't gonna kiss you big man. I don't want to start any rumors around here that you and I are a thing. Just kidding my man, what the hell happened in there?"

Tony sat in a chair. He finally made some effort to wipe the blood from his face. His nose hurt like hell, but it was not broken. He had a couple of broken noses in the past. A few more guys started to join in on the congratulatory party. Tony being a quick thinker and a real good bull-shitter started to talk. "Guys, let me just say that I did do some damage in that room. I think they are sorry they took the cuffs off me. There's blood in that room, and most of it ain't mine. All I can say about what happened in there is that they thought they could strong-arm me into saying who nailed Mandez."

The crowd around Tony grew to about half the inmates. There was a certain faction that didn't like Tony and his associates, so they stayed away. Tony made no effort to reach out to those inmates who were not in his inner circle of friends. Even though the tier wasn't that big, it did allow for groups to bond. From the day the CLEO Unit was opened, it didn't take long to see the groups form. When they were in the yard for exercise, it was the same. It was not quite like gang affiliations inside Pelican Bay. Most of the inmates in the CLEO Unit were just cops that went bad; they were not gangsters before they were sentenced. They were cops that looked for some easy money. They turned against the oath they had sworn to uphold which was to protect and serve the citizens of their cities and states.

In the prisons that they had come from, they needed to put on a façade of a tough guy. If not, they could find themselves in fights just to stay alive. Also in their former prisons, they were most likely in the general population with real hard core inmates; guys who had committed some of the most heinous crimes imaginable. Now they knew they were in with other cops that got caught doing bad things. The fear that they might have had in their prior prison was not a factor in the CLEO Unit. In any accommodations that were crowded on a daily basis, you would expect some disgruntled men.

After the death of Mandez, the staff of the CLEO Unit looked at the inmates in a different light. The guys that were just cops gone bad were now looked at as people with some of the same anger issues that the inmates in general population had. When you treat someone like an animal, you can only expect that person eventually to act like an animal.

Tony had cleaned up and was sporting a few bruises on his face. He continued to lavish in the attention he was getting. Down deep inside he knew he had to play the game if any subsequent release would happen. He also knew that he would want to leave the CLEO Unit with everyone thinking how tough he was. His release could not be discussed with anyone, even his closest cell mates. He wanted to leave the CLEO Unit with the inmates just thinking that he was granted an appeal and thus a new trial. If they had any wind of him making a deal with the government to get out, it wouldn't take long for the details to get around. These prior cops still had connections on the outside. Any leak of the information about Tony's deal could mean serious consequences for Tony and his family.

Pat Driscoll reported back to Thompson on the meeting with Gibbons. "Well, with a little persuasion I have convinced Mr. Gibbons to cooperate with us. I still don't trust that guy. He has had so many years working with the mob as their consigliere or as he would want to be called, their attorney. His connection with some of the most powerful Dons goes back many years. If this guy would ever consider working with us, we could take down the entire Camden mob. I really am skeptical of him."

"Pat, you did a good job. Let's not worry about Gibbons at this time. We need him to continue to represent Tony. Once we get Tony back on the street, we can think about getting an indictment on Gibbons. He is so underwater with his mob dealings, and we have enough on him to send him away for a long time. At this point, we have a judge that is worrying about his retirement. We have a lawyer that we need to work with, although we know all about his dealings with the mob. We are almost ready to make the move to get Tony out."

Driscoll thanked Thompson for saying he did a good job. He was well aware that if Thompson's methods of handling high-level investigations were ever uncovered, he might go down with the ship. He had thought about leaving the Justice Department and going back into private practice, but the money was good and he didn't have to seek out new clients, as he would have to do in private practice.

Thompson said, "I was considering talking to Hubbard, but I'm not sure I want him in on Spitlao's release. He's a pretty straight guy; he might not want to go along with it. I'll have to think about what I want to do with him. I get the gut feeling that he would just as well pack it in and go back to D.C. with his wife. I think the fewer people we have involved in this—the better our chances are of any success."

Driscoll paced the office while Thompson was talking. "John, I know how much you want the plan to work. I'm totally on board with you. We need to make sure that the people that we need to make it happen, don't get jittery later and go to the media to save their asses. The only one that will benefit from this whole ordeal is Spitlato. He gets out of prison, and the only thing he has to do is go back to his friends. I know he will have to report to us, but what if he decides to just feed us bullshit? We would be no better off with him on the street unless he takes this opportunity seriously. The only people I'm worrying about in this are me and you."

"Pat, we work for the highest law enforcement office in this country. I don't have to tell you that in the past we have dealt with some characters that needed to be silenced. We do this important work under the umbrella of what's best for the country. We know that when you fight organizations like the Mafia, you do not play fair. Over my years here in the Justice Department, I've dealt with subjects that we needed to eliminate. They could just disappear or meet with a terrible accident. We are not at that point yet, but do you get where I'm coming from?"

Driscoll knew exactly what Thompson was talking about. The power of the Justice Department was used in some nefarious ways in the past. It seemed that whoever was in charge, made it known that they had the power to do whatever was necessary to protect the integrity of the country. Thompson continued to stroll around the office, occasionally looking out the window at the great view.

Thompson stopped and looked directly at Driscoll. "At this level, we have immense power. I report directly to the attorney general, but I can filter what I report to him. That leaves him out of the fray. His job is more political than the real world of crime. He goes to the White House, he reports to Congress, and makes the department run.

It's my job to get real criminal work done. I knew that when I took the job. I have no problem with it. Don't worry about any of the other players in this plan. If it becomes necessary, they might just meet with the same fate as some other characters I have dealt with in the past. Do I have to lay it out any plainer for you, or do you get where I'm coming from?"

Driscoll knew exactly where he was coming from. He had heard this language a few times in the past. Driscoll sat on the couch as Thompson continued.

"This is serious shit. The Camden mob is responsible for so many murders over the years that I stopped counting. If we have to eliminate someone, we sure as hell have the ability to make it look like the mob did it. Those gangsters take pride in killing people. If necessary, all we have to do is leak something to the media that the mob did it. There are so many factions within the mob—they will be fighting to take credit. It's like a feather in their cap when they are accused of a murder, especially if it's a federal judge or a prominent attorney. I'm not saying that would happen. I am saying that in order to protect everyone at our level, we do what needs to be done. It's a dog eat dog business we're in. I like to think of us as pit bulls."

Driscoll listened to every word from Thompson. He knew how tough he was and wondered how far up the chain of command Thompson would have to go to actually get the okay to murder someone. How many times had they resorted to murder in the past? Driscoll knew that when it came to fighting organized crime, the Justice Department twisted the rule book on occasion.

"Pat, I don't think you know this…I'm actually a very religious guy. I participate in my church, and on occasion, I have preached to the flock. I've done a lot of reading in the Bible about justice. I'm not a scholar of theology, but I know that justice is a complex virtue. Since ancient times, it has been recognized that justice is a complex or multi-dimensional value that applies to a broad range of human endeavors in varying ways. Social justice deals with how goods and resources are justly distributed between parties. Criminal justice deals with how wrongdoing is identified and penalized. Much of what the Bible says about social justice has a direct correlation with criminal justice. Everything we do here at the Justice Department is legal and forthright in God's eyes. I do want you to understand that if people like you and I didn't have a passion for keeping this country safe, the elements that we fight against each and every day would take over."

"John, I agree with you a hundred percent. We're going to make this deal with Spitlato work. I can see us down the road standing in the media room announcing the biggest crackdown on the Camden Mafia in years. Let me know when you get the okay from the boss. I will be ready to make things happen."

Chapter 26

The CLEO Unit was fielding questions daily from the media. With the murder of Mandez still a hot topic, the media was now able to gain access to information that they did not have in the past about the CLEO Unit. The once mysterious unit hidden away within the walls of Pelican Bay was now being exposed. Why was such a unit needed in the first place? Couldn't this gathering of corrupt cops serve their sentences in the federal prisons where they committed their crimes? Why was there a need to create a special facility to house fifty of the most corrupt cops in the nation? Was it because the Justice Department needed to show its existence and power? Was it a scare tactic to law enforcement officers around the country? Was there a surplus of money at the federal level that needed to be spent? God forbid that a federal agency would ever think about turning money back into the big pot.

Was it political? Who was to gain by spending all the money and manpower to have such a unit? These questions and more seemed to appear in the newspapers on a daily basis. Over time, the media seemed to have more questions about the existence of the CLEO Unit than it did about the murder of a prison guard.

Hubbard tried to keep up with all the media requests his office received. His main concern, which he always told the media, was to bring to justice the person responsible for the death of Lieutenant Mandez. Convincing the media to keep the focus on solving a murder became

harder and harder. It would have been much easier for Hubbard to re-
fer the questions to the warden of Pelican Bay. He did not do it because he wanted to show he was in control. If the warden or the Justice
Department received inquiries about the unit, they simply directed
them back to Hubbard. Hardly a day went by without some news source
trying to get information.

Hubbard put out a memo to his staff that all request for information
be directed to his office. He wanted to do that to make sure the same
message went out after each inquiry. Maybe the press would get tired of
asking the same questions.

The investigation of the death of Mandez seemed to be winding
down, except that a murder of a correctional guard should never wind
down. Brewer and Sanders stayed on the investigation relentlessly.
Interviews had been conducted with all the inmates. Some of the interviews were done quickly. Some interviews that seemed to have the possibility of providing information into the death took longer; however,
none of the interviews proved fruitful enough that they would lead to
any possibility of charging someone with the murder.

It was frustrating for Brewer. He was accustomed to applying a heavy
hand to those with whom he had dealt with in the past, but now he was
under the watchful eye of Warden Hubbard. On a few occasions while
doing some interviews, Brewer made threats, and a few physical confrontations did occur. While conducting the interviews, Brewer had to keep
in mind the Justice Department's main plan of getting Spitlato out of
prison. In a couple of interviews with those on the tier that did not like
Tony, a few inmates told Brewer that if they had to pick someone capable
of killing Mandez, it would be Tony Spitlato. That's about as far as it went
with anyone coming up with information.

During a few of the interviews, Brewer got agitated, screamed, and
threatened, but he never used excessive physical force on anyone. As
the interviews went on, he became totally frustrated knowing that somebody on that tier had to know what happened. His screaming, threats,
and promises went by the wayside. On occasion, he even made some

promises he knew he could not keep, such as a reduction in their sentence, a transfer back to their home state, and extended visitation rights for families. He tried everything.

Could the murder of a prison guard in a small facility like the CLEO Unit go unsolved? Was Tony right when he told Brewer that Mandez was a real prick? Did he actually come on the tier that night drunk with the intentions of hurting someone? Was the pipe brought on the tier by Mandez? If all of these questions were true, did someone on that tier just simply defend himself? It would be much easier if that person would come forward and tell his story. That wouldn't happen because of the circumstances of where the murder occurred. It wouldn't happen because who would believe that an inmate was merely defending himself?

No inmates in the unit were serving life sentences; they knew they would be released one day. Some of their sentences were long, but if convicted of being involved in murdering a prison guard, they would either get the death penalty or life without the possibility of parole. It started to become apparent that this crime, as terrible as it was, might never be solved.

Hubbard was preparing his weekly report for Warden Dent. The usual was on the report: disciplinary problems, medical reports of inmates, staffing of the unit, unusual expenses, and, of course, the update on the Mandez murder. The update was always very short. Hubbard did not want to reveal anything to Dent that he could use at his weekly press conference. Since the retirement of Warden Scope, Dent had established the weekly press conference, something that was never done in the past. It was also highly unusual for a prison warden to hold a weekly press conference.

Hubbard was finishing the report when Marcia buzzed his phone. "Sir, Lieutenant Sanders is here to see you. Do you have time, or should I tell him to come back?"

Hubbard moved some papers around on his desk in an attempt to make it look a little neater. He told Marcia to send Sanders in. He had not had a chance to sit down with him since the promotion. It also seemed that wherever Sanders was on the prison grounds, Brewer was not far behind. They had become inseparable since starting the investigation into the Mandez murder. Hubbard liked Sanders. He knew that he would pick up some investigative experience while working with Brewer. He was well aware of Brewer's reputation from the past, but he felt confident that Sanders would not partake in any unprofessional behavior that Brewer might want to try. The meeting would be a good time to discuss the investigation with Sanders without Brewer hovering around.

Sanders seemed a little nervous and uncomfortable. He obliged Hubbard by taking a seat on the new leather couch. Hubbard came around from his desk and joined him on the couch. "How does the couch feel? It was delivered the other day, but I have not had a chance to test it out. The other couch was thrown into the dumpster; it was horrible."

Sanders made a couple of slight moves on the couch as if he were testing it for Hubbard. "Yeah, it's pretty nice. Sir, I don't want to take up to much of your time. I know how busy you must be. After you promoted me, I told you how much it meant to me and my family. I feel a sense of loyalty to you. I know how you feel about loyalty. That's why I came to see you. I'm sorry we have not been able to find out who killed Lieutenant Mandez. I want you to know that we've spent a lot of hours working on the investigation. I have learned a tremendous amount from working with Agent Brewer. Just by being in the room when he interviews inmates will make me a better investigator in the future."

Hubbard was listening, but by Sanders' nervousness, he knew that something was bothering him. He did not want to interrupt, so he asked him to continue.

"I have a problem that I need to discuss with you. I don't think you are aware of something that's going on. I really don't want to sit here and sound like a snitch. I have the highest respect for you, and I'm fully aware of the career you had prior to coming to Pelican Bay. I have also learned a lot by watching the way you handle situations. I'm assuming that Agent Brewer will be leaving soon. When that happens I hope that you have enough trust in me to continue to handle investigations as they occur in this unit. Now that I have laid the groundwork, I want to inform you of something that is going on between Agent Brewer and the Justice Department."

Sanders now had Hubbard's complete attention. He squirmed a little in the couch—no screeching sounds like the old couch. Hubbard knew that whatever it was that Sanders wanted to say was really bothering him. From his observations over the past months, Hubbard felt that the connection between Brewer and Thompson was strong. He thanked Sanders for coming to see him. He told him that he was right; loyalty was the foremost quality he looked for in men he supervised. He sensed that Sanders was still trying to find the right words. "Ron, just relax. I consider you a very valuable member of my command staff. What is it you want to tell me?"

"I don't know all the intricate details, but the Justice Department is working to get Tony Spitlato out of this unit. Brewer received the go-ahead from Mr. Thompson to make a deal with Spitlato. I feel bad that I did not come to you sooner. At first I thought you knew about what they were doing. I later found out from Brewer that you didn't know all the details. When we were interviewing Tony, Brewer presented the idea to him. Of course, Tony jumped on it. We actually smacked Tony around a little to make it look good when he went back on the tier. I'm ashamed to say that I actually delivered a punch that drew blood from Tony's face. I guess being new at this I got caught up in the moment."

Hubbard did not tell Sanders that he had been made aware of some of the details on the effort to get Spitlato released. He wanted to hear what Brewer had told Sanders about the plan.

Sanders looked uncomfortable as he continued talking. "The deal that Brewer offered Tony was that they would make sure he won his appeal. He would be released pending a new trial. They feel that if released, Tony can make his way back in the Camden mob. All of this was discussed on a phone conference with Thompson, Driscoll, and Brewer. I was made aware of it after the conference. Brewer told me not to discuss the plan with anyone, especially you. I was shocked when he said that. At first, I thought he was kidding, but I soon realized he was serious. I told him that I could not go along with something that you were not on board with. He actually threatened me. He said that you would be gone soon, and my position here at the prison could be in jeopardy if I discussed their plan with anyone. I feel ashamed that I did not come to you immediately. I wasn't sure what to do."

Hubbard got up from the couch and paced the office. He turned a couple of times and appeared to be ready to say something. He raised his finger toward Sanders, not in a bad way; he appeared to be letting him know that he was thinking how to react to this news.

"At moments like this, I try to practice breathing techniques. Sometimes it works, and sometimes it just makes me worse. As you can see from my actions, the breathing exercise is not working right now. Okay, I'm settled down to the point I can think straight. First, I want to thank you for coming to me. You did the right thing. I want to promise you that nothing will happen to you. When you leave this office, I want you to continue working with Brewer until he's out of here. I'm not quite sure what I will do, but I will keep you in the loop. I would also appreciate you getting back to me on anything you hear about their plan. Those bastards don't care anything about the murder of Mandez. You can tell by what they are doing that the only thing they care about is making themselves look good. It doesn't matter who they hurt, they are ruthless."

Hubbard shook hands with Sanders and walked him to the door.

"If the media only knew what goes on at the Justice Department level, the public would be shocked. I've had a taste of their bullshit when I was with the Bureau. They do things that would disgrace this country. It's supposed to be in the name of justice. If the truth were ever told, a lot of those shitheads would be in prison."

Sanders stood by the office door. Being recently promoted to a job that he had longed for, kept him thinking he could possibly be losing it. He knew he had done the right thing. Sanders respected Hubbard. He believed that no matter what happened he would be okay. The main thing now was to try to act normal when he was around Brewer. He knew that Brewer had extensive training in interviewing and body language and would most likely pick up on any changes in behavior.

"Ron, I want you to call me at my condo every night. I would rather you not be seen coming in my office. When you call me and have information, I will meet you somewhere to talk. Don't say too much on the phone. I would not put anything past them; they could have my phone bugged. Thanks for coming in. I will be indebted to you for giving me this information. Don't worry about anything; I have lots of friends at the Bureau in Washington. If necessary, I will call in some favors that have been owed to me by some people high up in our government."

When Sanders left the office, Hubbard went to his desk and made some notes. Before writing anything down, he sat back in his chair and smiled. I hope I convinced Ron that I was not aware of any deals being made by Brewer. He sounded so convincing, but I need to be careful. Is this a move by Brewer to send Sanders in to see how I would react? He continued with the notes. As he was leaving for the night, he could not help but think, *I need to really stay alert with these bastards. They are relentless.*

Chapter 27

A couple weeks had gone by with no communications from the Justice Department. It seemed strange for Hubbard not to hear from Thompson. He decided to just wait and see what move would be forthcoming from the very secretive Justice Department.

At times, he fumed over the situation with Spitlato. Was the Justice Department ever going to try and include him in the real plan to release Spitlato? He had the urge to call some friends in Washington to put some feelers out to see what would come back. He also tossed around the thought of calling Thompson and just flat out resigning. The haunting speculation of what they were trying to do kept him curious. What would the final outcome be? How are they going to pull Spitlato's release off? Getting a federal judge to go along with getting Spitlato out of prison might not be that far-fetched. Most federal judges had held their seats on the bench for many years. They would not jeopardize their lucrative retirements. If threatened, they would go along with anything. What the hell did they care if a crooked cop got out of prison?

Hubbard, during his many years of service with the Bureau, had seen a lot of shady deals made in the name of justice. We are a country of laws, but it appeared that sometimes those laws were broken, supposedly to protect the citizenry. It all sounds good, but it's a crock of shit. Who the hell would benefit by having Tony Spitlato back in the mob? Not John Q. Citizen—he could give a shit. John Q. is the guy who is barely making it.

He is probably going by the book when it comes to following the law. What is John Q.'s reward for doing the right thing? He continues to struggle, he continues to get shit on, and he will never know about the clandestine activity that his government does in the name of freedom and justice for all.

Hubbard was known in the law enforcement circles as one of the good guys. His career had spanned decades. He climbed the ladder in the FBI to become one of the Bureaus most trusted leaders. With a little more political pull and using some of those people in high places, he might have been nominated to be the director.

He has found himself in a position as warden of a unit that might not succeed as the model it was intended to be. He has the murder of one of his supervisors being committed on his watch, and he is being undermined in his position by the same people who put him there. He could say the hell with it, look the other way, and keep drawing the big bucks, or he could blow the whistle on the plan to get Spitlato out of prison.

He had a lot on his mind. His pride and dedication to duty were the forces that pushed him to continue to run the CLEO Unit. He knew no other way than to push forward in a professional manner.

Being a man who loved quotes, he drew upon one of his favorites from President Lincoln, "Better to remain silent and be thought a fool than to speak out and remove all doubt."

U.S. Department Of Justice 950 Pennsylvania Avenue N.W.
Washington, D.C. 20530 – Secure Conference Room
It was 9 a.m. Monday morning, and the conference room was already crowded. The Justice Department's security force had made a sweep of the room for devices. The sweep was always ordered when the attorney general himself was making a rare appearance in the very large secure conference room. The devices that were being looked for included: miniature recorders, any size camera, and pretty much anything that came under the title of device. All cell phones were checked at the counter before anyone entered the conference room. The uniform officers also used K-9 dogs in their sweep.

Most Justice Department personnel who attended these meetings on any regular basis thought the sweep to be a show of force by the attorney general, rather than thinking they would find someone using an illegal device. It was common knowledge to all that the attorney general loved the power he had. The sweep, just prior to his arrival, although unnecessary was a fear factor he enjoyed immensely. If folks thought that the department was not run like a military outfit, they only had to be around Oliver Paige for a period of time to confirm that issue. Paige played up the part of attorney general; you would think he was a military general the way he used his power. He had two agents assigned to protect him around the clock, and agents stationed outside his home in the D.C. suburbs. His bullet proof limousine was driven by an agent with two SUV's following him wherever he went. If he was traveling any distance in the D.C. metro area, his entourage was escorted by the D.C. Metropolitan Police with lights and sirens blaring.

Paige had been appointed attorney general by the President over several seemingly more qualified candidates. His confirmation before the Senate was turbulent at best. He was eventually confirmed, but it was known that the President had to pull some strings to make the confirmation happen. From the day he started, he changed many of the procedures that had been in place for years. The Department of Justice went from an advisory type of entity to an outfit that looked like the Pentagon. The security force was increased, and cameras were installed everywhere, including the bathrooms. Most employees thought that the phones were bugged. If Paige was walking the hallways with his security team, people literally jumped against the wall to get out of his way. It was sort of a pins and needles type of atmosphere. Nobody dared to be late for work or even think about leaving work early.

"Gentlemen, please secure those doors. I do not want any interruptions in this conference room for the next hour. Do you understand?"

Without even answering, the security guards closed the doors and left the room. Paige asked everyone to please have a seat. No one had dared to sit before he gave the order. The room was huge. The conference table could seat thirty people easily. The table had been a special request when Paige took over. It was beautiful. It had all the high-tech equipment needed to conduct business. It had a built-in video conferencing system. At the head of the table where Paige sat, was a red phone. The instructions were that no one under any circumstances was to use this phone. The lawyers on staff were told that it was a direct line to the White House.

Several of the assistant attorney generals were in the room for the first time. Paige adjusted some papers handed to him by his chief administrative aide. Coffee and croissants were served by the kitchen staff. The kitchen was off to the side of the conference room. It was a fully equipped kitchen that had been installed at the request of Paige. Many in the department thought that this kitchen was an extravagant measure that was way over the top. However, this was Paige's Justice Department, and if you thought otherwise, you didn't last long. He had dismissed assistants who had questioned his leadership and spending. Some employees left knowing they would probably be terminated anyway. The pressure to prove yourself worthy was always present. If you were going to make it in Paige's Justice Department, you had to be thick-skinned.

"Now that you all have your coffee, let's get started. If you have been invited to this meeting, it means you will have a part in what I am about to tell you. I would ask that you hold all your questions. I think I can make everything very clear in a short period of time. I don't think I have to say it, but this meeting is considered highly classified. You all have clearances, so consider the meeting to be extremely classified. We are going to implement a plan to get a former police officer out of prison. He is now serving a lengthy term in the CLEO Unit at Pelican Bay. His name is Tony Spitlato. The reason for getting him out is to have him go back into Pete "The Cigar" Calabrese's crime family in Camden, New Jersey. We have good reason to believe from our intelligence that he would be accepted in the mob with open arms. We have chosen this individual because he is the right person for the job. He's a tough guy who was deep into the Camden mob when we indicted him under the RICO laws. He was a good cop at one time, but he decided that the mob was more lucrative than being a cop, so he became a made man in the Calabrese crime family."

The attorney general was enjoying every moment of his talk; he loved to see the faces of his subordinates. He knew that some of them would be with his office for a long time, and some would be weeded out. He glanced around the room as if he was taking mental notes on which attorneys were true believers in his system.

"Tony Spitlato was so good while working undercover that they made him a "crew chief". He took his orders directly from his capo and had complete access to Pete Calabrese. As you know, we have been trying to take down the Calabrese crime family for several years. We know that there is a lot of infighting in the Jersey mob families right now. It seems to be the best time to get him back in the mob and working for us. This whole plan could be very dangerous for a lot of people. I have confidence that if monitored properly it can be one of the largest hits against the Mafia in years. Basically, what we are planning is to have Judge Wallace Sharper grant Spitlato his appeal. His attorney is Howard Gibbons, who has been mob connected in Jersey for years. We talked to Gibbons, and he has no choice but to work with us. He has enjoyed the profits of being the consigliere for the mob for a long time. We will deal with him after we get his cooperation."

The attendees in the conference room were now on the edge of their chairs. Several had questions, but they dared not ask them until Paige finished. They took notes or just scribbled on their pads as if they were taking in every word from the boss. Some had been involved in similar covert operations in the past, but nothing quite like this one. To get someone deep into the mob working for the Justice Department would be a huge undertaking. Some mobsters had given information in the past after they were arrested to save their asses, but this was different. If it worked, there would be no telling how many Jersey mobsters would go down.

Paige, after a short pause and a sip of coffee, called upon John Thompson to continue to brief the group.

"I think you all know John. I have asked him to head up this operation. He is very familiar with Tony Spitlato. John has also been very instrumental in overseeing the start-up of the CLEO Unit at Pelican Bay. John will be calling on some of you for your expertise during this operation. I'm sure you will do your best to assist him. I want the operation to go off without any glitches. John will report directly to me. If you have any reporting to do, it will be to John's assistant, Pat Driscoll. I do not want to know the progress of this operation unless it comes directly from John. The less people we have in the chain, the better our chances of maintaining complete secrecy. Pat is John's right-hand man and will play a big part in making it all happen. I will now turn this meeting over to John. I need to be at the White House to brief the President on another matter."

As Paige rose from his chair, you would have thought it was the Pope getting up. The chairs screeched in unison as everyone bolted to their feet. Paige left the conference room with a smirk on his face, his two security people following like ducks on the way to the pond. He shook hands with Thompson on the way out. As he approached the door, which was opened by one of the security guys, he turned and gave a little hand wave to the group. The wave was like the one that President Nixon gave to the crowd as he boarded the plane after resigning the presidency.

The group seemed a little more at ease after Paige left. There was some mumbling amongst the group. Thompson immediately pulled it together. He took the seat at the head of the table where Paige had been sitting, and he tapped his pen on his coffee mug. The mumbling stopped, and he had their attention.

"Gentlemen, some of you in here will play an intricate part in this operation. Some of you were invited to this meeting by the boss. To be honest with you, I'm not sure why he invited so many. I will break this group down into a small handful that will be involved. The rest of you will be called upon as needed. I want to reiterate what the boss said—this is a touchy operation. If it is to work, we need complete silence about what you have heard so far. If I ask you to stay in this conference room, it means that you have been handpicked to work with Pat Driscoll and myself. If I do not call your name, it means that we may call upon you at a later time to assist us. Each of you has something to offer this operation. We will need assistants to work on the tax implications involved, the intelligence gathering, the forensics, surveillance, wire taps, and other things as they pop up."

With much anticipation the assistants in the room waited to hear their names called. Knowing how Paige ran the department, it behooved everyone in the room to get picked. Thompson pulled a list from his attaché case. He read out each name, and as he did, he nodded to that person. The list was much shorter than everyone expected. He read off five names. He then thanked the others and asked them to leave the conference room. The group now consisted of seven people. Thompson told the smaller group that they were picked because of their expertise in the areas that he had mentioned. He told them that any conferences in the future would be held in his office.

"Pat and I personally picked you guys because we have worked sensitive cases with you before. We know that you can be trusted. There may be some things done in the future that will be done solely in the interest of taking down a large criminal element. I intend to make the plan work, and I will use whatever means I need to get it done. We will be part of something special. I hope that we are all back in this room down the road when the boss is thanking us for taking down the Camden, New Jersey Mafia."

Chapter 28

Life in the CLEO Unit was starting to look like any other correction facility. The inmates knew the rules. When there were infractions, they paid the price. Since the death of Lieutenant Mandez, some privileges had still not been fully restored. Time in the yard was cut by fifteen minutes, family visits were cut to two days a week, movie nights were eliminated, and shakedowns were common and unannounced. Still no new information concerning the death of Mandez had surfaced. There were times when the rumor mill produced something that sounded good, but it always turned out that the information coming from the tier could never be corroborated.

Tony continued to be looked upon as a guy that had the most power in the unit. He kept his close ties with Louie Tusta, Donny Napolitano, and Bernie Wells. They went to the yard together, they played cards together, they ate meals together, and they appeared always to be watching each other's back. Louie and Donny had expressed to Tony that they didn't really trust Bernie. According to Tony, they had no legitimate reason not to trust him, other than him being a black guy. Tony himself was not a big fan of blacks, but he needed Bernie on his team. The other blacks in the unit would often go to Bernie with problems. Bernie, in turn would bring the problem to Tony, but he always allowed Bernie to appear to get the credit for solving their problems.

As the days rolled by, Tony was getting anxious to talk to Brewer. He did not want to bring any attention to himself, so he just waited. He had thoughts every day about when he would get out. Now that he knew the release might happen, he was getting antsier as each day passed.

Tony had no alternative than to wait it out; however, he didn't have to wait long. He got a notification from a guard on Friday that his attorney was coming to visit him on Monday morning. He was doing everything he could to keep cool. Being with his buddies around the clock every day, made him draw on all the willpower he had not to slip and say something about getting out. As close as he was with Louie and Donny, keeping the secret wasn't easy.

The weekend for Tony was one of the longest he had ever spent. Monday morning was slow coming around—but it did. Right after breakfast, he was informed that he would be seeing his attorney at 10 a.m. Louie was around when the guard gave Tony the news. He wasted no time asking Tony what was up with the lawyer coming to see him. Tony told Louie that he forgot to tell him that his lawyer was pressing the appeals court for a new trial. Louie just nodded his approval. He told Tony that if he got turned down once by the appeals court, his chances of getting another trial are slim. Tony just grinned and told Louie that it never hurts to keep trying.

"Tony, it's so good to see you. How the hell you been? Have you had any more trouble from the goons that run this place? I got some great news. That asshole federal appeals judge has re-opened your case and is considering your appeal. I think it looks good, Tony. I'm hoping that if he reviews it soon, you might be out of here in a short time."

Tony knew that the possibility existed that the room was bugged. He smiled at Howard Gibbons and gave him that Italian goomba look. He was about to say something when Gibbons slipped him a piece of paper. Gibbons kept talking about how great it would be to get Tony out. He was talking loud and fast to allow Tony time to glance at the note.

I'm working with the Justice Department to get you out.

"Well, Howard, you've certainly brought me some great news. I knew that the appeals court would come through for me. After all, this is America, and people can't be kept in prison for something they didn't do. Have you notified my family about this great news?

"Tony, this is all happening now. I don't want to notify anyone until I see the papers from Judge Sharper. It's going to happen; you just need to be patient for a while. I wanted to come here and deliver the news in person. Tony, there are a lot of people in Camden that will be glad to hear about this. Gibbons leaned in close to Tony and whispered, *"Especially Pete."*

Gibbons and Tony continued with some small talk. Tony was excited and wanted to ask questions, but he kept the conversation to personal matters. He had heard what he wanted to hear. He knew that the process was moving forward. Gibbons had already told him that he was working with the Justice Department—what else did he need to hear? After the recent conversation with Agent Brewer and now some great news, he was sure that his release would happen.

The visiting time was up. The guard escorted Tony out of the room and back to the tier. On the way out, Tony thanked Gibbons for coming and bringing good news. Gibbons gathered his papers into his briefcase and was escorted out of the room. As he was heading for the main exit to the parking lot, he encountered Warden Hubbard. Both appeared to be a little shocked to see each other. Gibbons acknowledged Hubbard and reached out to shake hands with him. Hubbard shook hands and asked Gibbons what was the occasion for him to be at the prison, as if he didn't know.

Gibbons, who was a master at words, seemed a little taken aback by the statement. Was Hubbard in on the plan to get Tony out? Didn't the Justice Department trust him enough to include him in the plan? Did he know about the plan, but did not know Tony's lawyer would be involved? Should I just say my visit was an attorney/client visit? Do I keep my mouth shut like I was told to do? Was Hubbard just screwing with me and was well aware of the plan? In what seemed like a long time, but was probably a minute, Gibbons asked if they could talk in Hubbard's office. Hubbard obliged and could not wait to hear what Gibbons wanted to say in private.

"Have a seat Mr. Gibbons. Can I get you something to drink?"

"Mike, my visit to Tony was business. I have good reason to believe that we will prevail at the federal appeals level, and he will get a new trial. I also feel that while waiting for that trial, he will be released. I came here to advise Tony. He is excited at the possibility of being released. I think at a new trial he will be exonerated. He didn't do all that bullshit they convicted him of. Tony was caught between a rock and a hard place."

Hubbard let Gibbons talk. When he had heard enough, he put up his hand. "You know what, Mr. Gibbons? You're a real crock of shit. Do you take me for a fool? You fuckin' lawyers are all alike. You think that we peons who don't have a law degree are dummies. I know exactly why you are here. You and that corrupt Justice Department are scheming to get your client out of my facility. You know what? You are just a small fish in the big pond. You have no say in their plan; they are using you like they do other people to serve their purpose. When they get what they want from Spitlato, they will come after you. I don't know about your dealings with the Mafia, but you can bet that your ass will be indicted after they are done with you. I have kept quiet for too long. I think it's time I make some waves of my own. I don't need all this aggravation from Thompson and his Justice Department flunkies."

"Mike, I assumed that you were aware of the situation. I guess I was mistaken. You might be right about what they are going to do with me after Tony gets out, but I will worry about my future when it happens. There have been attempts to indict me in the past. I'm only doing what they told me to do. I didn't really have much choice in this matter. I was threatened by the Justice Department to work with them. I'm pretty sure they have the federal judge in their pocket. By the way, how did you find out about the plan to get Tony out?"

"It's not important how I found out. You might not believe it, but I still have some employees that are loyal to me. You need to be very careful, Mr. Gibbons. The people you are dealing with at the Justice Department are treacherous. They make things happen and don't care who gets hurt. In all my years in law enforcement, I have never seen anything like them. You don't owe me anything Mr. Gibbons, but I would appreciate it if you don't mention that we had this conversation."

"Mike, I came here to tell Tony about the possibility of getting out of here. Those were my instructions. As far as I'm concerned, that's what I did. It baffles me why they don't want to include you in their plan. As a lawyer who has been around for a long time and has seen a lot of strange things happen, I would also advise you to watch your back."

Hubbard escorted Gibbons out to the main exit. They shook hands, and he watched the attorney walk to the parking lot. Hubbard wanted the last word. "I wouldn't trust that piece of shit. Watch yourself, Gibbons."

Returning to his office, Hubbard sat and contemplated how he would move forward. He was pissed. He decided to call Thompson. It was now a game, and he wanted to hear from Thompson. He would make no mention of what he knew about the plan to get Tony out. He would have to acknowledge that Gibbons came to the prison to inform Tony of the appeal process. Having thought in the past of resigning his position, he now had that pride thing working. He was the only one not doing anything wrong. However, if he just played along with them, it might appear later that he was involved. So far the people involved in trying to get Spitlato out were Thompson, Driscoll, Brewer, and Gibbons.

Hubbard hooked up his recording device to the phone. As he did it, he was thinking…I'm recording the deputy attorney general of the United States. What the fuck is this world coming to? I had a great career in the FBI. I tried to always play by the rules. I believe in the rule of law, and I believe in the Constitution. Now, I am faced with my own government pulling some shit that could take me down with all those assholes involved in this silliness. It's time to play hard ball. I will only stay in the game as long as I feel comfortable. I will pull the plug when I think it is time to get out.

"Hi John, we haven't talked for a while. I just wanted to let you know that Spitlato's lawyer was here at the prison today. He met with Tony and told him that the appeals court has decided to look at his case. He feels strongly that Judge Sharper will grant him a new trial. He also thinks that Tony will be released pending the new trial. I think it's a crock of shit. Have you heard anything?"

"Well, Mike, I have heard that his lawyer filed an appeal on the grounds that he did not get a fair trial the first time around. I know the federal judge and would not be surprised if his motion is granted. Judge Sharper is a weak judge. I guess we will just have to wait and see what happens. How is the Mandez investigation coming along?"

Hubbard was steaming. You could almost see the steam coming off the top of his head. He could not help but grind his teeth. He smacked his open hand on the desk loud enough for Thompson to hear it. He was loosening his tie and ripped the top button off his shirt. He made sure the tape recorder was running. Before he could answer Thompson, he took a sip of water. How in hell could this guy who hand-picked me for this position, now be finagling behind my back? This has to be the greatest breech of loyalty ever committed on a fellow law enforcement officer. He cleared his throat.

"Nothing new has come to light on the Mandez murder. We have worked with the local detectives, we have interviewed all the inmates, we have gone over all the forensics, and we have nothing. I'm not sure if you have talked to Brewer."

"Why would I talk to Brewer? You're in charge, and you are who I rely on for any information coming from your unit."

The steam from the top of the head continued, his teeth grinding like a cement drill. He wanted to pound his fist on the desk, but he feared he would smash through it. This bastard is lying to someone who has been in the business of detecting lies for over thirty years. *Who the hell does he think he is talking to? I'm embarrassed for him to think that he can pull this off. I would like to reach through this phone and yank this bastard toward me so I can punch the shit out of him. The nerve he has. I need to control myself and let this asshole think he is getting over on me.*

"I only mention Brewer because he is your man. He has a reputation for going over the people he reports to. I thought maybe he has talked to you about the investigation. While I have you on the phone, I think Brewer can go back to whatever he does. I don't need him here in my unit. Whatever happens with the investigation can be handled with the people I have."

"Mike, if you think that Brewer talks directly to me, you are mistaken. I believe in the chain of command as much as you do. If you think Brewer's services are not needed any longer, I will let him know.

Mike, you called me. Is there anything else that's important on your mind? If not, I have to be at a meeting in a few minutes. I will keep you posted on what we hear about Spitlato's appeal."

Hubbard did not have anything else to talk about. He was fighting back the notion of just letting it all out; instead he hung up the phone. As he played back a portion of the tape to make sure he had it all, he could feel the sweat beads on his neck. He was now very hot. Thoughts raced through his head. Losing an inmate like Spitlato might be a blessing in disguise.

Hubbard figured that it was the old mentality of the Justice Department to view everything they got involved in as some mighty clandestine venture. He still felt that he was holding the upper hand. He could walk away from this job anytime he wanted to. *I guess it's the thirty years of doing the right thing. I'm still the same guy that was sworn into the FBI a long time ago thinking that I can make a difference.*

It was a new ballgame in law enforcement these days. So much secrecy and deceit, but it shouldn't be that way. As he packed his briefcase to leave for the day, he thought of a quote by George Bernard Shaw that was appropriate for the moment…

We are made wise not by the recollection of our past, but by the responsibility for our future.

Chapter 29

One Month Later – Warden Hubbard's Office

Hubbard received an e-mail informing him that Federal Appeals Court Judge Wallace Sharper had signed the order granting Tony Spitlato a new trial. The message came from Pat Driscoll. The e-mail stated that Hubbard would be receiving the official paperwork shortly by way of a federal marshal. His instructions were to keep the information confidential. No sooner than he read the e-mail, Marcia called and said there were two federal marshals in the outer office.

The paperwork was no real surprise to Hubbard; he just didn't know when it was coming. Remaining calm, he called Lieutenant Sanders and asked him to come to his office. Sanders knew about the Justice Department's plan; he just didn't know when it would go down. Hubbard wanted to see if he had talked to Brewer lately. The short meeting with Sanders proved fruitless. Hubbard called the tier and requested that Spitlato be brought to his office immediately.

Tony strolled in handcuffed. He had that smile on his face—seemingly not a care in the world. Hubbard told the guard to take the cuffs off and wait outside. The guard looked at Hubbard and asked him if he would be okay alone with the prisoner. Hubbard waved the guard off. "I think that what Tony and I have to talk about won't be anything that will provoke him."

Tony seemed more at ease than ever. He was confident that what was about to happen would be life changing. Before being asked to sit, he flopped down onto the new couch. His weight did cause a few screeches from the leather. The nickname he carried while working in the Camden mob, "Big Tuna," was a name he was living up to. Since coming to the CLEO Unit, he had not lost any of his two hundred and forty or more pounds. It appeared that most of it moved to his stomach. The short walks in the yard weren't enough to get anyone in shape. Everyone, including Tony bitched about the meals. He may have bitched, but it didn't look like he missed any.

"Warden, I was wondering if I could get a soda. Whatever that shit is we drink with our meals can't compare to a real Coke."

"Sure, Tony, anything for a guy of your stature. I'm excited to be in the presence of a man who knows people in high places...a model federal prisoner who can get the attention of the big shots at the Justice Department...a guy that people want to just put back on the streets of Camden, and a guy who did some terrible shit while he turned on his police agency. Not a problem, Tony. I'll get that Coke for you right away. Is there anything else I can get you? I sure as hell would not want you to complain to the Justice Department that I didn't treat you well."

Hubbard called Marcia and asked that she bring a Coke to his office. He walked over to the couch and smiled at Tony. The smile was returned. It seemed like Tony always had that smile on his face. It obliviously worked in his favor to fool people over the years. It gave the appearance that he was always under control and feared nothing.

That smile had also got him into many brawls when growing up. His smile was a natural barrier that allowed him time to figure out if he were dealing with a friend or foe. Even now as he sat on the couch, you would never guess that he was a federal prisoner; one that was about to get great news.

The Coke arrived, and Tony stood to get it from Marcia. "No, just sit there Tony, I'll get it for you. After all, you're my guest today. Whatever you want just let me know."

"Okay, Mr. Warden, although I appreciate your generosity, you are killing me with this pretend kindness. I would love to spend the rest of the day with you, but I have a card game in about an hour. My luck lately with the game has not been good. I'm hoping my overall luck is about to change. I don't mean with the card game; I mean with getting out of this hellhole. You didn't call me in here to pamper me with goodies and sweet-talk. Can we be frank with each other and get to the point? I do respect you, but I would appreciate you doing away with all the bullshit niceties."

Hubbard walked back to his desk, picked up a large envelope, and put it up to his ear. "Tony, do you remember on the Johnny Carson show years ago when Johnny would put the envelope near his ear? He would then predict the answer to the question in the envelope. It was really funny. Let me try this with you. I think the answer to what is in the envelope is—*what has Tony been waiting for since he got to this prison?* Now comes the part where I rip open the envelope, just like Johnny did, and read the question. Are you ready Tony? Here we go."

Hubbard waved the envelope around and was having a good time watching Tony's reaction. He paused with the envelope outstretched toward Tony. With a motion that resembled a magician pulling a rabbit from a hat, he ripped the envelope open. He pulled a paper from the envelope and stared at Tony. "Well, what do you know? It's a letter from the Justice Department. I can't imagine what this letter is about. What do you think Tony? Do you have any idea what this is about? Do you have any idea why I asked you to come to my office? Should I read it or do you want to tell me what it's about?"

The smile on Tony's face got bigger. He was actually enjoying the act being put on by Hubbard. He squirmed several times while Hubbard was performing; the new couch made very loud screeches. He sipped on the Coke as if he were drinking some fine wine from one of the top Italian restaurants back in Camden. He finished the Coke and sat it on the table. When he thought Hubbard was finished with the charades, he tried to speak, but was abruptly interrupted by Hubbard.

"Tony, I've had some fun with you today. Now I'll get serious. I don't need to read this letter to you. You don't need to read it either. We both know what it says. I wouldn't be surprised if I get a phone call shortly from my dear friends at the Justice Department. The conversation will go something like this—*Hi Mike, this is John Thompson. You have been doing a great job running the CLEO Unit. I'm sure you have the official papers concerning the release of Tony Spitlato. I would appreciate it if you expedite his release.*"

Even with the natural smile on his face, which was now looking a little strained, Tony knew that Hubbard was not real happy about his pending release. This was no time to get in a pissing match with Hubbard. Just play the game, go along with Hubbard's rant, and freedom would be forthcoming.

"You know, Tony, I would love to respond to Thompson by saying— screw you John. There ain't going to be a release. I guess if I said that it would get real interesting. I would be bucking the system. The corrupt system that is undermining all that this unit was set up to be. What do you think Tony? If I said that, what do you think Thompson would do? What if I said I would go to the media about this scheme? I could blow the lid off this ridiculous plan of theirs."

Hubbard had Tony's attention. The smile was now almost gone. He sat up on the couch. "Mr. Hubbard, I'm not sure what you're getting at. I was told about this plan by my attorney. I would think that the Justice Department has plans for me on the outside. I'm not sure why you would give a shit about my release. I'm no saint, but I can do more for law enforcement on the outside than I can do sitting in this shithouse. If you weren't included in the plan, that's not my fault. You need to take that up with the Justice Department. I'm pretty sure that the papers in that envelope are crystal clear about my release. If you have a beef with someone, it sure as hell ain't me. I'm not trying to be a wise guy, but I would appreciate you moving forward with me getting out of here."

Hubbard let Tony talk. He sat at his desk and was thinking that Tony might be right; Spitlato was merely the recipient of a gift from the Justice Department. He didn't initiate it; the Justice Department did. Tony is just a bad guy in prison. He was getting a release to do something that the justice people are hoping will take down bad guys that are considered worse than Tony.

Hubbard looked over the papers again. "Tony, I'm not going to keep you any longer. I don't want you to miss your card game. You will be released when I say so and no sooner. I've got some thinking to do and some calls to make. You might not think so, but I can squash this nonsense in a New Jersey minute. You were convicted and sentenced by a jury. You should serve every minute of that sentence. You violated the trust placed in police officers. You are a felon, and it's my job to see that you do the time handed down by the courts."

As the guards came to escort Tony back to the tier, he turned and looked at Hubbard. He started to say something but stopped and presented that smile. Hubbard smiled back. "Good luck with the card game, Tony. I hope you guys aren't playing for money…you know that's against the law."

When the door to the tier shut, Hubbard grabbed the envelope. He pulled out the papers. He stared at them as if something would change. They were all in order. A lot of legalese in the document, but the bottom line stated that Spitlato would be released from the CLEO Unit. Feeling drained from the exchange with Spitlato, he put his feet up on the desk. If it were not the middle of the day and very unprofessional, he could fall asleep right there in his office. He thought about what Tony had said. *Why should I care so much about his release? If it were not for the fact that I care deeply about the court system, I could probably put my stamp on his release with no problem.*

Hubbard threw the paper on the desk. With no one in the room, he started to talk out loud to himself. "Who do these bastards think I am? Are they confident that I will sit back and say nothing about releasing one of my prisoners? Well, I think I will test the waters. I have nothing to lose, but I have everything to gain…like keeping my integrity. I will probably lose this job, but I feel like I want to go down swinging. They can't mess with my pension from the Bureau. I have enough money to go back to my beautiful wife and do retirement things. I just can't sit by and let this stupid idea go forward."

He caught himself talking out loud to no one, but it felt good. It was like getting it off his shoulders and out in the open, even if no one was listening.

He walked around his office and continued to talk out loud. "Down the road when it blows up, I can at least be on record for opposing it. Let me strap on those brass balls that have gotten me through all those years in the Bureau. Hell, anyone that ever worked with or for me in the Bureau would expect nothing less than Mike Hubbard stirring the pot. I don't want to make it sound like a game, but that's exactly what those assholes in Washington are doing…playing a game. Well, I guess I need to stop talking to myself and make my move."

He dialed Thompson's private line. He was nervous, but it was a good nervous. He knew what he wanted to say. He knew what he wanted to hear from Thompson. He reported directly to Thompson, so that's who he wanted to talk to, not Driscoll or any other flunky under Thompson.

Thompson answered the phone which was not the norm. He preferred to have people leave messages. He would then prioritize them and return the calls. As second in command at the Justice Department, he could be on the phone most of the day. Having the ability to see who was calling made it easier to let the call go to voice mail. Knowing that Hubbard would be upset about the papers being delivered, he had expected the call.

"Hello, Mike, I was expecting your call. If it's about Tony Spitlato, I will listen to what you have to say, but I can tell you upfront it's a done deal."

Hubbard flipped on the trusty recorder. He knew that down the road he might not be able to use the recording. In most states you need to have the permission from the person you were recording. He nevertheless felt secure in recording people. He knew the laws and would act accordingly when the time came. He knew that what he was about to tell Thompson would likely end his tenure in the CLEO Unit. In the past, he had always been apprehensive when talking to Thompson. He knew from past experiences with him that he had only one thing in mind and that was to look good in the eyes of the attorney general.

"John, I did receive the paperwork from the appeals court. I would think that any plan like this would have to go through me. I actually did find out before I got the official papers. What the hell was the reasoning to keep me in the dark? I don't like what you are doing. I think it is a slap in the face to the judicial system. It's an affront to all the good law enforcement people all over the country who put their lives on the line every day. I'm pissed. I don't know if I can stay on in this position. My gut feeling tells me to call the media. I feel like I want to blow the lid right off this stupid plan."

"Mike, let me stop you right there. What we do here in the Justice Department is usually very secretive. We have operations going on right now around the country and the world. If information leaked out on those operations, lives would be on the line. It's my job under the direction from the attorney general that I make every effort to protect those that decide to do covert operations. I take my job very serious. I make decisions every day that affect our country. In this particular plan, I did not think that you needed to know. Your position at Pelican Bay was to run the CLEO Unit. I have told you on many occasions that you're doing a good job. This plan will move forward with or without your blessing. Do I make myself perfectly clear?"

From the tone of the conversation, it was clear to Hubbard that his options were becoming clearer. He could either go on as the warden of the CLEO Unit or hang it up; however, the decency and integrity in him was pushing him toward just putting a stop to the crazy plan. Did they really need Spitlato back in the mob? They could obviously get another operative to infiltrate the mob. Something was missing from this whole crazy situation. What was it?

"Mike, let me say this to you—I want to see you succeed, but I will not allow you to prevent this plan from moving forward. I really need to hang up and go to a meeting. I want you to give it a few days. Calm down and we can talk again. I'm sure it will take a while to process Spitlato for his release. I know you had many years at the Bureau, but you are questioning the highest level of our government. There is more to this release of Spitlato that I can tell you about. Let me just say one more time for the record; I will not allow you to bring any light on this plan that would cause us to abort it. Do I make myself perfectly clear?"

"John, if I didn't know that I was dealing with the deputy attorney general of the United States, I would think that I was being threatened. I will give it a couple of days. We want to be perfectly clear with each other and that's about the only thing we both agree on at this time. I'll tell you that I do not handle threats well. I will make my decision based on ethics and morals. I'm not sure those characteristics exist in your office. Have a nice day."

CHAPTER 30

Carlo's Restaurant – Camden, New Jersey

The special table in the rear of Carlo's Italian restaurant was always reserved for the Camden Mafia family. The tradition surrounding that table went back many years. The owner, Vinny Vitale, can't remember anyone other than Camden mob guys ever sitting there. This night it was no different. You would think the President was coming in for dinner. Vinny and the staff were used to the procedure.

If the table was going to be used by high up members of the mob, a couple of wise guys would show up about an hour ahead of the bosses. They would check the entire area around the table. Vinny would also assure them that the same chef was on duty as always. The two waiters who attended to the table had to be the same. After all was checked out, the two wise guys would sit at a table near the main table until the arrival of the mob bosses and their guests. When they arrived for dinner, they were always accompanied by an entourage.

Vinny did not mind the inconvenience caused by all the special needs of the mob bosses. He was paid well. He never joined them for dinner; he knew they were talking business. In all the years he had operated the restaurant, he did not have to pay protection money like most businesses in the area. He had been through a few mob bosses in his time, but this one, Pete Calabrese, was his favorite. In all the years that he had known Pete Calabrese, he never greeted him as Pete; it was always Mr.

Calabrese. When notified that Mr. Calabrese was coming for dinner or just having a meeting, he made sure everything was in place. His reward for being so efficient was that he received mob-controlled jobs for many of his family members. It was also not unusual for him to get large sums of money at Christmas and other special occasions.

Vinny got the call that Mr. Calabrese was coming to the restaurant at 7 p.m. with a group of five. Vinny started to make the calls to get everything ready. Calabrese was a neat freak. If he picked up a glass from his table and saw a spot on it, he would throw it against the wall. He had, on occasion, when he had seen dirty silverware, put it to the neck of a waiter.

The two waiters assigned to his table were very efficient at making sure they did not piss off Mr. Calabrese. It was also understood that they would approach the table only when beckoned by him. They were never to be in hearing distance of any of the mob's conversations.

At the table with Pete Calabrese were his capo regime; Alfonse "The Butcher" DiNatale, consigliere Howard Gibbons, the Mayor of Camden, Nick Adamo, and two lieutenants working for DiNatale. The Mayor of Camden had no problem meeting with Mafia associated guys. He was already under investigation by the state prosecutor for corruption in office. He was not the only mayor that had accusations of corruption. The prior two mayors were indicted for corruption and had served time in federal prisons.

It was Pete's custom to eat and drink before any business was discussed at the table. Everyone looked over the special menu except Pete. He always ordered the same thing. It was prepared his very special way. His order was bruschetta alla muffuletta as an appetizer, followed by a main course of roasted vegetable cannelloni. The wine flowed before, during, and after the meal.

While enjoying the meal, the talk covered sports, local politics, and family matters. It was Pete's custom to hear some of this talk before he discussed mob business. Pete loved to talk about family. He was a very religious man. For a guy that was known to have murdered so many people that the FBI dubbed him Pete "The Cool Killer" Calabrese—you would question how religious could he be.

If you didn't know that these guys were Mafia, you would just think it was a group of business men out for a good dinner. Because of the seclusion of the table and the bodyguards, Vinny knew that some of his other regulars wondered who they were, but none dared to ask. When you have five guys eating, while four big guys were standing around watching them, it became very obvious who they were.

The dinner party was not just a casually dressed bunch. When you dined with Pete Calabrese, you wore your finest. He was known around Camden, not just as a very spiffy dresser...but as the best dressed man in New Jersey. He wore Brioni suits that cost between five and ten thousand dollars. His dress shirts cost six hundred and his ties were two hundred. His suits, shirts, and ties were tailor-made at the Brioni factory in Rome. His shoes were Ferragamos and they cost two thousand dollars. His leisure clothes usually consisted of Sergio Tacchini warm-up suits that cost a thousand dollars. He did not usually wear any rings, but he was never without his forty thousand dollar Rolex Masterpiece, which was an eighteen karat gold watch.

If you showed up for dinner with Pete Calabrese and he thought you didn't look good...he would let you know. He had, on occasion, sent people to his personal haberdashery to be fitted for expensive suits. He footed the bill. He found pleasure in seeing that person later wearing outfits that he had paid for.

The meal was winding down. The mayor was talking about the raw deal he was getting from the state prosecutor. Pete knew that any talk of a raw deal was all bullshit; he had been paying off the mayor for years. In Camden, it was a known fact that nobody ran for mayor to make $49,000 a year. They ran for mayor to stuff their pockets with all they could get in a four year term. If they got caught like the two prior mayors, they did a couple of years in prison. When released, they usually landed some made-up position either in the mob or a phony company set up by the mob.

"Gentlemen, I hope you all enjoyed your meal. I have certainly enjoyed your company tonight. I'm not going to get into a lot about our operation. I do have something that has come to my attention. I know you all remember Tony Spitlato. Tony is one of us. He may have been a cop at one time, but he proved himself to my organization, and I want him back. We got some good news from the court. I will let Howard tell you about it."

Howard Gibbons had played the mob game for years with very lucrative results. He had been at these dinners with Pete and associates on many occasions. He knew his position as consigliere. He had made a pretty good living getting mob guys off of charges ranging from tax evasion to murder. Although a very outspoken person, Gibbons knew his role was to speak up only when called upon. The regular business of the mob was not something he got involved in.

He was now faced with the dilemma of going along with the Justice Department and convincing Pete Calabrese that the motion he filed with the appeals court was his work. He knew that he had to be very convincing to Pete about winning the appeal for Spitlato. Prior to the dinner, he knew why he was invited. He also knew that he was now between a rock and a hard place. If he would let it be known that the release of Spitlato was actually the brainchild of the Justice Department, he would be in serious trouble. If he could be convincing enough to assure Pete that the granting of the appeal was just a normal procedure pulled off by a good lawyer, he would live to play another day. He would also be somewhat of a hero in Pete's eyes.

Gibbons could worry about the ramifications of his involvement with the Justice Department down the road. He knew that he had enough money to live comfortably on a small island somewhere, even if it was in the Witness Protection Program. If he told them in simple terms that the federal appeals judge granted Spitlato's release, they would not have any questions.

"Gentlemen, first of all I want to thank Pete for a wonderful dinner. It has been a pleasure to get together and share such quality time. Now, the very good news I want to share is that Tony Spitlato will be released from that hellhole of a prison on the West Coast. I have been notified that the appeal I filed for his release pending a new trial has been granted by Judge Wallace Sharper. That's the good news. I have talked to Tony, and he is aware that we were granted the appeal."

Gibbons was thinking that so far so good. Being a lawyer, he had the gift of convincing people that what he said was the truth. He sipped his gin and tonic and continued.

"A little bit of bad news that I really haven't had the time to share with anyone is that the warden of the unit holding Tony might be fighting the release. This guy is a former FBI agent and has been butting heads with the Justice Department since he took the job as warden. They call it the CLEO Unit; that stands for Corrupt Law Enforcement Officers."

Before Gibbons could continue, Calabrese threw his drink against the wall, drawing the attention of his bodyguards and the other patrons in the restaurant. He stood and motioned as if he were going to turn the table over. But he stopped, and apologized to the mayor. He sat down and looked around the table.

"Mr. Mayor, I think I'm going to ask you to leave. We will be discussing something that you might not want to be a part of. I will be in touch with you soon."

The mayor did not hesitate. He excused himself and headed for the exit. He knew that when Pete Calabrese gets mad, nasty things can happen. When the mayor was gone, Calabrese continued.

"What the fuck is this guy's name that's in charge of that silly unit? I don't give a shit if he was a FBI agent or not. He can be eliminated. Why in the hell would he fight Tony's release?"

Gibbons moved to a chair closer to Calabrese. "Pete, this guy has had a few problems since he took the job as warden. One of his guards was murdered on the tier where Tony stays. It was a big deal because the guard was a lieutenant. He was beaten to death with a pipe. He was on the tier one night, and the reports are that he was drunk. They interviewed all the inmates, but no one has been charged. I think that this warden believes that Tony either did it or knows who did it. Tony is well-respected on that tier. He is the leader. I think that the warden and Tony actually got along at first. The problem now is that the warden is a stickler for punishment, especially when it comes to corrupt cops. He wants to fight any release for Tony. I received information that he has threatened to go to the media."

Pete Calabrese lit a cigar, a very expensive cigar. There was no smoking in the restaurant, but he was Pete Calabrese, the capo of the biggest crime family in New Jersey; he smoked wherever and whenever he damn well pleased. "Do you mean to tell me that this warden guy could possibly stop the release of Tony? Let me tell you something, Howard. You keep the pressure on with making it happen. What else do we know about this warden?"

Gibbons felt comfortable lighting up a cigarette. He took one drag before Calabrese knocked it out of his mouth. "I'm talking to you, asshole. I want to know more about this guy running the clown unit or whatever the hell you said it was called."

"Pete, all I know is that he was high up in the FBI, and he is well-respected in the law enforcement community. He has lots of ties in the D.C. area. He was hand-picked by the Justice Department for the job. The unit is actually called the CLEO Unit, not the clown unit. I think that if he wants to make some waves, he could do it. He has a home in the D.C. suburbs where his wife lives. I think he has a son on the D.C. Metro Police Department. If you're thinking about getting to him with some money, you can forget about it. This guy is as clean as they come."

"Howard, I never mentioned anything about money. Why do you lawyers always think that the only way to get someone to change their mind is with money? As you know, Howard, my organization has a reputation of making things happen, and most of the time it does not involve money. Whether we like it or not, we have been accused by the government of getting our way by force. Some of the shit I have read about me makes me out to be worse than Al Capone, Machine Gun Kelly, and the fuckin' Grim Reaper... all wrapped into one. I guess if they think that way, then we should not ever let them down. I want to know everything about this guy. If he's standing in the way of Tony's release, we might have to take him out."

CHAPTER 31

It had been two weeks since Hubbard had talked with Thompson. The paperwork from the appeals court did not actually specify a time for the release of Spitlato. Hubbard had read the court decision enough times that he nearly had it memorized. Each time he read it, he became more incensed. Spitlato had inquired through the guards every day, asking about his release. The standard answer that was relayed to him was that it was being reviewed.

Spitlato had also made several calls to his attorney. Gibbons always assured him that his release would be soon. Tony was not happy and expressed his unhappiness in harsh words to Gibbons. He did not want to use names on the phone, so he simply asked if the boss was aware of the situation, the boss being Pete Calabrese. He was told that the boss was aware of what was happening and was furious.

Tony had made numerous requests to talk to Warden Hubbard, but they were always denied. It was becoming very obvious to others on the tier that Tony was going through something. He was irritable and quick to jump on those he had always been friendly with. He, however, continued to maintain his silence about getting out.

The word on the tier had gotten around that Tony may have won his appeal. It was something that Tony tried to keep secret, but secrets were hard to keep in prison. He thought that on a late night conversation with Donny Napolitano, it may have slipped out. Tony confided in Donny because he needed to talk to someone he trusted. When it slipped out, he told Donny not to talk about it with any of the inmates. He knew as soon as he had mentioned the release, it would get out. Donny loved to talk about his wrongful incarceration to anyone that would listen. He had a big mouth and Tony regretted telling him anything about the possibility of a release. He knew it would get around. In no time at all, he was being approached with congratulations from inmates. When he asked Donny why he told others about his possible release, he simply said it wasn't him. Tony knew that was bullshit. At this point, he figured it didn't really matter who knew. It was either going to happen, or it wasn't.

Having recently retired from the Bureau and having many contacts still at the top in the agency, Warden Hubbard decided to make some calls. His first call was to Al Gluskow, the top attorney in the FBI. He and Al had worked together for many years on some high-level investigations. They were very close and shared a professional and personal relationship that had bonded over many years.

"Al, this is Mike. How the hell have you been? Are you still talking about retiring, or did you find another reason to stay on the job?"

"Well, Mike, I have thought about retiring. I keep saying one more year. I have been saying that for the past five. We all can't bail out of here and land a gravy job like you did. It's great hearing from you. What brings a busy man like you to call me?"

Hubbard knew that he did not have to build up to why he made the call; he could get right to it with Al. Their relationship was such that they could say anything they wanted to say, knowing each would give the best answer he could muster.

"Al, I'm going to really cut to the chase. I'll fill in the blanks later. Hear me out and then give me your opinion on how you think I should proceed."

Hubbard commenced to tell Gluskow the entire story about Tony Spitlato. He started with the basics. He quickly included the part about not being informed of the plan by the Justice Department. He explained that he found out about the plan from a guard. He talked about the conversations he had with John Thompson and Pat Driscoll. Gluskow was well aware of Thompson and Driscoll. Hubbard talked for about fifteen minutes, and during that time, Gluskow could sense the frustration in Hubbard's voice. Hubbard paused and asked him if he understood the problem up this point.

"Mike, I think I get the gist of what happened. I must tell you that I am not surprised about anything coming out of the Justice Department. I can't believe that from the beginning they did not include you in their plan. I assume that you are against the release of Spitlato?"

"Al, I am totally against the plan. You have known me for a long time. I have participated in many covert operations over the years, but getting this guy out is something I'm against. I have no fondness for cops that are corrupt. This Spitlato guy is one of the worst. He started undercover in the mob in Camden, and in no time at all, he was a made man in that organization. He's a suspect in the killing of a federal judge while in the mob. I feel that he is also a suspect in the killing of one of my guards. I see no real purpose for going along with him getting back on the street."

"Mike, I have known you for a long time. From what you have told me, I agree with you. On the other hand, I know that you are in no position to fight the Justice Department. The guy running the show over there now is thinking of only one thing, and that is to impress the President. I know for a fact that he will do anything to accomplish whatever makes him look good. If you try to block the release, they could smear your name all over the place. If you do go to the media about this, be prepared for the backlash. They are powerful. Thompson won't let anything stand in his way."

Hubbard listened intently to Gluskow, whom he respected immensely. He knew that the conversation would stay between them. He also knew that Al had made some good points, but he just couldn't get the release of Spitlato out of his mind. It would take putting on his big-boy pants if he wanted to go to the media. There would be no turning back once he did it.

"Al, I appreciate your advice. I'll think it over for a while. Whatever I decide, I will let you know. Before I hang up, let me just say that if anything happens to me or my family, you'll know who the suspects are."

Hubbard stayed late at the office. He pondered whether or not to bring Spitlato out for a talk. He decided against it and left the office. He sat in his car for a long time. He didn't start it or play any music; he just sat and thought about the ramifications if he tried to stop Spitlato's release. He was well aware of the power of the Justice Department. He knew in the past they had used tactics that were downright criminal acts to get what they wanted.

After eating dinner at one of his fast-food spots, he went home. He was tired and he needed to get some sleep; the situation with Spitlato was draining him. He parked in his numbered spot and walked to his condo. He fumbled with his key in the dark. When he placed the key in the lock, he pushed, and the door opened without turning the key. He backed away from the door. He drew his five shot Smith &Wesson from his briefcase. Of all the guns he had over the years, he preferred to carry this one when he retired. He had purchased the gun over thirty years ago. He thought about calling the police. He hesitated, and thought maybe he had left the door unlocked when he left earlier that morning.

In any case, he was reverting to his law enforcement training. He entered the condo; he did not hit the light switch. He had just enough light coming in from the street. As he slowly walked toward the kitchen, he had the sense that someone had been in his place. The condo was not ransacked, but it had the appearance that some things had been moved. When he felt comfortable that no one was in the condo, he flipped on the light in the kitchen; it illuminated his office area. On his desk was his personal laptop. The cover was closed with a white envelope protruding from it. He pulled the envelope from the laptop. It was addressed to Warden Hubbard. He sat down with his revolver not too far from him. He opened the envelope and pulled out a letter. He could feel his heart racing. He remembered that all his training told him to breathe under these circumstances. He moved the revolver within reaching distance and read the letter...

Mr. Warden,

We came in your condo earlier. As you can see, we did not disturb anything. We could have destroyed your place if we wanted to. We left the door unlocked just to put a little fear in you. We would greatly appreciate you not trying to block the release of Tony Spitlato. It would be a shame if you didn't get to enjoy your retirement. We hope you take our effort to get Spitlato released, serious. Please do not involve law enforcement. By the way, does Donna still live alone at 2212 Valley Ridge Lane, Rockville, Maryland? Is the phone number at her house still 240-365-9298?

We hope we didn't ruin your night. This letter is just a forewarning that if you make any attempt to block Tony's release, bad things might happen.

Have a nice night.

After a couple of stiff drinks, Hubbard decided to call his wife. It was late, but he needed to hear her voice. He would not tell her about the letter. He only wanted to make sure she was okay. He would try to convince her to come and stay with him for a while. He also thought about calling Gluskow. He could get the Bureau to provide protection for Donna. He also thought about his son who was a D.C. police officer. David could stay with his mother until things calmed down.

He had the phone in his hand, but slammed it down on the table. He needed to back up a little. He had a letter put in his house by people he didn't even know. Everything revolved around him trying to stop Spitlato from being released. Before he made calls and asked for protection for his wife, he needed to decide what he was going to do.

He knew they would be monitoring his moves. Calling and asking for protection was going to start a whole bunch of activity to begin, but he was not going to be bullied around by the Justice Department. His whole career had been based on the fact that he believed in the system.

"I'm not going to change anything. To let these people threaten me is not something that will sway my decision either way. I will do what is right. I won't be able to live with myself if I don't stop this craziness," he said aloud before pouring himself a drink.

CHAPTER 32

One Week Later

The meeting took place at the Horizon Hotel in downtown Crescent City. Hubbard had made arrangements to meet with a reporter from the Crescent City Times. Dennis Mitchell had been with the newspaper for thirty years. He had the reputation of writing the hard stories. The stories that he reported on dealt with topics such as political corruption, government overspending, and wrongdoing in the police department. He was a hard-nosed reporter who had the reputation of finding out things that others could not.

When he got the call from Hubbard, he thought he was getting the first scoop on identifying the person who murdered Lieutenant Mandez. When Hubbard called him, he asked only that they meet; he did not tell him the reason.

Hubbard arrived first. He found a seat in the very large lobby area. He was nervous. The meeting reminded him of the times with the Bureau when he worked some undercover investigations. This encounter was much different, but he still had the same feeling as in his undercover days.

On the drive to the hotel, he thought about cancelling the meeting. Was he doing the right thing? Would he be blackballed in any endeavor to get another position in law enforcement? Would he and his family be in any danger over what he was about to do?

Mitchell walked into the hotel, and Hubbard spotted him right away. Hubbard had never met him before, but Mitchell's appearance and demeanor said he was a reporter. Without even knowing for sure if this guy was Mitchell, Hubbard waved to get his attention. Mitchell acknowledged him, and they greeted each other. Mitchell asked Hubbard if he was comfortable in the lobby or would he rather ask for a conference room. They both agreed that the far secluded corner of the lobby would be fine.

"Mr. Mitchell, I appreciate you meeting with me. I know your reputation as a reporter. I have something that might be of interest to you. I'm sure from the message that I left, you are aware of my position at Pelican Bay."

"Why don't you just call me Dennis, and I'll call you Mike. I'm aware of your position at the prison. I covered some of the stories about the murder of your guard. I assume that's what you want to discuss with me."

Hubbard pushed forward in the very cushy chair to get closer to Mitchell. He leaned in and told him that he did not have anything further on the murder at the prison. He told him that he asked to meet with him to talk about something else.

"Dennis, I will give you the short version of what I want to discuss. If you have questions later, I will fill in the blanks. I have a situation in my unit that bothers the hell out of me. You know my background, so I will skip all of that. I have an inmate in the unit that may be one of the worst corrupt cops in the nation. At one time, he had worked undercover and made his way into the Mafia in Camden, New Jersey. He was involved in all types of crimes while working in the mob. It turned out that he liked the mob more than he liked police work. He turned on his department. Over a period of time, the government had enough to indict him under the RICO act. I'm sure you're familiar with the RICO act."

Mitchell acknowledged that he was familiar with the RICO Act. He asked Hubbard to slow down a little; he wanted to take some notes. Hubbard apologized and waited for Mitchell to get his notepad from his briefcase. Hubbard took a deep breath and continued.

"The Justice Department, led by the number two man under the attorney general now wants to get him out and have him work his way back into the Camden, New Jersey, mob. I know what I'm telling you probably all sounds silly, but bear with me. They have somehow finagled a federal appeals court judge to grant him his appeal and release him from my unit. There are others involved in working on his release, but you get the gist of the story. I found out about their plan from a guard who reports directly to me. Now let me just add my take on this before we move on."

Mitchell asked Hubbard if would like to get a drink. The drinks were ordered, and after they arrived, Hubbard picked up where he left off.

"As you know, I'm retired from the FBI. I had a great career with them. I had a reputation when I was there of someone who despised any form of corruption in law enforcement. Maybe that is why they wanted to leave me out of their plan. I just can't, with a clear conscience, go along with the Justice Department. I know by giving you this story, I could be cutting my throat. I also know that if you print this story, the Justice Department will deny everything. They have a way of covering their asses pretty good. I also know that at times they have ways of shutting people up. I have given you the gist of the story. I have kept very good records as their plan has moved forward. I can provide you with that information at a later date. I guess what I need to know now is this something you want to take on."

"Wow, Mike that was a mouthful. Yes, you bet, I'm certainly interested in the story, but I need to know if exposing their plan is something you really want to do. I have also been around a long time. I know that things can get a little nasty when a story like this one hits the newspapers. If you're sure this is what you want, I'm your man."

"Dennis, I ask only one other thing. I want you to prepare your article, but you need to wait for me to give you the nod to move forward."

They shook hands, and Mitchell offered to buy dinner. Hubbard accepted, and they moved from the lobby to the restaurant. Hubbard felt comfortable talking with Mitchell. During dinner, they shared stories as if they were long lost buddies. When they parted, Mitchell said that he would wait to hear from Hubbard before he proceeded to compile the story.

On the way back to his condo, Hubbard was feeling good. The few drinks he had at dinner relaxed him. He felt confident that he was doing the right thing. *If I'm going to fully retire and spend quality time with my wife, I want to go out knowing that all my values are intact.*

Hubbard arrived back at his condo. He was still feeling the effects of the drinks. He decided that before he hit the sack, he would call his wife. After preparing another gin and tonic, he made the call. He realized that he had missed a day of not calling her. It would have been the first time since he took the new job. He would make a sincere apology. Telling her that he was seriously thinking about retiring would have to wait, until he was certain that is what he wanted. He knew that even over the phone she would be able to determine from his voice if anything was wrong. The drinks would hopefully help him disguise any outward signs of distress. Being married for all those years and having lived through so many investigations that took him away from home, she accepted the life of a FBI agent. The new job was different; she wanted him back home.

The phone conversation covered all the family issues that husbands and wives talk about. He let her talk for quite a while. Just hearing her voice and listening to her was comforting to him. He did tell her that there were some issues on the new job that he didn't like. He also hinted that taking the job might have been a mistake. She had listened to problems in the past—she was a good listener. Before hanging up, he told her that he missed her very much. He promised that he would not miss any more calls to her. The conversation ended with him mentioning that retirement would mean that they could spend every minute together. He told her that he loved her. They both hung up their phones, not knowing that someone else was listening to their conversation.

CHAPTER 33

Two Days Later

The morning was uneventful for a Monday. No incidents had occurred over the weekend, so the paperwork was minimal. Marcia made it a point to come in early on Monday mornings. She compiled what reports there were from the guards. Any documents that needed Hubbard's signature were neatly positioned on his desk. The coffee was brewing. The few plants around the office had been watered. She had the muffins on a tray next to the coffee. Hubbard enjoyed Mondays. He called her efforts, the Monday morning munchies. He had made it a point to always tell Marcia that he could not get by without her help.

"Good morning, Marcia. Other than the coffee is there anything hot that I should know?"

"The only thing that appears to be pressing at the moment is that you need to return a call from Mr. Thompson. He left a message on your phone early this morning. The message was brief. He only said for you to call him when you got in."

Hubbard decided to have his coffee and muffin first. He was in no hurry to make the call. He knew what it would be about. He browsed the morning paper, reviewed some reports, finished his muffin, and made the call. The phone rang four times. He waited, knowing that the office phone switched over to Thompson's cell phone when not answered. "John, this is Mike. Seems a little early in the morning for you to be calling. Have you changed your mind about Spitlato?"

"Mike, you do understand that the decision to release Spitlato was made by a federal judge, not me. He will be released, and there is nothing you can do about it. I'm calling to tell you to have the papers ready for his release by tomorrow. I'm also calling to ask why you felt the need to talk to a reporter from the Crescent City Times. Listen to me. I want to be very clear, if you continue with your stubbornness... you might regret it."

Hubbard made sure the recorder was on. He was not surprised when he heard that Thompson knew about his meeting with Dennis Mitchell. After all, this was the Justice Department; they had all the resources they needed at their disposal. He was surprised that Thompson would come right out and say he knew about the meeting. That meant that he had been followed. It also probably meant that they were monitoring every move he made. When they follow people for no reason, and tap their phones for no reason, they say it's done in the best interest of the nation. And they call themselves the Justice Department.

"John, are you threatening me? For a minute there, I really thought that the second in command at the Justice Department was threatening me. Let's be clear—I don't take threats lightly. I can blow the lid off your plan with one phone call. I don't think your boss wants that kind of publicity. He has his eye set on bigger and better things."

"Mike, I'm going to end this conversation by telling you that the paperwork on Spitlato needs to be completed by tomorrow. I have nothing further to discuss with you. If you think you can fuck with me, you're sadly mistaken."

The conversation ended and Hubbard hung up the phone. He checked his recorder to see if he got the conversation. His next call was to Dennis Mitchell.

Later That Day At Thompson's Office
Thompson called a few members of his team together. He had limited the group to those that had a need to know. "Gentlemen, I have a little problem with our plan to get Tony Spitlato out. It seems that the warden

of the CLEO Unit wants to go to the media. He wants to expose what he feels is a travesty of justice. He doesn't seem to give a shit that we have a federal judge on our side. I could easily replace him at the prison, but that would only add fuel to his fire. He's a pretty tough guy, but I'm sure we can come up with a way that would make him cooperate. You know— sometimes playing fair just doesn't work with some people. Let's start off with putting a little heat on something that is near and dear to his heart. Pat, let's make a call to one of our operatives in the field. Let him know where Hubbard's house is located in the D.C. suburbs. Instead of adding fuel to his fire, we can add a little fuel to his house... sort of like firing a warning shot. I want it done when his wife is out of the house, and I want it done as soon as possible."

Thompson ended the meeting by telling the group that things might get a little dicey down the road. He emphasized that getting Spitlato out of prison was more important than worrying about Hubbard's future. He told them that anyone could operate the CLEO Unit, now that it is up and running. He was furious, and assured them that getting Spitlato back in the Calabrese mob would be a huge opportunity for the Justice Department.

Hubbard's Office

The second set of papers from the appeals court arrived by way of the U.S. Marshals. The new documents clearly stated that Tony Spitlato was to be released to their custody by 4 p.m. the next day. Hubbard knew that although the federal judge was in the pocket of the Justice Department, he had no choice but to release Spitlato as directed. He could not delay it any longer. The only option left on the table would be if Mitchell's story hit the paper before the deadline to release Spitlato. Maybe there would be enough outrage about his release that the New Jersey prosecutors who tried the case would file some kind of motion with the courts to keep him in prison. It was a long shot, but the release of the story to the media was something that had to be done.

Chapter 34

The late news was something that Hubbard watched faithfully every night. That was his point of no return as far as trying to stay awake. Getting up at 5 a.m. each morning came around much too soon. If he didn't get to bed after the 10 p.m. news, he would be dragging the next morning. Usually it was the same old mundane news...the crime in the county, politicians talking about how they wanted to pass certain legislation, local sports, and finally the weather.

Hubbard frantically reached for the remote. It fell to the floor, and he literally dove on the floor to retrieve it. The news anchor started the program by saying...*A prominent local newspaper reporter was gunned down in the Mount Vista area of Crescent City tonight.*

Hubbard pushed the volume on the remote so hard that the news anchor's voice vibrated throughout the condo. He turned it down in time to hear the anchor go on to say that a veteran reporter, Dennis Mitchell, was shot several times as he approached his apartment. Hubbard was shocked. He didn't know whether to make phone calls, and if he did, who would he call?

The news reporter went on to say that Mitchell was a highly respected veteran reporter for the Crescent City Times. The on-scene reporter was reporting from behind the yellow police tape. The picture on the TV screen showed police officers milling around. It also showed a white sheet on the sidewalk. Hubbard knew from his law enforcement background that the white sheet usually covered a body. The reporter said that there were no witnesses to the shooting, and Mitchell had been shot multiple times. He reported that he died on the scene.

Hubbard had lots of questions running through his head. They must be sure it's Mitchell, or they would not release the name. Did they notify a next of kin that fast? Did they recover anything from the scene? Was Mitchell carrying a briefcase? One big question that bugged Hubbard… were Mitchell's notes about Spitlato among the things recovered at the scene?

Hubbard pushed the power button on the remote and threw it across the room. Was it just a coincidence that Mitchell gets murdered the night before he was going to write the story about Spitlato? Would the Justice Department go that far to kill Dennis Mitchell, to keep the story out of the paper?

Hubbard paced back and forth. A gin and tonic was in order. *Who the hell do I call? It would be a waste of time to confront Thompson. Do I call the local police and ask them what they recovered from the scene? Hell, that's crazy to even think about doing that. I'm the warden in a prison, not an FBI agent.*

I need to be calm and think this out. I put Mitchell in a bad spot. I would never have thought that Thompson would go this far. I'm jumping the gun. I need to wait and see if this was a street robbery, before I draw any conclusions.

The gin and tonic settled Hubbard down a little. As he stretched out on the couch, he was dozing in and out when his cell phone rang. It startled him. *Who in the hell is calling at such a late time? Is something happening at the prison?* He fumbled for the phone which had fallen between the cushions on the couch. "Hello, this is Mike Hubbard."

"Mr. Hubbard, this is Sergeant Alvarez with the Montgomery County police department. I hate to bother you so late at night. I'm afraid I have some bad news for you. There was a firebombing at your house tonight. The explosion caused severe damage to your home. Your wife was in the residence at the time, but she made it out okay; she's fine. She was taken to Bethesda General Hospital for precautionary measures. She has some scratches on her and may have suffered some smoke inhalation. She wanted me to emphasize to you that she is fine."

"Are you sure my wife is okay? I can't believe what you're telling me. Is my home destroyed? Screw the home. You are definitely assuring me that my wife is fine."

"Sir, your wife will be fine. She's alert, but very shaken up. She would have called you herself if it were not for the fact that she is receiving treatment for smoke inhalation. Our arson investigators are still on the scene. It appears very obvious to them at this point that some type of explosive device was thrown through the front window. Neighbors reported that they did see a vehicle driving from your development after they heard the explosion. We are working on that lead at this time. I will let your wife know that we talked. I'm sure if you call the hospital in the morning she will be able to talk to you. I do know that our investigators will want to take a statement from you. Do you have any thoughts on who would do such a thing?"

Hubbard had many thoughts running through his head, but it was not the time to share them with anyone. Enough damage had been done for one night. It was time to step back and assess the situation…that's what all the years at the Bureau taught him. He needed to get the next flight back to Washington. If the Justice Department was behind these two incidents, that could wait. The thought of his wife being alone in their home and experiencing that explosion was tearing at him. He needed to be with her.

Hubbard decided to call Lieutenant Sanders. For the first time since coming to the West Coast, he felt vulnerable. If Thompson was behind this craziness, he needed to take measures to protect himself.

"Ron, this is Mike Hubbard. I need you to do something for me without asking any questions at this time. Make some calls and get the first flight that will get me back to Washington. After that I need you to come to my condo. Make sure you have your weapon with you when you come here. I know this sounds crazy at this time, but I will explain what's going on when you take me to the airport."

After being assured by Sanders that he would do as instructed, Hubbard flopped down on the couch; he was mentally drained. He bounced back up and started to throw some clothes in his carry-on bag. He unlocked his gun safe and retrieved his Smith & Wesson revolver. He put the maximum five rounds in the gun.

While packing his bag, he was thinking that even though he was retired law enforcement, he did not have a California gun carry permit. He did have a D.C. and a Maryland permit. He decided that on the way to the airport he would strip the weapon down and place it in his carry-on bag. He would then check the bag, instead of taking it through the metal detector. He wanted to make sure that he had the weapon when he landed in Washington.

Lieutenant Sanders arrived at the condo. He informed Hubbard that he had booked a flight to Reagan National Airport and the flight left from Los Angeles International Airport. They had two hours to get to the airport. Sanders asked Hubbard what was going on and why did he need to fly back to D.C. Still throwing things into his bag and briefcase, Hubbard told Sanders that he would explain the situation on the ride to the airport. Sanders noticed that Hubbard was carrying a weapon, but he didn't ask any questions.

On the ride to the airport, Hubbard told Sanders about what happened to his home. He also told him that he had been working with a newspaper reporter about doing a story on the release of Tony Spitlato. He told him that the reporter was gunned down earlier that night. Hubbard told Sanders that the events seem to be very sketchy at this time, but he thought that the Justice Department was sending a signal that he should back off on trying to block the release of Spitlato.

While they were talking, Hubbard was breaking the gun down. He told Sanders that he would put the gun in the bag that he would check at the counter. He also asked him to show up for work in the morning and act as warden until he could figure out what he was going to do.

Upon arrival at the airport, Sanders dropped Hubbard off at the main entrance and assured him that he would take care of things at the prison. When Sanders pulled away and was clear of the airport, he pulled to the side of the road. He dialed a number and turned down the radio.

"Mr. Thompson, this is Ron Sanders. Hubbard is on flight 1837 which will be leaving LAX in about thirty minutes. He should be getting in at Reagan Airport in about six hours. He has a Smith & Wesson revolver in his luggage. I will be in his office in the morning if you need to talk to me."

CHAPTER 35

The release of Tony Spitlato went off without a hitch. U.S. Marshals arrived at the prison in the morning, about the same time Lieutenant Sanders arrived. He made it known to the guard staff that he was now acting warden in the absence of Hubbard. He requested that Spitlato be immediately brought to the warden's office along with all his personal items.

Spitlato threw all his belongings in a duffle bag. While being escorted to the warden's office, he shouted his goodbyes to those that were awake. He made a special point to give a shout-out to Donny Napolitano. "Hey, Chee Chee, hang tough *paisan*. You have been a great friend to me. I will not forget you. Tell the guys I will always be thinking about them."

Donny hollered as loud as he could, "Be well my friend – *Vivi Bene, Ama Molto, Ridi Spesso*." As Tony passed the cells, hands reached out to slap his hand and wish him well. Tony tried to slap hands, and say something to each person as he passed their cell. As they approached the door to the warden's office, the guard asked Tony what Donny had said to him in Italian.

"Well, Donny was just saying something that all you fellows should try. He said, '*Live well, Love much, and Laugh often.*' I intend to do just that when I get out of this shithouse."

Tony was turned over to the marshals. Lieutenant Sanders signed some papers, and as simple as that, Tony was heading out of the prison.

He was not even handcuffed as he got in the backseat of the marshals' vehicle. He attempted to engage the marshals in conversation, but they only nodded when he talked.

After driving for about thirty minutes, one of the marshals told Tony that he would be put on a plane and flown to Philadelphia International Airport. When he arrived at the airport he would be met by his attorney, Howard Gibbons. Then he would be driven to Camden where arrangements have been made for him to stay at a hotel. He was told that any direction from the Justice Department would come through Howard Gibbons. He was also told that he would not be allowed to make contact with anyone until he got the okay from Gibbons. They informed him that a U.S. Marshal would be on the plane going to Philadelphia. The marshal would not identify himself, but would be watching him. Upon arrival in Philadelphia, the marshal would make sure he hooked up with Gibbons. The marshal asked Tony if he understood what he was to do.

"How long do I have to stay cooped up in the hotel? Is it okay if I phone my family and let them know I'm out? What am I supposed to do for cash?

The marshal turned and handed Tony an envelope. "Mr. Spitlato, do you understand everything I have told you? All I want to hear from you is yes, or no."

"Okay, I understand. What the hell is in this envelope?"

"The envelope contains two thousand dollars. I think that should hold you until you can get back with your mob buddies. I have answered the question about the envelope. As far as you calling your family, that's a no-no. The only calls you should be making is to your lawyer. You will be told when and who you can call at a later time. If you didn't figure it out yet, we will be monitoring the phone in your room. I hope you don't try to do anything foolish, Mr. Spitlato. You need to remember that you are now working fulltime for the Justice Department. You seem to be a pretty intelligent guy, so my advice to you is…don't blow it. If you do what we expect you to do, there will come a day that you will be able to lead a normal life. That is, if you call being in the Witness Protection

Program a normal life. However, I'm sure it beats the hell out of prison life."

The rest of the ride to the airport was quiet. Tony didn't say anything; he didn't want to piss off the marshals. He sat back and took in the scenery. He rolled the window down. Even though it was a bit chilly, the cool breeze felt great on his face. It had been a long time since he had experienced freedom. He breathed deeply as if he were taking his last breath. He could not believe he was out of the infamous CLEO Unit. As they drove, the sights that would be everyday normal sights for anyone else were being taken in by Tony as if he were a child at Disneyland.

Tony was driven directly to the tarmac at the airport. The plane was fired up and ready to go. Tony thanked the marshals and tried to shake hands. Neither marshal obliged him. They had a job to do, and that was to deliver Tony to the plane. Being friendly was not part of their assignment. Tony walked up the steps to the plane. When he got to the top and before entering the plane, he stood tall with his arms stretched out. He looked at the marshals. He gave the best Richard Nixon impression he could muster. With his thumbs in the air, he said, "I'm not a crook."

He boarded the plane and introduced himself to the pilot. If anyone saw his actions, they would think he was some rich dude boarding his private jet. Tony was feeling good, and he knew how to take advantage of a good situation. He stretched out in the very comfortable seats. After the quarter inch mattress at the prison, these plush seats felt like floating on clouds. As the plane taxied the runway, Tony, who was wearing a headset with direct communications to the pilot, asked if he could have something to drink. The pilot responded by telling Tony that there were no drinks on the plane. He was further advised by the pilot just to sit back and relax.

When the plane landed in Philadelphia, two marshals met the jet on the tarmac. Tony was put in a black Lincoln Town Car and driven to the hotel. The marshals could have been clones of the other marshals from the West Coast. They were silent on the ride to the hotel. Tony had a few questions, but he got no answers. When they arrived at the hotel, one of the marshals told Tony that he was already registered. He was instructed to go to the desk and get his key. He was told that he would be getting a call in his room in about fifteen minutes with further instructions.

The room was plush. Tony looked around and spotted the bar. He went directly to it, but it was locked. He realized that he had not tipped the bellhop, who stood by the door. He asked the young guy if he knew how to open the bar. "Sir, if you just punch in your room number, the bar will open."

Tony put the room number in and it opened. "Holy shit, look at the all this good booze. I can't fuckin' believe these bastards left all this shit for me."

The bellhop kept standing at the door. Tony, feeling like this kid had given him the key to paradise, opened the envelope and gave him a hundred dollar bill. "Sir, I appreciate it, but that's not necessary."

Tony put his arm around him. "Young man, today is the start of the rest of my life. Take the money and treat yourself. There's plenty more where that came from."

With his hands nearly shaking in disbelief, Tony pulled several miniatures from the bar. The phone rang, but he ignored it. He poured two miniatures of William Chase gin into a glass and added a little tonic water. Hell, the hotel even had some fresh limes.

He stirred the drink and plopped down onto the huge white leather wrap-around couch. He looked for the remote for the TV, but he couldn't find it, so he gave up. He sipped the drink. He made sounds that would lead the people in the next room to think he was having sex. When he finished the drink, he made another one. The phone rang, and again he pretended he didn't hear it. As he savored the new drink, his thoughts took him back to just ten hours earlier when he was sitting in a cage. This wonderful moment was like nothing he had experienced in years. He loved it and wanted more.

He was about to make his third drink when he realized that he hadn't answered the phone. He needed to get back on track, or all this new excitement could end. He had made a deal to work with the government. "If that damn phone rings again I need to jump on it."

"Hello, this is Tony Spitlato."

"Tony, this is Pat Driscoll. Allow me to introduce myself. I'm the assistant to Deputy Attorney General John Thompson at the Justice Department. I hope you are enjoying yourself. Did the phone ring a couple of times before you answered?"

"No sir, it only rang once, and I picked it up."

"Well, Tony, let me be the first to call you a fuckin' liar. We don't want to play games with you. We have cameras in that room and recording devices. I hope you've been enjoying your gin and tonic. You need to take it easy; three drinks might be a little too much for a guy who just got out of prison. The hundred dollars you gave to the baggage handler was a little overboard, but what the hell. It ain't your money, right Tony?

Even with the drinks taking effect, Tony knew that he better start playing by the rules. He looked around the room, but could not see any cameras. He put the drink down and apologized to Driscoll for not answering the phone when it rang the first time.

Driscoll continued, "Let's get something straight before I go any further. You are out of prison for one reason and one reason only. If you don't play by the rules we set up, your ass will be back in that stupid CLEO Unit as fast as you can say Mafia. Do you understand?"

Tony, knowing that he was being recorded, sat up straight on the couch. He didn't really give a shit if they were watching or listening to him; he was out of prison and living large. He smiled and waved as if he knew where the camera was. He held up the gin and tonic. "Here's to you, sir, and the Justice Department. I'm all yours. Just let me know what's expected of me. By the way, what did you say your name was?"

"My name is Pat Driscoll, but that's not important. You will not be dealing with me after this phone call. I want to explain some things to you before you drink that whole cabinet. So listen up Tony; I don't like to repeat myself. You are not to leave that room until you hear from your attorney, Mr. Gibbons. You can order meals off the menu and eat in your room. You have everything you need in that room. Later this evening, a man who works with us at the Justice Department will be coming to your room. He will call you before he comes up. His name is Andy Brewer. When he calls, he will tell you his name. He will then ask you how far can you run into the woods. You will respond…half way, because the other half you are running out of the woods. I know it sounds like child's play, but this is what we do to protect people. When he meets with you, he will have some material for you. He will be there for quite some time filling you in on what has been happening with the Pete Calabrese crime family."

"Sir, could you just stop for a minute? I understand most of what you have said. Did you say that the guy coming here is Andy Brewer?

Is this the same Andy Brewer that gave me a raft of shit when I was in the CLEO Unit? Is this the tough CIA agent that first talked to me about getting out of prison? Is this the guy that thinks I know who killed that prison guard?"

Driscoll seemed to pause for a moment. He knew that Brewer had been the guy who first told Tony about the plan to get him out. He was now wondering if sending Brewer to meet with Tony was such a good idea. "Tony, to answer your questions, yes, it's the same guy. Do you have a problem meeting with him? If so, we can send someone else. I would really like to send Brewer. He has been involved in the process from the beginning. He's a very capable guy."

At this point, Tony was thinking…*what the hell do I care who they send. I'm out of prison, sitting in a nice hotel, drinking very expensive booze…shit, send anybody you want to.*

"Sir, I have no problem meeting with Brewer."

Chapter 36

The house was literally on the ground. What little that was left after the fire bombing was taken down by the city, as being unsafe for human habitation.

Hubbard stood on the lawn talking to the fire marshal. He asked if he could go through the rubble to try to find any remnants of the life he and his wife had led. Could he find any photos of the kids or trophies they had received over the years? Could he find their wedding album, his awards from the Bureau, the videos they had taken, his small gun collection, newspaper accounts of cases he worked at the Bureau or anything that was salvageable? He thought about the few pieces of expensive art that they were so proud of buying over the years.

The fire marshal was aware of Hubbard's background with the FBI. His first question to Hubbard was, "Do you have any idea who would do something like this?" Hubbard just looked at the fire marshal and dropped his head. He did not answer. The question was posed to him again.

"Sir, at this time I'm just happy that my wife made it out okay. I have dealt with some unsavory characters over the years. I need some time to think about your question. My concern now is to be with my wife. I need to think about our future. I know you have a job to do. I will cooperate, but at this time I'm filled with so much anger that I might say the wrong thing and live to regret it."

"Mr. Hubbard, I can certainly understand how you feel. My job is to investigate this incident. I will need to take a statement from you and your wife. I will be finishing up here on the scene with the forensics. With what we know now from witnesses and fire patterns, this is definitely an arson investigation. I will give you some time, but I will need to meet with you in the morning for your statement."

Hubbard acknowledged the fire marshal and agreed to meet with him. He shook hands and started to walk around the property, or at least what was left of it.

Hubbard met up with his wife at the hotel they were staying at in downtown Washington. For having been through such a traumatic incident, she appeared to be handling it quite well. Over the years with Mike working in the Bureau, she had been through a few scares. There was the time when he worked to convict a member of the Black Panthers. The investigation dragged on for months. Toward the end when the indictments came out was when the scary part started.

They were living in an all-white neighborhood in D.C. While Mike was at work, she noticed a car parked in front of their house with several black men in it. She could see from her front window that they were taking photos of the house. The kids were younger at the time and playing outside. She scrambled to get the kids into the house and called the police. Before the police got there an object was thrown through the front window. The car drove off.

The object turned out to be a large rock with photos of Huey Newton and Bobby Seale wrapped around the rock. On the photo was written, *Power to the people...enjoy your kids.* Newton and Seale were leaders of the Panthers at the time. It was believed that neither was actually involved in the incident. Nothing further happened, but it left Hubbard knowing that there could be retaliation from those he investigated and sent to jail.

Hubbard knew his wife would have a lot of questions; that was her nature. He decided to have the talk over dinner. She insisted that before they ordered their dinner, she wanted to know what was going on. He tried to assure her that everything would be okay. She stopped him and told him that they had been through a lot, that nothing he would tell her would shock her. He proceeded to tell her about his displeasure lately while running the CLEO Unit. He was apologizing in a way for even taking the job. He did not want to leave anything out. She had been his sounding board for all the years while at the Bureau. Even if he wanted to try and sugarcoat the story, she would see right through him. When the waiter asked if they were ready to order, Mike asked if they could have a few more minutes.

He went through the entire scenario from the time he found out the Justice Department wanted to get Spitlato out of the unit, until he got the phone call about the explosion. She did not interrupt him, but he could see that she would have questions...she always did.

The waiter returned, and they decided that they would order. Hubbard finished talking and as expected, she started with the questions. They were simple and basically what anyone would ask if they heard the story for the first time. Her first reaction was asking him why she was hearing all of this for the first time. Hubbard apologized and told her that it was all happening so fast. With the death of Mandez, trying to get the unit up and running in a cohesive manner, and the Justice Department working to get Spitlato out, he thought it best not to burden her.

The dinner came, and they tried to have some pleasant conversation other than about what was happening in the CLEO Unit. In the middle of the meal, she put her fork down. "Mike, you should never have taken that position. I wish I would have been more forceful and stopped you. We both knew that working in a prison was not your forte. You had a stellar career with the Bureau. We have earned the right to enjoy our retirement. I can't believe the Justice Department would think that they could use you to set up that unit and then try to pull something like that. Where do we go from here?"

"I'm not sure at this point. They are a treacherous bunch that I'm dealing with. Getting Spitlato out of prison took a lot of finagling on their part. They had to have a federal judge on their side. I'm sure Spitlato's attorney is involved. I would not be surprised if they even had some of my people working for them. The second in command at the Justice Department is John Thompson. This guy has a reputation of doing whatever it takes to get something done. That includes breaking the same laws he is sworn to enforce."

Hubbard's wife did not stop him, even if she had questions. He seemed to be explaining what happened in much detail. Hubbard ordered another drink and continued talking.

"I would not be surprised to find out that Attorney General Paige is involved. He probably knows about the initial plan. I would doubt it if he knows what Thompson is doing. Paige has his sights set on a higher office. He leaves all the dirty work to Thompson. That way when the shit hits the fan he can say he didn't know about it. I never thought they would go this far to keep me quiet."

When dinner was over, Mike asked Donna to have a drink with him at the bar. From what she had heard, she agreed that a drink was needed. At the bar, Mike tried to assure her that he would be okay. She took no time in coming back at him. "Why do you think that? The story you told me sounds like something I've seen in the movies. You feel that they killed a reporter to stop him from writing a story. Our house has been firebombed apparently to send a message to you. I could have been killed in that house. You are up against a formidable foe here. I think you need to go to someone in the Bureau. Forget about the newspaper for now. We need to get some help before they decide to quiet everyone that knows about the Spitlato deal."

Back at the hotel and after another round of drinks, Hubbard decided to call his office. It was getting late by Washington, D.C. time, but it would only be 6:30 p.m. on the West Coast. He called his office, and Lieutenant Sanders answered the phone.

"Ron, I'm glad you are still in the office. How are things on your end? I did receive a message from Marcia that Spitlato was released this afternoon. I'm probably going to stay in D.C. for a while. Some weird things have been happening. I know it all revolves around my objection to releasing Spitlato. The reporter from the Crescent City Times was gunned down because he was going to put a story in the paper. My house has been firebombed here in D.C. My wife is shaken up, so I will be staying here for a while. I will have to make a decision on whether I will come back to run that unit. I appreciate you taking over for me. You can call me anytime if you need me."

"I'm really sorry to hear what's going on. I can handle things here, so don't worry about anything. What are you going to do about all this craziness?"

"Well, I need to think about it. I will probably reach out to someone high up in the FBI. I still have contacts over there. In the meantime I will be spending time with my wife. We have a lot to do about our house. I will stay in touch with you."

"Mike, I hope everything works out for you. By the way, where are you staying?"

"I'll be staying in a hotel in D.C. I need to work with the insurance company in the morning to make arrangements for housing."

"What hotel are you at? Under the circumstances, I think it best to let me know where you are."

"I'm not sure I should let anyone know where we are. I guess it's okay to tell you. We're at the world famous Watergate Hotel."

Mike hung up and joined his wife on the couch. She gave him a very inquisitive look...one that he had seen many times. She stood up and faced him with her drink in her hand. "Mike, I'm a little surprised at you. We both feel that your life might be in danger, and you tell some-one where we are staying. Do you think you can trust anyone back there at that CLEO Unit? Since you left the Bureau have you lost your prowess for being one of the best agents the Bureau ever had? I can't believe you just told someone where we are staying."

Mike stood up and put his arms around his wife. He stepped back from her and gave her a sly look. "Honey, what does it say on the glass you are drinking from?"

"It says, Embassy Suites. I take it all back. Let's get some sleep, gumshoe."

Chapter 37

Tony was getting used to the elaborate digs at the hotel. His day of freedom consisted of watching television—lots of television. He surfed until he found the channel that was running the old shows. The meals were great, and the bar was restocked. He was thinking that just a short time ago he was in a cage at Pelican Bay.

Dinner at the prison usually consisted of mostly unidentifiable stuff. The inmates ate to survive. Now at the hotel, Tony ate to run the bill up on the government, the same government that put him in prison. He would never say it out loud to his new handlers, but he kept thinking, *what a great country.*

The reruns consisted of two of his favorites, *All In The Family* and *The Rockford Files.* He absolutely loved Archie Bunker, who reminded him of his Uncle Tomaso. If only Archie was Italian, he would be the spitting image of Tomaso. They talked alike and hated pretty much everybody. Tomaso was from the old country. Tony loved Tomaso and in many ways felt closer to him than to his father. He could always go to Uncle Tomaso and talk things out. If he was in trouble, Uncle Tomaso seemed to come up with solutions. He always gave Tony money. He made Tony swear that he would never tell his dad.

As far as *The Rockford Files,* he thought that James Garner was the best. He was a smooth talker and always found a way to solve his investigations. When Tony started as a cop in Camden, he thought about how Rockford would solve the crime. What would Rockford do?

So Tony's new freedom consisted of the reruns, good booze, great food, and a view of Philadelphia that made him yearn for the days when he would be back on the streets of Camden.

In between watching Archie and Garner, the phone rang and this time he answered it. Howard Gibbons was in the lobby and would be coming up to the room. Tony was excited because he was told that he would take his instructions from Gibbons.

He was waiting at the door for Gibbons. When he entered the room Tony hugged him and kissed him on the cheek. Tony made a drink for Gibbons, and they sat on the plush couch. Gibbons seemed a little up tight. He put his drink down, grabbed Tony, and hugged him again. "Damn Tony, it's great that you're out. This all doesn't seem like it's real. Sit down, my friend. We've got to talk about some things."

Gibbons cleared his throat and loosened his tie. He moved his neck and it reminded Tony of Rodney Dangerfield. Tony told him to just relax and let me know what was happening.

"Tony, this is great for you, but I feel like I'm walking a tightrope. I've been on edge for a few weeks in anticipation of your release. I'm in a place where I might screw up and either get my ass whacked or go to prison. I'm sure you know what I'm talking about. I'm here to give you instructions from the Justice Department. I'm also here because I talked to Pete last week, and he is looking forward to having you meet with him as soon as possible. Do you know what I'm saying?"

Tony got up and walked toward the huge window overlooking the city. "Howard, you're a very smart man. You've been in this business for a long time. I understand how you feel. You just need to keep telling Pete one story. Just tell him that you filed for an appeal, and it was granted. Pete doesn't have to know anything about you cooperating with the Justice Department. I'm sure as hell not going to say anything. You will look like a miracle worker in his eyes. On the other hand, the Justice Department will hang this over your head. I don't trust any of those bastards. Just so you know, I got a call earlier, and they are sending Andy Brewer to update me on what they want. This Brewer guy is supposed to be a former CIA agent, or at least that's what I was told. He worked at the prison and tried to get me to talk about the murder of that Mandez dude. Do you know anything about this Brewer guy?"

"Tony, I don't know anything about Brewer. I'm here to let you know that Pete Calabrese is excited that you're out. It doesn't have to be soon, but he made it known that he wants to get together with you. After my meeting with you, I'm going to try and stay out of things. I will need to be playing along with all the bullshit they created. If you call me, make sure you talk about your appeal. I'm sure those bastards have my phone juiced. When you meet with this Brewer guy, play along with him. You really don't have much of a choice; you agreed to work with them. Be careful, Tony. Sometimes, I'm not sure who I fear the most…Pete Calabrese or the Justice Department."

Gibbons left the hotel room with another big hug and kiss from Tony. As Tony was getting back into his television shows, the phone rang again. Brewer was in the lobby and coming up to the room. Tony did not know what to expect from him. His only prior contact was at the prison. Tony paced the room and was hoping that Brewer did not cross paths with Gibbons in the elevator.

The talk with Brewer didn't take long. He seemed a whole lot more congenial than he was at the prison. Tony offered him a drink, but Brewer turned him down. He told Tony that he worked directly for Pat Driscoll at the Justice Department. He gave Tony a little of his background. Tony asked him what his role at the Justice Department was. Brewer told him that he is just a guy that gets things done. He did not seem to want to elaborate any further.

He gave Tony some paper work and a verbal update on what the Justice Department knew about the current situation with the Calabrese crime family. Nothing he said was new except that the family was branching out more into the drug business. Tony was a little surprised that the family would branch out into the drug racket. Prior to going to prison, he knew first hand that some guys within the family wanted to get more involved in the drug business in Camden and other parts of Jersey.

When Tony was in good standing with the family, he often talked to Pete about staying away from drugs. He told him that the money was so easy in all the other areas, such as; selling stolen property, gambling, loan sharking, political corruption, and money laundering. Also one of the biggest interests of the Calabrese family was controlling the unions. The drug business, according to Tony, would only lead the family in the wrong direction. He told Pete it would bring to much heat from law enforcement.

Brewer told Tony to be very careful when he got back into the Calabrese family. He told him that times had changed a little and while he was in prison, some wise guys moved up the chain of command. He told him that there might be some animosity towards him. Brewer suggested that when he was ready to travel to Camden, he might want to contact Pete Calabrese directly to see how he wanted to meet.

The meeting with Brewer lasted about thirty minutes. It ended with Brewer telling Tony that he would not be wearing a wire during his stint back with the Mafia. He said it would be too dangerous. Tony agreed that a wire would not be the way to go. If it was detected, it would not only end the investigation—it would end Tony. He was told that he should call Brewer at least once a week, especially if he had information on something big going down. He would be provided with a new phone number to call after each conversation. Tony was told that if it became necessary to meet, they would meet at the Philadelphia Zoo in downtown Philly.

Brewer ended the meeting with wishing Tony well. It seemed unusual for this alleged bad-ass CIA agent to actually be wishing him well. Tony walked him to the door. "Hey, let me ask you something. If you're a CIA agent, why are you working with the Justice Department? Don't they have enough people over there to handle something like this? What's up with that?"

"Tony, let me tell you something, and I want you to remember it. I have been all over the world doing jobs for the Justice Department and the CIA. I have no real family life to talk about. I have dedicated my life to handling situations that our government seems to think needs to be done. I'm not going to go into what I have done for my country. I will say that I'm back in the states because a few of the countries I've done jobs in, have a price tag on my ass. I'm good at what I do."

For a guy that was leaving, it seemed like Brewer wanted to let Tony know that he was an extremely valuable asset to both the CIA and the Justice Department. He opened the door and turned toward Tony. He told him that he only had one more piece of advice.

"You seem to be a pretty smart guy, Tony. I would only caution you to remember that down the road, there are only a few ways you can come out of this. You might be a hero and take down the mob. You might get back there with your mob cronies and think…I like this kind of life. Whatever happens depends on you. You are in a very dangerous position. I don't have to tell you what could happen. I can tell you this…if you decide to renege on your deal, you will be getting a visit from me, and it won't be a social visit."

It seemed as if Brewer was going to stand by the open door forever. Tony said nothing, he just listened. He was hoping that he would end his lecture and get the hell out.

"By the way, Tony, my name is not Andy Brewer. I have used so many names over the years, it's hard to keep up with them. So down the road, if you try to play cop and check on me, it won't get you anywhere. The next time you see me, I could be Samuel L. Jackson. Well, maybe not; he's a black dude. I could be Stonewall Jackson. You get the gist of what I'm saying, right Tony?"

Brewer left the hotel room, and Tony just shook his head. *What the hell was that all about?*

He made a drink and caught the ending of *All In The Family*. He tuned in just when Archie was talking to meathead about religion. Archie says, *"I ain't got no respect for no religion where the head guy claims he can't make no mistakes, like he's waddyacall…inflammable."*

Meathead just stands there, squinting his eyes, and Archie comes back at him and says, *"Like the good book says, let he who is without sin be the rolling stone."*

Life was good again for Tony Spitlato.

Chapter 38

Hubbard took a cab to the FBI headquarters in downtown Washington, D.C. He had spent many years working out of that building. He could have driven there and would have been allowed to park in the executive parking lot. Instead, he chose to take the cab and be as inconspicuous as possible. The headquarters had been at 935 Pennsylvania Avenue, Northwest D.C., since the mid-seventies. It was an enormous structure that housed the executive branch of the Bureau, and other specialized units. About four hundred people were employed in the headquarters building alone. The budget was eight billion dollars, a far cry from the budget when the Bureau started in 1908.

As Hubbard approached the entrance, he felt a bit of pride coming over him. He had so many great memories from his days with the FBI. He loved working in the Bureau. At times like this, he wished he were still there. He had participated in some of the most complex investigations ever conducted by the Bureau.

At the entrance to the lobby he stopped to look at the motto: *Fidelity, Bravery, and Integrity...FBI.*

The meeting was with Al Gluskow. Hubbard had called him at his home and asked for the meeting. He had talked to Gluskow previously about the situation with Spitlato. Gluskow's office was enormous, a perk for the top attorney at the Bureau. Although he had a scheduled meeting with Gluskow, the young receptionist asked him to have a seat in the waiting area. She did ask if he wanted something to drink, but he passed. He was hoping he would not be sitting long. He wanted to get in Gluskow's office as quick as possible to avoid speaking with anyone that might recognize him.

"Al, I want to thank you for taking time to meet with me. I must say that since I left the Bureau they must have upped the ante on what kind of office furniture you can have."

Gluskow came around from his desk and shook hands with Hubbard. After directing him to a couch and offering him coffee, he asked Hubbard about his wife. "How is Donna doing? I heard about the fire at your house. Are you guys okay? If there is anything I can do, please don't hesitate to ask. We have plenty of room in our home. You are certainly welcome to stay with us until you're back in your home."

Hubbard appreciated the gesture. He thanked Gluskow and told him that he and Donna would be just fine.

Even though he had known Al for many years, he felt a little uncomfortable having to ask for an official meeting. When Gluskow poured coffee, Hubbard decided he would have a cup…maybe that would calm him down.

"Al, I won't take up much of your time. I have told you the situation at the prison. Since we talked last, it has been a nightmare. In all the years I worked here in the Bureau, I have never seen anything like what I'm seeing over this release of Tony Spitlato. I haven't informed Thompson yet, but I have decided to resign my position at the prison. Too many things have been going on. I need to look out for myself and my family."

Gluskow listened intently to Hubbard and let him finish before telling him that he was aware of what was happening. He told Hubbard that before he went any further, he had a couple of people he wanted him to meet. He asked Hubbard to follow him.

They walked down a long hallway to a conference room. When they entered the room, Hubbard immediately knew that the room was something he had not seen before. It could be described as more of an auditorium than a room. It had stadium seating for about fifty people. In front of the seating area was a huge conference table that could seat at least thirty. The room was equipped with screens, maps, cameras, and many more bells and whistles. Gluskow led Hubbard to the large conference table.

"Mike, this is all new. It's state-of-the-art as far as intelligence goes. We can run any operation from this location. It is the most secure part of this building. I'm sort of old school, so most of what goes on in this room is sometimes mind boggling to me. The director usually conducts all classified business in this room. I will wait until the people I want you to meet get here before I go any further. If there's anything you want, we can have it brought in. I think after the meeting we have today, you will understand a whole lot more about what's happening. I will probably hear some things for the first time also."

As they were catching up on some small talk, two men entered the room from an area that seemed like they came out of the wall. Hubbard knew immediately from their dress and the way they carried themselves that they were agents. Both shook hands with Gluskow and took a seat at the table.

"Mike, let me introduce these agents. Bud Nagle is new here at headquarters. He's the SAC of our intelligence division. Everything you see or will see in this room is under his purview. Larry Harms has been in headquarters and working in the intelligence division for about two years. I'm sure you don't know these agents; they were on different assignments around the country when you were here. Both agents also work in the Special Operations Unit. I'm sure you are familiar with that unit. It has changed a lot since you were here. Believe me, Mike, the technology associated with this unit is evolving every day."

Mike Hubbard had seen a lot of technical advances when he was with the Bureau, but this had him in awe. He could not help but to continue gazing around the room.

Gluskow smiled at Hubbard and said, "Before we start, I want to assure both agents that they can speak freely. Everything talked about will be kept in the strictness of confidence. You may be retired, but I know you are still one of us. Just so you know, Mike, they are very familiar with all that has been going on at the prison. They also know what has been happening in your life. I'm glad you called. You deserve some closure. What the Justice Department is trying to do, is getting a little crazy. I will let Bud take over from here."

Hubbard, being a former top-level supervisor, knew from the talk that Gluskow had just given that he was about to hear something very interesting. He watched as Agent Nagle pulled material from his brief-case. Agent Harms turned and faced an enormous wood paneled wall. He had a remote device in his hand. He directed the remote toward the wall, and a huge screen slowly dropped from the ceiling. He hit the remote again and the lights dimmed in the area of the screen. Nagle turned and faced the screen. Hubbard and Gluskow were facing straight ahead and did not have to move. Nagle looked at Hubbard and told him that if he had any questions he should hold them until he finished. Harms nodded to Nagle and clicked the remote.

"Mr. Hubbard, before I proceed with the slides, I want to let you know that we are aware of all that has been happening in the CLEO Unit. We know all about Tony Spitlato, the people at the Justice Department, Spitlato's attorney, and, of course, Pete Calabrese. We understand that you have been through a lot while in your position at the prison, but I feel confident that when we get done here today you will see the entire picture. We're confident this whole incident is coming to an end. It could have dragged on for quite some time. I know that Mr. Gluskow and the director agree that it needs to end. Now, let me have the first slide."

Harms clicked a button and a photo of John Thompson filled the very large screen. Nagle pulled a laser pointer from his jacket. While directing the pointer at the photo, he commenced to tell everyone that they were looking at the second in command at the Justice Department. He gave a brief bio on Thompson and explained that the entire op-eration that he will talk about has been sanctioned by Thompson. He asked for the next slide and the photo of Pat Driscoll appeared on the screen. He said that Driscoll was the guy who took orders directly from

Thompson. Before he requested the next slide, he confirmed with Hubbard that he knew these two. Hubbard acknowledged that he had met with Thompson before taking the job at Pelican Bay. He also told Nagle that he knew Driscoll and had worked some investigations with him in the past.

Before requesting the next slide, Nagle walked closer to Hubbard and Gluskow. He told them that before he went any further, he wanted to make it clear that the Bureau had no evidence that Attorney General Paige was involved in any wrongdoing. He said that it didn't mean he was not aware of what was going on, but they just didn't have any evidence that he was involved. Nagle emphasized that Paige was more of a political figure. He left the covert operations and criminal investigations to be handled by Thompson. Nagle stated that if the Bureau thought that Paige had first-hand knowledge of what was happening, the director would have to put the White House on notice.

The next slide was of Tony Spitlato. Nagle said he would push past this slide as he was sure that Hubbard certainly knew all about Spitlato. Before asking for the next slide, Nagle said that Spitlato was just a pawn in this endeavor by the Justice Department. He said that he would get back to Spitlato. The next slide was of Howard Gibbons. He asked Hubbard if he had any dealings with Gibbons. Hubbard explained that he did talk with Gibbons at the prison. The next slide was of Pete Calabrese. The slide was a photo taken by surveillance cameras; it was of poor quality, obviously taken from a distance.

Agent Harms pushed some buttons on the remote and the face of Calabrese came in clearer. Nagle talked about Calabrese for a few minutes. He said that the crime family under him in Camden, New Jersey, was thriving. The Bureau's intelligence showed that they were getting deep in the drug business. He revealed that the Bureau now had an undercover operative inside the Calabrese family. He also pointed out that there was a lot of turmoil in the ranks of the family.

His last slide shocked Hubbard. He stood up to get a closer look. Before Nagle could say anything, Hubbard said, "That's Andy Brewer."

Nagle snickered a little. He looked at Gluskow and then back to Hubbard. "Mike, that guy might be the Andy Brewer that you know, but his name is not Andy Brewer. He's a real nasty character. He was formally with the CIA. When he returned to the states from working covertly overseas, the Justice Department took him on board. He's as treacherous as they come. When you talk about someone that would kill you at the drop of a dime, he's the guy. He goes by many names depending on what they have him doing. His real name, according to CIA records, is Leanderthal Wisnowski. I guess with a name like that he probably doesn't mind assuming other names. They referred to him when he worked covertly at the CIA as '*The Buzzard*'."

Hubbard was smiling at the sight of the picture. He now knew why he had nothing but trouble with the guy he knew as Andy Brewer.

Nagle continued, "We know that he was sent to your CLEO Unit by Thompson. We also know that while he was there he convinced one of your trusted employees to work with him. He's a real con artist, one of the best. He has no real life other than creating havoc when called upon. The employee he got to turn on you is Ron Sanders. We know that he convinced Sanders that if he would work with him, he would make sure the Justice Department got him a promotion within the prison. Some of the information coming back to the Justice Department was provided to Brewer by Sanders."

Hubbard had heard enough to make his head spin. He looked at Gluskow and just shook his head. He asked if he could get something to drink. After drinks were brought in for everyone, the short break ended. Before Nagle could start up again, Hubbard said, "I'm really shocked about Ron Sanders. I promoted him…I trusted him. I'm starting to look like a real idiot in this whole mess. I should have taken my retirement from the Bureau and rode off in the sunset like my wife wanted me to. I'm sorry to interrupt you…please continue. I can't wait to hear the rest of the story."

Nagle moved away from the screen and joined the group at the conference table. He told Hubbard that he had other slides, but he would like to continue for a while without slides. He said that the Bureau's intentions were to indict Thompson, Driscoll, Wisnowski, Sanders, Gibbons, Judge Sharper, and Tony Spitlato. Nagle asked Gluskow if wanted to add anything to what he had said.

"Mike, I know you're sitting there wondering what the hell the Justice Department was thinking. I can assure you that when we first got involved, we thought the same thing. There are a lot of tangibles connected to this investigation. When it first started, we were sure that Spitlato had killed a federal judge who was presiding over a mob trial in New Jersey. Tony might have been a good cop at one time, but when he was undercover in the mob he turned out to be a pretty bad actor. As far as Thompson and the others at the Justice Department, they got a little greedy."

Hubbard pushed back in his chair. He was thinking that it was all making sense now. If they wanted to pull this off, why did they pick someone with integrity like me? They could have just put anyone in that position.

Gluskow stood and walked around a little. "Mike, when Spitlato was sentenced in federal court under the RICO Act, the people at the Justice Department tried to make a deal with him prior to the sentencing. The deal would have been a very light sentence. He would get out early and end up back in the mob working for them. For some reason Tony balked on the deal. The Justice Department then made sure he got the lengthy sentence. He always said that he was framed. I guess he thought he would win his appeal. We assume that's why he turned down the deal."

Gluskow continued walking and Mike followed his route by maneuvering his swivel chair. Gluskow said that he only had a few more things to say.

"The next best thing for the Justice Department was to trump up this crazy idea about the CLEO Unit. It is now believed that Thompson thought that if he could get the worst corrupt cops in one place, he would have more control and make deals. He probably thought that he could work his magic and get people to cooperate with him in exchange for the promise that they would get released. We know from our intelligence that they have worked with a few others in your unit. I'll let Agent Nagle take over from here."

Nagle went back to the area of the screen and asked Agent Harms to put up the next slide. Hubbard just sat there wondering who in the hell would be popping up on the screen. He ran that thought through his head. He could not think who else could be involved. He didn't have to wait long. The next slide appeared on the screen. He had to maneuver his chair again to recognize the guy on the screen. As he moved his glasses to get a better look, Nagle spoke up. "Mike, this is Donny Napolitano. This is where it gets real interesting."

Before he could go any further, Hubbard slapped his hand on the table. "Damn, how could I miss that guy's name? I'm really slipping. I can remember the time when I could remember just about everybody I had seen in a day. I should have recognized Napolitano. He came to the CLEO Unit from the Otisville Federal Prison in upstate New York.

During my stay at the prison, I had a few private conversations with him. He's quite a character, a real mean son of a bitch."

Hubbard got up from the chair and walked to stretch his legs.

He stretched out a little, took a deep breath, and said, "I remember the eyes on that guy. You could look at him and see there was no feeling or emotion. I don't think anybody on that tier messed with him. He was friendly with Spitlato. They were a lot alike. He was also convicted under the RICO Act. He did the same thing in New York that Spitlato did in New Jersey. I guess they got along in prison because they had a lot in common."

Agent Nagle told Hubbard that he agreed with everything he said about Napolitano. He used his pointer to direct everyone's attention back to the screen. "Mike, you are right about Napolitano. He was very friendly with Spitlato. They formed a bond in prison, and from what we understand, they enjoyed leadership roles on the tier. Even though he's a nasty bastard, he ain't a dummy. He's been working with us ever since we found out what the Justice Department was trying to do. We have an agreement with him that we would simply get him back to Otisville. He just wants to be closer to his family."

Nagle told Harms to shut down the slide show. He came back to the table and sat across from Hubbard. He adjusted some of his papers and asked Gluskow if it was all right to continue, or did they want to take a break. Hubbard insisted that they continue.

"Mike, we have gone over a lot today. I want to go a little further because we are dealing with a very serious situation. We have had things go down that we did not think would happen. We feel bad about the reporter being killed; that was a senseless act on their part. The firebombing of your house just shows how far these bastards will go. We do feel that you are in danger. Whether you go back out to run the CLEO Unit or not, they would take you out just to prove their point. I'm suggesting that you stay here under our protection until the indictments come out. The protection would include your wife. We have made arrangements for you to stay at a place that you are very familiar with."

Before Nagle could continue, Hubbard stood and walked across the room. He returned to the table and shook his head. "Gentlemen, I appreciate your concern. I have been threatened many times in the past and I'm still standing. I really don't think it's necessary to provide protection for me or my wife."

Gluskow intervened, "Mike, we have thought about you and your wife. As we speak, your wife has been informed of the situation. She knows that we are meeting. She has agreed to go with our agents to the location we think will be the best for the both of you. When we are done, you can call her and talk to her. As a friend and former colleague, I really want to insist that you do what we think is best for you."

"Well, if you're telling me that my wife has agreed and is on her way to this great location, I guess I can't object. Now, where's this place that I'm familiar with? I hope it's not in one of those third world countries that I've had the misfortune of working in. Since my retirement, I have been getting used to fine dining and the many luxuries of life. Will we be living in a mud hut in Bangladesh? Where is this place?"

After a good laugh, Gluskow put his hand on Mike's shoulder. "You will be staying at the FBI Training Center in Quantico, Virginia. I'm sure you have fond memories of the training center. You also know that we have several guest houses there that are very nice. I'm sure you and Donna will be safe there. I think that a five hundred and forty-seven acre Marine Corps Base can do the job quite well. Along with the Marines, we have over a hundred agents at the facility involved in training. I couldn't think of a safer place than there."

Hubbard could only shake his head and smile at Gluskow. He asked how they convinced his wife to go along with them. Gluskow told him that she was not a problem. When she was informed of the investigation, she agreed that staying at the training center for a while would be in your best interest. Agent Nagle told Hubbard that he and Harms would personally transport him to Quantico.

As the meeting was winding down, Nagle said that he wanted to conclude the meeting with some final thoughts. "Mike, it was a pleasure meeting you. I have heard nothing but good things about you when you were with the Bureau. It appears that they took advantage of your good reputation when they asked you to head that unit. I can assure you our investigation will be over soon. We have been in touch with the legal people at the White House. This is a very delicate situation, and when it hits the media, there will be a field day by reporters. It's not every day that people in positions like Thompson and Driscoll are indicted, and that includes a federal judge. Before we leave for Quantico, I need to let you know one more thing."

Hubbard extended both of his hands toward Nagle. "Agent Nagle, I can't imagine there is more. But whatever you have lay it on me. I had no idea when I came here today that I would be finding out so much about these people."

"Mike, a final piece in this investigation is something that has probably been bothering you since it happened. We have two different sources inside the CLEO Unit that have confirmed who actually killed Mandez. I'm sure you know that one of them is Donny Napolitano. The other has come forward with information on the murder to work a deal for himself."

Mike Hubbard was all ears now, just when he thought he had heard it all, there was more. "Please continue, I need to hear this."

"Do you remember when I told you that Ron Sanders joined forces with Brewer? Well, it seems that Sanders got scared. When he was interviewing Donny about the murder of Mandez, he got a little careless. He was trying to get Donny to say that Spitlato killed Mandez. The interview got a little heated. Eventually, Sanders got him to calm down. He promised to help him get back to Otisville, if he talked about the murder. Well, Donny gave in, and told him that Spitlato killed Mandez."

Hubbard dropped back down in his chair so hard that the swivel action almost caused him to fall on the floor. He caught himself and asked Nagle to continue.

"According to Donny, Mandez came on the tier late that night in his uniform. He had been drinking. He told the two guards in the booth that they could take a break, and then he told them that he wanted to walk on the tier for a while. The guards were intimidated by Mandez and did as he said. Mandez opened the cell doors of Spitlato's and Donny's cells. When he approached their cells, he started to belittle both of them. He called Spitlato a wop, a dago, and some other choice names. He screamed at Spitlato, telling him he was a piece of shit, and he was going to teach him a lesson. Mandez pulled a pipe from his uniform jacket. He started into Spitlato's cell. Being drunk, he stumbled, and before he could recover, Spitlato was all over him. Mandez dropped the pipe, and Spitlato got it and commenced to hit Mandez in the head and all over his body. Blood was everywhere. Mandez never moved after being hit with the pipe. Spitlato dragged him out to the center of the tier. It all happened so fast. There was very little commotion. Spitlato cleaned the pipe, wiped the blood from his cell, and threw the pipe next to Mandez's body."

Hubbard stood again and threw his hands in the air. "Holy shit, I can't believe you got all this information—I feel like a fool."

Nagle said there is more and continued, "Mandez must have stayed in that position for fifteen minutes before one of the guards came looking for him. They sounded the alarm, and the tier was locked down. It happened so quick that most on the tier weren't even aware of what had happened. We have talked to the two guards, and they confirmed what Donny told Sanders. The guards also said they did not hear or see anything. They left their post because Mandez told them to. Also, both have confirmed that Mandez appeared to have been drinking."

Hubbard was speechless. He looked at Gluskow, wondering if there could be more. He looked at Agent Nagle and said, "Did either of you ever see the movie—*The Game*, starring Michael Douglas? He was given this adventure for his birthday. He went through a series of events that were life threatening and dangerous. At the end, when he almost died, it was revealed to him that it was all just a game and all the people involved were actually actors. Please tell me this is not a game, and you are not actors."

The meeting ended. The three of them left the building. The drive to Quantico would take about forty-five minutes. Hubbard sat in the back and listened to the two agents. When they pulled out of the building, Harms looked at Nagle and said, "That movie—*The Game...* sounds like something I should check out."

CHAPTER 39

Tony was returning from the lobby of the hotel. He just could not resist calling his wife. Knowing that the phones in the room were being listened to, he figured he would go to the lobby. The call to his wife lasted all of thirty seconds. It was a recording. It brought back memories; it was his voice on the recording. As he fought back tears, as he left a message: *It's Tony; I'm out. I'll call later. I miss you all very much.*

Being a former cop and also a member of the mob, Tony had the foresight of always watching his surroundings. He routinely made it a point to never take the same route when returning from a meeting or some activity. At the hotel, instead of the elevator, he took the stairs. He put the key card in the slot to open the door. Before he pulled it out, he noticed that the small pieces of paper were missing from the top of the door. He had always used a trick that he learned as a rookie police officer. Working the night shift, he was told by some old-timers to use pieces of paper or something small to put on a door. If he returned to check that door later, and the paper was gone, it most likely meant that someone had tampered with the door. This police technique also came in handy when he was with the mob, because he stayed in a lot of motels while doing mob business.

As he stood there, he could hear music coming from his room. He didn't remember leaving any music playing. He was considering his options when the door swung open. He reared back and was prepared to knock somebody out cold if necessary. He lowered his clenched fist.

Instead of knocking somebody out, he was staring at a very attractive female, something Tony hadn't see for quite some time.

Tony entered his room and looked around. He quickly shut the door. The woman was standing there with only a silk robe on. Tony looked around the room again to see if anyone else was there. The very attractive lady stepped back across the room and sat on the edge of the couch with the robe open, revealing her long shapely legs. She assured Tony that no one else was in the room; he looked again anyway. After he convinced himself that no one else was in the room, he went and locked the door. He put a chair against the doorknob.

"Who the hell are you?"

"My name is Mello. I hope I didn't scare you. Mr. Calabrese sent me here to welcome you home. I got in with a passkey from the front desk. Sometimes being a well-dressed, attractive woman pays off. It can get you almost anything you want, if you know what I mean."

"So Pete Calabrese sent you, and your name is Mello. I can see that you're not wearing much, but does Mello have a purse or any bags? I feel real good about this, but I would feel much better checking whatever you brought to my room."

Mello walked to the bedroom with Tony close behind. Tony was checking her out...all of her. She handed Tony her purse and a small travel bag. He checked the inside of both.

"Okay, Mello, let's continue. If I call Pete right now will he confirm that he sent you?

"Tony, you know Pete as well, if not better than I do. I think he would be offended that you did not take my word. Who else would send you something this good?"

"Well, I guess you're right. I actually loved Mello cups when I was a kid. I ate them all the time. I saved the cards that came with the candy. I'm sure my mom still has them in the basement at home."

"Tony, I'm not named after a candy. The candy was called Mallo, not Mello, but I'm sure I will be better than any candy you ever had."

Mello dropped the robe she was wearing. Tony stepped back and with wide eyes, he just took it all in. He was thinking that just a few days ago he was in a shower with a bunch of naked guys that were fat, ugly, and downright disgusting. Now here he was with the prettiest thing he'd seen in many years.

Mello played to Tony's lustful eyes. She asked him if he approved of the lingerie. She said it was called Pleasurements. "Pete paid for it. He got it at the House of Pleasure and paid three hundred dollars for it." As she stood and posed in the lingerie, she explained it was a high erotic brand made in Amsterdam. She finished by saying that you need an appointment at the House of Pleasure because it's made to size.

Tony knew what was eventually coming, but for now he just wanted to enjoy the fashion show. He thought he would have a little fun. "Mello, you do know that at one time I was a cop. We cops have the gift of observing and remembering people. Let me verbally describe you so I don't ever forget this moment. I want to remember you long after tonight. Let me start this way…you are about five feet seven inches tall, about one hundred and twenty-five pounds, full perky breasts, D cups, toned thin legs, a small tight ass, dark brown wavy hair, tan skin, big brown eyes, small button nose, full lips, pearly white teeth, and an absolute perfect smile. How's this former cop doing so far?"

"Wow, Mr. Policeman, you nailed it. You actually got me excited while you were describing me. I think we better take this in the bedroom before I ruin this very expensive lingerie."

"Okay, my little Mello cup. Let me just check this door again, I don't want anyone busting in on us. I've waited a long time for something like this."

Tony went to the door to check the chair. He was adjusting it when someone pushed the door open. He was shocked and surprised, actually more pissed off than shocked and surprised. Before he could consider throwing a punch, he was grabbed by two men. They dragged him backwards and threw him onto the couch. He started to get up and was pushed back. He did not recognize the two men. He assumed by them wearing suits that they were most likely law enforcement.

Mello heard the commotion and came out of the bedroom. One of the men told her to get her clothes and get the hell out of the hotel. She asked them who they were. She got no response until the taller of the men said it would be in her best interest not to know who they were. She gathered her clothing and her bags. She walked by Tony and kissed him on the cheek. "Sorry Tony, these assholes just ruined the absolute best day of your life. I'll tell our mutual friend what happened."

After Mello left the room, the men identified themselves as federal marshals. They produced badges, but told Tony their names didn't really matter. They said they were part of a detail assigned to watch him. They told him that they knew he went to the lobby to make a phone call. They also told him that they watched every move in the room when Mello was there.

"You sick bastards. You mean you were watching everything that went on between me and my Mello cup?"

The taller of the two marshals did most of the talking. He said that not only were they watching, but they were listening also. He informed Tony that he needed to follow the instructions that he was given, or his deal might just be terminated. He was told that they would be close by in the hotel.

"Do me a favor and find out when I can leave this place. When little Miss Mello goes back and tells Pete Calabrese what happened, he's going to have some questions. I hope you fellows know who we are dealing with when it comes to Pete Calabrese. How the hell do I explain you guys busting into my room and throwing Mello out?"

The two men didn't seem to be interested in what Tony was saying. They told him to sit tight for the rest of the night, and someone would be reaching out to him in the morning.

The men left the apartment. Tony made a very strong drink. As he savored the drink, he had visions of his Mello cup dancing in his head; he was glad that he had taken mental notes about her.

Now let me see if I can remember that vivid description of my little Mello cup.

Chapter 40

Three Weeks Later–FBI Headquarters

The FBI conference room was overflowing with personnel from law enforcement and a few government agencies. FBI Director, Morris Toranfo, was presiding over the meeting. The director had briefed the President's Security Council prior to the meeting. He had also met with certain members of Congress. The highly classified meeting was to start at 11 a.m. and everyone knew it would not start on time; it never did. The director was routinely late when he called for a meeting.

The details that were to be unveiled at the meeting would most definitely be one of the most news worthy events in the tenure of the director. For now, the press would have to wait. All media outlets were barred from the meeting.

Toranfo had been in the director's position for six years. Nothing during those years would come close to what was about to take place at this gathering. As usual, when the director was running the show, all of the upper echelon of the Bureau attended. The deputy directors took their seats in the front row. It was reminiscent of a state of the union address, except there would not be any sporadic applause. The deputies had been briefed earlier on what would be covered.

Most of the attendees from law enforcement agencies and a few government officials would be hearing what the director had to say for the first time. The buzz around the room was in high gear. It was not that often that the director himself called for a meeting of such high-level people. Everyone knew that whatever was about to happen was big.

The director entered the room accompanied by three agents carrying booklets. He moved swiftly, outpacing the agents. Alongside the director was his top legal adviser and personal confidant, Al Gluskow. The director stood behind the podium. Gluskow took a seat to his right. The conversing in the room came to a complete halt as the director positioned the microphone and cleared his throat. He took a sip of water and asked everyone to get comfortable. He told them they might be in the room for a while. He informed them that everything he would talk about would be available in print form and distributed by his agents at the end of the meeting. He also told them that a separate press conference would be conducted by his staff later in the day. Toranfo looked at Gluskow and asked if there was anything else he needed to say before he got started. Gluskow whispered in his ear that he should mention that the President, members of the Security Council, and certain members of Congress had been briefed earlier.

"Gentlemen and ladies let me start by saying that I appreciate all of you coming here today. I will forgo any introductions. I think that most of you in this room know each other. I will introduce my senior legal adviser here on my right, Al Gluskow. The distinguished looking men in the front row are my deputies. Before I proceed, I will ask that no one leave the room until I have finished. As you have noticed by now there are uniformed officers stationed at each exit to this conference room. I will also tell you that some of you here today will not like what I say. If you are starting to squirm in your seat, you may be who I will be talking about."

Most of the attendees laughed…some a nervous laugh. They stopped when they saw that the director was serious. There was some mumbling, but for the most part the room became very quiet.

The director continued. "I'm going to cover a lot of ground, so stay with me. What you are about to hear could be categorized as the dark side of blue. This is a sad day for law enforcement. Some time ago, the

Justice Department had the idea of starting a unit within a prison that would house the worst of the corrupt cops from around the country. On the surface, you would all agree that this would be a good idea. The unit was formed and located at the Pelican Bay Prison on the West Coast. The unit was aptly named the CLEO Unit, which stands for Corrupt Law Enforcement Officers. One of our distinguished retired FBI deputy directors, Mike Hubbard, was asked to run the unit. Mike accepted and got the unit up and running. Needless to say, running a wing in a prison was a major undertaking for him. He was persuaded by officials at the Justice Department to take the position. Mike is here with us today."

Mike Hubbard did not stand, but he raised his hand. Several of the FBI directors looked his way and he nodded to them. Director Toranfo also nodded toward Hubbard, and then he continued.

"As the unit was forming, fifty of the worst corrupt cops, one from each state, were transported to Pelican Bay and placed in the CLEO Unit. This was a major undertaking with many logistical concerns. Mike picked his staff to assist with running the unit. He was recruited and eventually appointed to this position by the second in command at the Justice Department, John Thompson. Mr. Thompson is also here with us today. Also, assisting in overseeing the establishment of the unit was Pat Driscoll, a deputy under Thompson. I'm not sure why he is not here at this meeting. There were others at the Justice Department that participated in the start-up of the unit."

When Thompson heard his name, he did not flinch. His two assistants sitting with him looked at him, but he maintained a stern face and looked straight ahead.

"Let me try to get to the crux of this meeting. As I mentioned, the men held in the CLEO Unit were all former law enforcement officers that turned their backs on their profession in some way or another. Most were convicted in federal courts around the country under the RICO Act. They were all serving their sentences at federal prisons in all fifty states. Some committed more egregious acts than others. It seems that the Justice Department had a real interest in one particular prisoner named, Tony Spitlato. This guy was not only convicted under the RICO Act, he was a suspect in the killing of a federal judge that presided over the trial of a Mafia figure from Camden, New Jersey. They wanted to get this guy out of prison with the intention of getting him back in the mob in his home town of Camden. The FBI has firsthand knowledge that Spitlato, after turning on his police agency, became a mid-level lieutenant in the Pete Calabrese crime family in Camden."

Mike Hubbard was in a position to see the reactions of most in the room. Some were taking notes, but most were fixated on the director. Toranfo would pause once in a while from his written material and glance over the room.

The director continued, "The Justice Department through some underhanded tactics worked diligently to get Spitlato out of prison. They threatened a federal judge to make him agree to grant Spitlato a release from prison pending his appeal. They sent a former CIA agent, Andy Brewer, to the prison to work with Mike Hubbard. The agent's name is not Brewer. We have his real name in the pamphlet that will be handed out. Brewer while at the prison befriended a guard by the name of Ron Sanders. He promised Sanders a job at the Justice Department in exchange for information on the daily activities of Mike Hubbard. Prior to Sanders hooking up with Brewer, he was a trusted employee in the unit. Brewer's original instructions were to work in the unit as an internal investigator. He was instructed by the Justice Department to use whatever methods he needed to get information from Spitlato. During his interviews with Spitlato, he found that he was a lot tougher than expected. That's when they decided to use different tactics to get him out of prison."

For the first time since the director started, Thompson showed some nervousness. He began to move his head from left to right as if to relieve some tension.

Director Toranfo moved his glasses down a little on his nose. "It should be noted at this time that shortly after the unit was up and running, a guard was murdered. The guard, Lieutenant Oscar Mandez, according to all reports was not a very nice person. Brewer, thinking he could use Mendez the same way he used Sanders, lured him over. Mandez was tough on the prisoners. His nickname was "The Pincher." That will also be explained in the handout. Brewer and Mandez were a team for a while. They both had a mean streak in them, so they got along just fine. The murder of Mandez took place on the tier of the CLEO Unit. No one has been charged with that murder. It seems that Mandez came on the tier one night and had been drinking. He apparently told the guards in the booth to take a break. What happened after that was a mystery for a while. Most of the prisoners on the tier were interviewed by Brewer and Sanders. I'll get back to the murder of Mandez a little later."

Hubbard knew most of what the director was saying. He knew that shortly he would probably be hearing some things that he was not aware of. He knew one thing for sure, this whole situation was coming to an end, but he just didn't know what the end game would be.

Director Toranfo removed his glasses and continued, "When Brewer interviewed Spitlato about the murder, he also approached him about getting out of prison and working for the Justice Department. Spitlato jumped at the opportunity as would be expected. The Justice Department then solicited the help of Spitlato's attorney, Howard Gibbons. He was told to file the appeal for Spitlato to the federal appeals court presided over by the less than honorable, Judge Wallace Sharper. Gibbons was threatened that if he did not cooperate, he would be indicted. Gibbons has been the attorney for the Calabrese crime family for years. He probably should have been convicted years ago of tax evasion and money laundering. When Gibbons filed for the appeal, the agents from the Justice Department visited Judge Sharper. They reminded him that he was approaching his retirement, and he needed to cooperate. He was instructed to grant the appeal as soon as he got it. Judge Sharper did grant the appeal and ordered the release of Spitlato. Judge Sharper is not here today. He has been visited by members of the Bureau and has agreed to cooperate with this investigation."

Toranfo looked directly at Hubbard and said "It should be noted that Mike Hubbard, being the loyal and dedicated public servant that he has been for many years, was totally against Spitlato getting out of prison. When he was made aware of the scheme, he approached Dennis Mitchell, a reporter for the Crescent City Times, the local newspaper. Mitchell agreed to write the story for the paper. Looking back on the whole situation, Mike has regretted going to the reporter. The reporter was murdered. He was shot several times as he was walking to his apartment. Shortly after the murder of the reporter, Mike Hubbard's residence was firebombed. His wife was home at the time, but got out without any injuries. The home was destroyed. I hope you are feeling the ruthlessness of the people carrying out these dastardly deeds. Their desire to get one person out of prison overshadowed all the harm they were bringing to people in their way. I have been around for a long time. I never thought I would see our government go to such lengths for a despicable person like Spitlato."

The director took a brief moment to drink some water. As he did, the room filled with a quiet buzz. It was obvious from what he had said that he was directing his remarks at Thompson and others at the Justice Department. Thompson was sitting in the second row. Even though he and his people were the target of the FBI investigation, he continued to show no emotion. He looked straight ahead. He was known for his arrogance and his attitude of superiority. He had run the Justice Department by snubbing anyone he thought would hinder his career. It was well known throughout other federal agencies that he called the shots, not Oliver Paige. Even sitting listening to the FBI Director talking about him and his office, he was probably thinking that he was untouchable…Paige would protect him.

Mike Hubbard sat in the second row on the side behind the FBI deputy directors. He could see Thompson from his peripheral vision, but he made it a point to stay totally focused on the director. As the director went through the litany of the events, it was still hard for him to comprehend what had happened. The thought of his wife and a long future retirement with her kept him going. The nightmare was finally coming to an end. It didn't really matter to him who got indicted. He knew from the seriousness of the investigation, that Thompson and others would be out of their high positions in government.

The director positioned his papers and told the attendees that he would only take a few more minutes.

"I would like to continue by saying that the President is aware of this investigation. He has informed me that he and his staff take these allegations very serious. He has ordered an investigation of Oliver Paige to see if he had first-hand knowledge of this scheme. He has also ordered the House of Representatives to conduct an impeachment investigation on John Thompson. The President and his legal staff feel that Thompson has violated the Tenure of Office Act. If that investigation shows criminal acts, he could be charged criminally."

This finally seemed to get to Thompson; he was looking around the room. He made a motion as if he was getting up to leave. He saw the uniform guards at the doors. He also was noticing the stares from everyone in the room.

Director Toranfo asked Gluskow if he would take the podium and continue with the presentation.

"The FBI will be filing charges against Pat Driscoll for malfeasance in office and conspiracy to commit murder. As the investigation continues, he could be charged with other offenses. As far as Judge Wallace Sharper, we will be referring his involvement to the federal judges' oversight board for violations of the Judicial Conduct and Disability Act. He could also be facing criminal charges. As far as Howard Gibbons, we will be referring his involvement to the American Bar Association for violation of their rules of professional conduct. Mr. Gibbons has been skirting the law for many years. We are looking to bring a case against him for tax evasion and money laundering. His days representing the Calabrese crime family are over."

Gluskow continued, "Andy Brewer, whose real name is Leanderthal Wisnowski is currently in custody, and is being held in a very secure place. As expected, he is not cooperating. He has been a menace to society for a long time. We are working to bring charges against him for the murder of Dennis Mitchell. We feel that he was also involved in the firebombing of Mike Hubbard's home. Now as we get near the end of this meeting, I want to let you know that agents in the field are rounding up members of the Calabrese crime family. We have been working our investigation on that group for several years. Through our on-going investigation, which included intelligence from undercover operatives, informants, surveillance, wiretaps, and some good old field work, we are ending the reign of terror that the Calabrese crime family has bestowed on the citizens of Camden. The arrest will include the head of that family, Pete Calabrese."

Upon hearing the news of the demise of the Calabrese crime syndicate, there was some rumbling from the group. A few of the directors in the front row actually started to clap, but they caught themselves and stopped. Thompson and his entourage remained stoic.

The director stood up, sipped water, wiped his brow with his handkerchief, loosened his tie, and rolled his neck to both sides. He appeared to be maneuvering his legs to get comfortable. He told Gluskow he would take over.

"Gentlemen, I promise you we are getting to the end. We have talked about most of the players in this investigation. We have probably skipped by the main character, Tony Spitlato. We had obtained federal indictments for him long before he got his short stay back in the mob. While the Justice Department was working their voodoo magic, the Bureau was getting attainable concrete information to indict members of the mob. We have been very lucky on many fronts. I told you I would get back to the murder of the prison guard. Well, because some prisoners in the CLEO Unit want to get back to their home state prisons, we have received very credible evidence. Ron Sanders, who I told you was working with Brewer, has also talked to our agents. He wants to work with us. He told us that CLEO Unit inmate, Donny Napolitano, told him in an interview that Spitlato killed Mandez. We have interviewed Napolitano, and he confirmed what he told Sanders. We have also received information from another inmate in that unit, Bernie Wells. He told our agents that he did not see Spitlato hit Mandez with the pipe, but he did see him drag his body to the center of the tier. With the information from these three people, we have obtained an indictment of Tony Spitlato for the murder of Mandez. The indictment is a mere formality at this point. It will clear the case, but it will not bring Spitlato back. He was gunned down while leaving his favorite restaurant three days ago. We have worked with the Camden Police Department and the medical examiner's office to keep his death quiet until now. We have good intelligence that Pete Calabrese became disenfranchised with Tony and ordered the hit. When Tony returned to the Camden mob, by all accounts, he got out of hand. He was making deals that were not okayed by Pete Calabrese."

The director paused. He looked over at Gluskow to see if he missed anything. Getting no response from him, he asked the agents to pass out the documents. He asked if there were any questions. No hands went up, but no one was in any hurry to leave the conference room. It seemed as if the news had mesmerized some of them. The first to stand were the directors. The others waited for their pamphlets. Most directed their attention to John Thompson and his people, who still seemed unfazed by all that they had heard.

Thompson took his pamphlet and started to walk toward the door. He turned and asked the director if he would be detained. He was informed that he could leave. The director told him that it would be in his best interest to go back and report directly to Attorney General Paige.

As the room was emptying, Mike Hubbard was approached by the FBI Director. "Mike, I just want to thank you. I know that you have been through a lot. When I first learned of all this foolishness, I could not believe that someone that we worked so closely with would attempt to pull off something like this. It makes you wonder what else that crew at the Justice Department has been up to. I'm glad that the President has ordered a thorough investigation."

Mike Hubbard visited with Gluskow for a few minutes and thanked him for all his assistance. He left the conference room and walked around the lobby for a while, looking at the articles displayed in the museum. There were artifacts and stories of decorated agents that dated back to the beginning of the Bureau. He had looked at this museum many times when he was active in the Bureau. Today, he took time to read some of the plaques; he hadn't done that before. He was more proud of the Bureau than ever before.

He walked toward the exit and paused to take his last look at the emblem of the FBI. The words on the emblem meant as much to him now as they did throughout his career...FIDELITY-BRAVERY-INTEGRITY.

As he approached the security guards manning the entrance and exit, he noticed a photo of John F. Kennedy. He stopped to read the wording under the photo.

Our problems are man-made; therefore they may be solved by man. And man can be as big as he wants. No problem of human destiny is beyond human beings.

Made in United States
Orlando, FL
19 October 2024

52872216R00127